Crow Of Thorns

Crow Of Thorns

Richard Mosses

Chapter 1

The tent arches above me. I sit up, breath pounding into steam. Grey day leaks through the nylon flaps. I feel like crying. Perhaps my prayers were answered after all.

Thankfully morning has come. I am empty, shallow, hollow, fragile.

From within the warm cocoon of my sleeping bag I grab at my clothes, dress quickly and crawl out into the bright, grey day.

As usual, I'm one of the first to rise. I stretch, breathing in the cold air. All around me, the sea of tents stretches – canvas and nylon, of many colours and hues, billows and flexes with the thin breeze. From makeshift drying lines, left-out clothing hangs stiff, rimed with frost.

I shiver and stoop back inside, pull on a jumper and coat, find my wash things and head across the grass, avoiding guy lines. As I pass between the giant Victorian greenhouses on my way to the toilet block at the back of the Botanic Gardens, only the yap of Janice's wee dog, protecting its owner and her stuff, breaks the silence.

I wash and shave in icy water, and brush my teeth. We're lucky to have any kind of facilities at all, but just the same I long for a hot shower, to stand in there until my skin wrinkles, until I've washed the ache out of my joints, until I can feel the ends of my toes again.

The smell of espresso and the warmth of the café are adequate compensation. I slide into my usual seat just as Sindi appears to take my order.

"Howdy stranger." Sindi runs her fingers down her pen, before flipping it over and starting again. "How you?" Her Northern Irish accent could dent metal, which might explain the piercings – shards of shrapnel.

"Not bad." I look up at her pretty, disfigured face. "How's work?"

"Things are picking up again. You're here, for a change."

I smile. "I've got some time, and some cash."

"Sure, you look like you could do with a good feed. What can I get you?" Her pen is poised over the pad.

I wonder what I can afford. "I'll have a bacon roll and mug of tea, please."

"That'll be a tenner."

Fuck. "Really?" But my stomach groans.

"Sorry. New management policy. We've had too many runners."

I find my phone and wave it in front of Sindi's terminal.

"I'll be right back now." A few moments later scalding tea is banged down on the table along with a chipped plate holding a morning roll stacked with bacon – sunshine yellow oozing out of it like a cartoon gunshot wound. The breakfast of kings.

"Charlie was feeling generous," she says. "Since you're a regular."

I smile wide and it infects Sindi, but she leaves as soon as some customers with real money come in. I wolf the roll, wash it down with the tea sugared until there are no packets left in the little ceramic pot. I glance at the time and run out of the café, wiping yolk from my face.

Chapter 2

I check each server core. All the lights are blinking a comforting fluorescent green. I could stay in like everyone else, read my diagnostics or sit in a nearby pub or hotel and start a new set of simulations using a borrowed Wi-Fi link. But I prefer the comfort of routine, and the cooled server room is still warmer than outside.

I miss putting on my suit every day, tearing away the protective film from a freshly laundered shirt. It felt like being a superhero leaving behind a secret identity, showing my true face to the world. But I have nowhere to keep a suit now and no access to an iron. And anyway, wearing my civvies protects me too. Would people be as kind if they knew what I had done?

I used to dig out information, analyse the data, understand what was and predict what could be, and ended up inventing, purely as a side effect, new ways of assessing risks. Someone else packaged that risk, turned it into a product. It was too abstract for the salespeople who simply sold another way to make money out of other money. They didn't know it could take just one guy defaulting on a payment for the whole house of cards to come crashing down.

I was one of the lucky ones. I got a new job, in a smaller firm, doing what I do best – even if it's only for a third what I made before. And I live in a tent. It's odd that the stains on the pavement outside the old offices never seem to wash away.

I gather data and make models. But that kind of work requires a number of powerful machines, dedicated iron, and with everyone else working from home someone needs to keep the systems running.

I sit down at the only desk the company owns, surrounded by black and grey, plastic and glass, the hum of hard drives and cooling fans, and enter a password – data might want to be free, but sometimes it needs help escaping its prison.

The view of the Clyde is always impressive. I get lost looking at the steel waters lapping against the walls. Dr Reynolds coughs to gain my attention.

"How are you getting on?"

These sessions have been an unexpected benefit of my severance package.

"I had the dream again." The couch creaks beneath me. I avoid eye contact. "It was much worse this time."

"Tell me about it."

I try my best to explain. As I speak, Reynolds scribbles in her notebook. What is so important? I turn my head and she finds my eyes.

A hand moves across my chest, clammy and pale. Fingers curl around my ankle. A third hand grasps my thigh. I struggle but the hands tighten their grip. There are screams directed at me. I shout, and a fist is pushed into my mouth. I can't move. Bound and powerless, mute, I'm pulled down into the earth, through dirt and bedrock, passing worms and stones, falling into caverns of fire.

I land on my back on a stone slab. Hands still hold me, arms slither over me. This is when I normally wake up. But something is different tonight.

Shadowed figures approach, their voices distinct above the chorus of hate.

- Can you see it?

- No.

- What about here?

My left arm is pulled behind my head. It feels like something wants to drag me from the stone slab, but the hands stop them. My shoulder pops as the bone is torn from its socket. My cry is stifled by the fist as tendons tear and muscles rip. An electric blue flash fills my mind obliterating all thoughts except one: I want to wake up.

But I am dead, and this is Hell, with no escape for sinners.

The severed arm is held over me, its warm blood dripping onto my chest. The skin is peeled, each muscle stripped away, and all is thrown into a bubbling pot until only the bones remain.

- Is it there?

They are looking for something. I pray to all the gods I know that they find it. Soon. What did I do to deserve this?

- No.

I confess.

- Is it there?

I confess to every shameful moment.

The bones are tossed into the pot. A shaft of dark metal lances my right leg, sending more electric bursts into my brain. Hands pull at the edges of the wound, widening it. The skin is stripped back, exposed flesh sifted and separated. The lance is withdrawn, and the skeletal leg wrenched from its socket.

- No.

I confess to each unintended slight.

- Maybe there.

Lances pierce my torso, ringing when they hit the slab beneath. A butterfly pinned while fingers burrow, ribs snap, and the chest is exposed. I feel a terrible pity for my beating heart, my airless lungs. It drives me to one last desperate prayer, to confess the smallest, pettiest things. I empty myself.

Still they persist.

Each organ, each part, is lifted, examined, rejected, and thrown into the pot, until only the head remains – barely conscious.

- Is it there?

- No.

Fingers scoop out the eyes, yet I still see, my jaw removed, my tongue torn away, my skull cracked open and the brain squeezed out.

A hand finds something, something small, and holds it between thumb and forefinger.

- Is this it?

- Yes. Put it back.

Like a film in reverse, my body is put back together. Vessels, lymph nodes, nerves, tendons, veins, muscles, fat, skin, all gathered from the pot, clean. Dislocated limbs sewn back together, organs replaced. Last of all the small bone, glinting in the flames, is forced back into my head through my nose. A final agony, then nothing.

"What do you think accounts for the change?" she says.

"It's been the same since I was a teenager. But never like this."

"So, what then?" Her eyes focus on me. "What do you think it could be?"

"I was eviscerated last night." I tear my eyes away. "It has fuck all to do with a guilty conscience."

"Maybe you should think about that. I'm sorry this will be our last time, it looks like we were just starting to make some progress."

I walk home. It's already dark. Am I really torturing myself to make up for my past actions? Absurd, but I have to consider it. It's weird thinking I don't have to go back to see Dr Reynolds. It felt like a millstone, but it was also good to have someone to talk to.

A car horn blares, shocks me out of my stupor. I grin like an idiot and half-wave an apology, then watch as the Merc speeds off towards Park Circus. I used to have one just like it.

Along Woodlands Road, a grey squirrel, which probably ought to be hibernating, crosses the path in front of me, darts up a tree and then, clinging to the trunk, tries to pretend it isn't there. The camouflage might work were it not for the nervous micro-movements of ear and eye.

A shadow swoops down, sending the squirrel scurrying higher into the tree, and a bloody great crow lands on the pavement in front of me. I step back, then feel like an idiot. It's huge, it might be a raven. It's looking right at me, its head tilted slightly, with a dark empty eye. I stare back. No bird is going to better me in a staring contest. Only when the bird shifts its feet, do I realise that I can see through it.

There's a haze around the bird so that its outline is ill-defined. It appears to be made of thorns – tangled, twisted, barbed. A multitude of spines stick out from its body, making it look like an intricate statue made from coat hangers.

This isn't possible. It's a trick of the winter light.

It walks towards me. Fixes me again with its eye. "Hi. Nikolai Munro?"

Did it really speak? I try walking around it, but the bird blocks my path, causing me to stop and change direction. I want to kick it. "Get out of my way."

The crow flaps its wings and moves out of leg reach. "Go on then, walk on by. I just wanna talk."

I've not had alcohol or drugs in a long time, so it can't be that. I've not eaten in a while, so maybe I'm hallucinating. I cross the road.

The crow, with an easy flap of its wings, glides over the road, and is soon alongside me. "Look, Niky - can I call you that? You think this is your imagination. I get that. But I'm not – well, technically I am. But whatever way you look at it, I'm here. I'm not going away, so you'd be better off accepting that."

Its voice is rough, like it's been smoking forty a day since it was a kid. A Noo Yoik accent. If my subconscious is talking to me, it's chosen a weird way to express itself. It's like being in a Disney cartoon. I don't want to end up dancing with animated candlesticks, but I decide to play along. "If you're my friend, then what's your name?"

"Corbie."

"Of course. Twa corbies sittin on a wa. So what do you want?"

The crow cocks its head to one side, like it can't believe what it's hearing. "I'm here to train you."

"For what? The London Marathon?"

"Good one. Not bad. You were chosen. They found the shaman's bone in you, man."

The small metal thing is shoved back into my head. There is pain between my eyes. The fear of the nightmare returns in full force. I'm going to be sick.

I understand now that my mum was right – all my life I've been called. I don't want her to be right.

I walk past the bird, aiming a kick that it easily avoids. "Piss off and leave me alone."

Chapter 3

For the first time in as long as I can remember the alarm wakes me up. Not just a signal to get out of bed. I slept right through the night. No dreams. Some sort of miracle. Yet I still feel shattered.

I get myself together and leave the tent. There's a commotion a few rows over, near the road. Someone probably tripped on a guy line and woke people up. But it's Albert's tent they're standing round and something wrong wafts its way towards me.

Out of all of us Albert shouldn't be here – he's seventy odd and should be enjoying retirement. Instead he's putting in who knows how many hours at the local supermarket and still finds time to help people out.

The sweet foul stench grows as I get closer to his tent.

Janice is in tears, and there's no sign of her yappy wee Jack Russell, which is odd. Big Malky is comforting her but it looks more like he's trying to cop a feel. Young Silk, skinny and pale is on his knees looking through the tent flaps. He stands up when he hears me coming. I wouldn't trust him as far as I could spit him.

"He's deid," he says, confirming what I had already guessed. He shifts from one foot to the next, his red-rimmed eyes look for exits. "Janice said that Brutus wouldnae leave the tent alane. Me an Malky couldnae reach him so we opened it up... Jeesus, the smell."

He hunches over, hands on his knees and dry wretches.

"Anyone called an ambulance?" I take my phone out and catch a flicker of appraisal from Silk.

Malky shrugs. "He's deid. An ambulance is nae use. Besides none ae us could afford one."

"Where's Brutus now?" I say to Janice.

"I tied him up outside the park." She points in the direction of Queen Margaret Drive. "He wouldnae shut up."

Albert must have died a few days ago, when it was colder. I didn't notice his absence. Today it's warmer, so the natural processes must have hit his corpse hungry.

I look out over the tent village. "We need to find somewhere else." Then I start dialling, even though Malky is right, this is hardly an emergency. "Otherwise none of us will make it through January."

I wait for the police to arrive, mostly so no one borrows anything from Albert. I call Kathryn to tell her I'm running late. We discuss a feeble excuse to give the kids, one that won't spook them – though Lucas would probably find it cool and Samantha would be indifferent. Kathryn needs to protect her illusion of their innocence and it's easier to play along.

It's nearly eleven by the time I get there, making me regret stopping to help out. I have my own illusions – that our tent city is a community.

Fiona opens the door. "You made it then?" I always thought we got along, but then things went south, and I knew better.

"I couldn't just leave."

"The living are more important than the dead." Fiona had high hopes once, that didn't involve shouldering the burden of her daughter and grandchildren.

She leads me through to the kitchen. The kids are upstairs in gadget oblivion. Kathryn sits at the round table, hands wrapped around a mug of tea. A look passes between the two women and Fiona disappears. I take a seat opposite Kathryn and get my excuses in early.

"It's not that." Kathryn puts down her mug and looks me in the eye. "I can't go on like this. This weird twilight life."

"I'll get back on my feet again soon. They say things are looking up."

"When did you last eat?" Her tone softens. It isn't an accusation.

I shrug, I can't think of anything worth saying, so the silence lengthens. "I want to move on," Kathryn says.

"What? You mean you've met someone?" I can't believe it. I'm struggling to pay for us all, literally freezing my ass off, and she's out playing.

"It's not like that." Kathryn takes a sip of tea.

"So what is it like?" I can't sit. I need air. I slide open the patio doors.

"Niky. It's cold."

"Really? I barely notice it anymore."

"My lean wolf-man." She smiles. "I'm sorry it's come to this, but I want a divorce."

"You know I can't afford that."

"Mum will give me the money."

"That is exactly why I'm in a tent and not living here."

"That is exactly why I'm asking for the divorce. Don't drag this out for another year out of spite."

"Have you told the kids?"

"Of course not. There's nothing to tell them, yet."

Everything I thought I was working towards is slipping away from me. My pride kept us from living together, but I thought we still loved each other, that we had an understanding – as soon as I had the means we'd be back together again. I can't recall the last time I stayed over, though. A year already since we left the old house? Who am I fooling here? "Okay," I say. "If that's what you want."

"I'll get the papers drawn up for next time. Nothing else will change, I promise." She gets up. "Here's some money." When I don't take the notes, she puts them on the table. "And the car keys." She drops them on top of the money. "Take them to McDonalds and the cinema. I'll see you later."

Kathryn leaves the room. I stare at the space she filled just a moment before.

Chapter 4

Back at the tent city there are a lot of people hanging out by Albert's tent, which has been sealed up with police tape. There are a number of yellow rectangles around it, like death has crept into the grass. No one had come to take the body away and the wait has turned into a vigil. People have been coming to pay their respects all day, telling stories. A small shrine has formed, with meagre offerings.

I join them. Maybe it will help me with my own loss. Silk and Malky aren't here, but Janice is about. Brutus must still be chained up elsewhere. A half-bottle of rough vodka is being passed from hand to hand. I think twice then take a mouthful.

A woman standing next to me says, "Did you know him?" She brushes a stray hair back behind her ear. It has become a ritual invitation. It's no surprise to see a stranger. The tent city has a core, but some people come and go.

"We used to say hello to one another," I say. "He helped me out. More than I ever thanked him for."

"Do you know where they took the body?" She wrinkles her nose.

I thought everyone knew by now. "That's why we're here. Waiting for someone to come for it."

"Jesus Christ." She shakes her head. "The whole fucking system is falling down."

I nod. "I live in one of these tents. You don't need to tell me."

"The police called, told me to come and get his stuff. I didn't even know he was living here."

The penny drops. "You're his daughter?"

"Granddaughter."

"Sorry. He never said. We all figured he was like us."

"Too pig headed and proud."

"That too." I didn't have to sleep here before. Now I do. "I'm Nik," I say, and offer her the bottle.

"Rachael." She takes a swig.

A flutter of dark wings and a *crawk*, and the crow of thorns glides in and lands on the roof of Albert's tent. An estate vehicle painted white drives slowly towards us. People make way for it but no one tries to shoo the crow away. I decide to ignore it like everyone else, then I realise that I'm the only one who can see it.

Something is really wrong with me, something that can't be blamed on an empty stomach or the vodka. So much for therapy.

"It's alright, Boss." The crow turns its head to one side, dark eye catching the headlights of the car. "The sooner you accept this, the easier it will be."

"That's easy for you to say."

Rachael frowns "What? I didn't say anything."

"Sorry." I try for a smile, just about manage it. "I was just running through a conversation in my head and that popped out. My wife asked me for a divorce today."

"She lives here too?"

"No, at her mother's. We've been separated since I started living here. You know how it is. Pig-headed and proud."

Rachael nods her head. "Look, I know this is kind of random, given we've just met. But would you come with me to the morgue or wherever they're taking him?"

She looks over my shoulder as a stretcher is taken out of the back of the estate, wheels concertina-ing onto the grass. Two men begin to get into bunny suits and masks.

"Okay… sure." Clearly I'm non-threatening. Corbie takes flight as one of the men cuts into the tent and it collapses. "Look this isn't going to be good. You can sit in my tent for a few minutes while they work. We can pick up Albert's stuff later, at the morgue."

"Okay." Rachael looks green. She takes another swig of vodka and passes it back to me. I try to wash away the sweet rot clinging to the top of my palette. We need a stronger solvent. I pass the bottle back to the crowd then we walk away, Corbie gliding after us over the eaves.

I unzip the flaps and hold out a hand. Rachael stoops and crawls in.

"You got all the mod cons here." She waves a hand toward my small pile of stuff.

"The tent was a gift from a charity. There are solar cells built into the fabric, even a crude heat pump in the floor that gives enough power for some light, or even a battery recharge in an emergency. Washing and other toiletries are reserved for the executive en suite bathroom. Sometimes, in summer, it even reaches above freezing. We're lucky, though, they used to lock the toilet block at night when they shut the park."

Rachael sits down on top of my sleeping bag. "How can you live like this? Aren't there homeless shelters or something?"

I crawl in next to her. It's a two-man tent but we're still close. Her perfume reminds me of fresh apples and summer grass. "They're all full. So are the hostels. From what I hear they're worse than this – sleep with your back to the wall kinds of places. I had benefit for a while, but there's a cap on claims after the first year. In any case the money went to feed and clothe my two kids. I had to sell my house, my cars, and ninety-nine per cent of my stuff to pay my debts. I refused to go bankrupt. The silver lining… I now have a job, no debts, I support my family, and I live here. No rent, no facilities."

"But why stay here at all? You could have stayed with your family. No need to be a hero." She's angry and her eyes are moist.

"There's no way I can give you a satisfying answer. I've tried." Her glare challenges me to try again. I dig deep, ignoring the nonsense about pride, about wanting to stand on my own feet, to fix what I broke myself, or even something feeble about the mother-in-law. I shrug. "Shame, mostly. Cowardice. Humiliation. I couldn't look in my wife's eyes, my kid's, without seeing a judgement, an accusation of failure. This is my punishment."

"Idiot. Didn't you realise that you've been punishing them too?"

Something dislodges inside me, like a heavy weight shifting. "I used to have bad insomnia. I was afraid I would lose everything. One day someone told me the only cure was to think through the worst that could happen. So what if you lose your job, you'll still have your health – that kind of thing. I never for one minute thought it would be like this. But you're right. I shouldn't be here. None of us should."

I cough, catch my breath and cough again. Must be the bad air.

"Are you alright?"

"Yeah. Guess something went down the wrong way. Let's get you to the morgue."

We hail a taxi from the top of Byres Road to the Saltmarket. Rachael winces when she looks at the meter, but she pays anyway.

"I have a car, but it's sitting dry since what was left in the tank got siphoned out. Couldn't afford to put petrol in it anyway."

"What do you do?" I say, pulling my coat tight against the thin wind coming off the Clyde.

"Primary teacher." She shrugs.

I clear some phlegm from the back of my throat and lead her to the wooden door. I'd heard they had planned a new mortuary at the Southern General. Guess it didn't work out. This place has been used for centuries. People were hung on the Green over the road, a short journey from the old High Court next door. I ring the bell and we wait in silence.

The door opens and a woman wearing blues nods and invites us in. She shows us to a small waiting area where there are only four seats. "We'll be ready for you in a minute." She brushes hair behind her ear, smiles briefly and leaves.

We wait for nearly twenty. I'm about to go and find someone when the woman returns.

"Sorry about that. They brought everything in the tent for some reason. We had to check it all, just in case." She looks how I feel. A bone-deep weariness has crawled into me.

"Just in case of what?" Rachael stands up.

"If it had turned out to be a suspicious death something in there may have been relevant to the enquiry. Are you ready to formally identify the body?" Her tone is soft, unthreatening. I forgot the people who work here are trained doctors. Good bedside manner for the dead.

"So what was it?" Rachael says.

"What was what?" the doctor says.

"If it wasn't suspicious, what did he die from?"

"Oh, right. We're putting it down to hyperthermia."

We follow her down the hall and into a side room. There's a large pane of glass between us and the steel slab. On top of the slab is a body draped in a green sheet. A man with a white beard and glasses walks over to the body and angles something hanging from a large light.

"If you look at the monitor, please." The woman indicates an ancient CRT TV bolted up high in our room. It shows the covered face. The man pulls back the sheet to show a skull with a thin veneer of flesh that just about looks like Albert. "Do you recognise this person?"

Rachael stares at the monitor. "He's so thin." Her voice breaks. "Yes. That's my Grandfather, Albert Morrison." Her composure starts to slip. I pass her my unused hanky.

"Thank you. Let me take you back to the waiting area. I'll get you the completed death certificate and your grandfather's personal effects. Can I get you some tea while you wait?"

Another hour seems to pass. I don't know what to say and Rachael stares at the mauve wall ahead of her, hanky in one hand, Styrofoam cup in the other.

"If it hadn't been for you, he wouldn't be dead," she says.

"I don't see what I have to do with it." I'm know I'm not responsible for the collapse of the finance sector, or her grandfather choosing to live in a tent in a park, but I feel a stab of guilt anyway.

"You let him stay there. You should have told him to go home. You could have checked up on him." Her eyes are hot while her cheeks are wet.

"Maybe I should go."

"And run out on your mess? Seems like a regular habit."

I push down my anger, stand up and open the door as the doctor comes in carrying two large carrier bags and a backpack. "Sorry, I didn't see you there," she says, as I brush past her and out into the cold. The raven is sitting on a railing waiting for me. "And you can piss off too," I shout. The night air hits my chest. I double over and cough up a large radioactive glob into the gutter. This isn't good.

I don't wait for Rachael. I'm not running away. I just don't feel like being a relative stranger's punching bag.

I walk home and can sense the bird gliding along in my wake, but I don't care anymore. I'm too tired and cold to care.

Back in my tent I think about calling Kathryn. It's late. Maybe I should leave it until tomorrow. I call anyway, and tell her I'm sorry, that I've been a fool, that I'll move back in. We don't need to do this. We can be a family again. The answering machine cuts me off.

Between fits of coughing I manage to fall asleep.

Sweat has soaked through my t-shirt and my sleeping bag feels damp. I have a raging thirst. My head is pounding and I can't breathe through my nose. My chest feels like a huge stone has been placed on it. I fumble around for some water, but the bottle is empty.

I put on some clothes and immediately start shivering. I make my way to the toilet block and need to cool down again. I've had the flu before, but never like this.

In a pained blur I go down to the Byres Road supermarket. I wait outside for it to open, like a junkie. Once inside, even the cheapest paracetamol is barely affordable. I dry-swallow two on my way round the aisles. I get enough dried soup for a couple of days, but I've almost no money left. I'll have to risk the water from the taps in the toilets. Maybe a little lead might help kill the bugs running through my body.

My limbs already feel like they're made from it – alternating between molten and cold.

My tent is more welcome than ever. I listen to the radio on my laptop and drift in and out of sleep, in and out of sweat. I'm sure the crow is in here with me, talking, but I can't make out what it's saying. Through the fog in my head it sounds like, "You're dyin."

"It's just the flu."

Is this what really took Albert, not the cold? I hadn't heard of any bugs going around. He's the first to get sick here. How long since anyone got typhus or cholera in Glasgow. Maybe it's bird flu from my new friend. I almost laugh, but it's more a gurgle in the back of my throat.

"No. You have pneumonia."

"You're not a doctor. How do you know?"

The bird stands on my chest, talons like little pin pricks, and says, "I'm a shaman. You will be too, if you want to live."

Chapter 5

I'm standing, fully clothed. At first I think I've wandered out of the tent in a fever, looking for water – I'm so thirsty I could drain a river and still not be satisfied. A mist covers everything, and there's no sound. Is this another dream?

I take a few steps but the fog is so thick I worry about walking off into someone's tent, or into traffic, or off the edge of a cliff. Something tells me I'm not in tent city, and this isn't a dream.

"Where am I?"

"Think of somewhere memorable, somewhere relaxin." Corbie's rough crawk sounds like he's on my shoulder, but he's nowhere to be seen.

The mist begins to clear, burned off by the noon-day sun. I'm on a rough beach next to a huge weathered tree trunk. Worn stones and broken shells cover the ground. Just ahead, a thick bar of fly-blown seaweed marks high tide. I turn around to where the dry grass starts and look to the top of the tall thin pines. The blue sky has a few light clouds and several distant gulls circle. The air is fresh, the sun is warm. I feel a smile growing.

Corbie lands on the trunk beside me. "Where are we?"

"Somewhere near Fort William. I think that's it, over the water." On the other side of the loch are houses, Ben Nevis towering over them.

"Childhood holiday?"

"Aye. We spent a week here in a wee cottage just up the road. I found a paperback of *Ice Station Zebra*." I pick up a stick and prod at the ashes of someone's fire – the black soot ringed by burnt stones. "Why are we here? And how do you know about the pneumonia?"

"I told you. I'm a shaman. I could tell just by lookin at your soul. In order to get better you'll have to begin your trainin. The Great Spirits are getting impatient with you, so they've made you ill."

"Great recruitment scheme they've got there. Conform or die."

"If it is any comfort it happens to most of us. No one volunteers for this."

"I feel really special. Just when I thought I was at the bottom, turns out I wasn't."

The raven makes a thick throaty sound and I realise it's laughing. "You're nowhere near bottom, yet."

I sit on the log and watch the water on the shore. The rhythmic lapping is calming. The light sparkles across the waves. "I'm a man of silicon and cities. These 'Great Spirits', who are they?"

Corbie lifts his wings up a bit – some kind of bird shrug.

I'm shocked. "You don't know? You're taking orders from them and you don't even know who they are?"

"Why should I? They're ancient, subtle, alien. I've never met them. Archetypes would define them too strictly. Demean them even. We could call them Bear, Stag, Anansi, Odin, Tenjin and it wouldn't make a difference."

"Subtle as a brick if you ask me. What do you mean alien? Are they ETs? Am I an abductee?"

"Maybe I should have said other." A cold breeze runs up the loch, ruffling the bird's feathers. "We should get started. We don't have much time."

"Make a start on what?"

"Find what's makin you sick. Usually there's a part of your soul missin. Maybe it got snagged somewhere. Or somewhen."

I laugh. "Now I know I'm really sick. Not only am being commanded by spirits, I'm hunting parts of my soul. This is some fever dream." I mark ashen circles on the rocks with the stick.

"If this was a dream you'd have little understandin and even less control."

Walking down to the water's edge, I stare at the stones at my feet. Picking up a perfect flat one, I turn it over a few times, feel its smoothness. Then I hunch down and skim it out over the loch. One, two, three, four, five, six, seven skips and it sinks down – a record. Never had more than five before.

Great Spirits. I laugh to myself. Having rejected all that religious crap when I was thirteen, I hadn't given it much time since. When the dreams started Mum insisted I was a shaman. She and my dad had blazing rows about it. He was a down to earth engineer; it was all in my head. No spiritual reality for him intruding into his son's consciousness. I just needed a good head doctor. Maybe he was right. But they looked hard enough, tried all the therapies they could think of. Still the dreams would come. Until last night.

Hallucination or not, perhaps this is just my body speaking to me, finding the mechanism to heal itself. "How do we find a piece of soul?" I say. "What does that look like?"

"You're going to hate this, but you'll know it when you see it."

"I always find things in the last place I look. Maybe I'll find it there."

Corbie blinks. "That's smart thinkin, but a bit too smart."

"Well maybe if you stopped being so fucking obscure that might help."

The bird flaps its wings, glides onto my shoulder, and whispers in my ear. "I'm not tryin to be obscure. I'm tryin to help you work things out for yourself. There's no Internet here to help you find the answers."

"Isn't there?" This is my dream, isn't it? "Computer, where will I find a lost soul?" To my surprise, a window opens up before me with a list of search engine results running down the pane. My mind is doing a good job of improvising. The Island of Lost Souls, The Bell of Lost Souls, Lost Souls the movie, the band, the game, the book, the album, some porno site with Goth girls – the list goes on. None of it very useful in itself, but it triggers the right connections. "The Land of the Dead. Where else?"

"Well done."

"Gee, thanks. How do I get there without, you know, actually dying?"

"It's also called the Underworld for a reason."

Feeling like a bit of an eejit, but not humiliated, I start looking around for somewhere to go down. Orpheus went in through a cave I think, but there was a dog and a ferry-man. In my pockets I have 30 pence, not bad for dream change. That wouldn't even get me through the turnstile for the toilets at Central Station. "I don't think I have enough coins for Chiron."

"That's okay. The route we'll take you won't be needin it. Just have to cross the hair bridge," Corbie says. "If you can't find a path on land, maybe there's one beneath the waves?"

At the edge of the loch, the salt water laps against my boots. Despite the sun, the water is slate-coloured and opaque. It looks cold. But I remember that childhood summer, disturbing crabs that lurked under the seaweed, and in and out of the water all day. I wade in. The water rises up over my boots, running inside, wicking up my trousers. It's cool and clingy and I shiver. I force myself to keep going. I may live in a tent, but I've grown up a soft city-dweller. The water rises up to my knees, my thighs, my hips and I go under. Full immersion. The salt stings my eyes, the water is cloudy with silt, but I can see well enough to find my way. Hopefully there are no conger eels or other large beasties lurking out here. A few meters out there's a hole where the raised beach falls off into the fjord. Clumsy in my clothes, I swim over to it and it looks like I can squeeze in. I look around for Corbie, but can't see him. I know what I have to do. I break the surface and take a deep breath then plunge down into the tunnel. Going in deep, my shoulders occasionally scrape the rock and then I realise I have no idea how far I need to go. The rock seems to push in on me and I have to hold in the air I have left. I push on, close to panic and then there is light up above. I kick upward, desperate. Bursting through the surface, I gasp for air. It is a few moments before I take in my surroundings. I am in a cave, a hole in the roof opens it up to the sky. A full moon hangs there perfectly illuminating the cave.

I pull myself out of the pool, water streaming down me, clothes a second wetter skin. The air is cool in here. I wring some of the water out of my shirt and trousers before peeling them back on again.

On the wall there are images, drawn in silver by the moonlight. Most of them are diamond shapes or the outlines of hands where paint has been blown over them. There are herds of bison. One or two are more complicated; a man appears to have been lanced by several spears, another has bird wings, a third has human rear legs, the body and tail of a deer, the arms and head of a human, but the face looks like an owl and antlers emerge from the head. All of them are done with perspective, like the Lascaux cave paintings. They look very real, rather than representative. Reflections from the pool almost seem to bring them to life.

Absorbed in these pictures, my clothes have dried, when I hear a scuffling noise. Could it be an animal coming home, or looking for a drink? I've not seen any bedding or bones. Maybe there are other people here, people trying to find their lost souls. I don't know what to expect, friend or foe.

Edging towards the slope leading up to the cave entrance, I feel nervous and afraid. I follow it up to the hole in the roof and poke my head out. The landscape is flat, empty except for a few weathered rocks and spiny bushes. Desolate is the word that comes to mind. Far in the distance mountains rise up, capped with snow. I'm almost glad that I can't see any dead people. Nothing is moving, except curls of dust, so I emerge feeling a little more confident. How could anything live here anyway? I must have heard the wind eroding rock or some loose stones finally losing to gravity.

There are no clues to which way I need to go, no river to follow, no handy signs. I start to miss Corbie. Where has the little bastard gone to? At least he knew what was going on. I must have been desperate or deluded to agree to this.

My body must have been found by now, given some antibiotics. I'll be better soon, come round. So who found me? Albert, who looked out for us in a way we clearly didn't look out for him, is in the mortuary or more likely a funeral home. Depends what day it is. He'll not notice anyone missing their routine now. What about Kathryn? She'll call me back, get worried when I don't pick up, come looking for me. Kathryn who's divorcing me. Moving on. Loyalty all used up, squandered while I slept in a park. There is no one at work. They'll only notice me gone if a server goes down and stays down. Maybe Sindi in the café? Sure, like she's going to miss a light tipper. This is my own mess, and I'll have to do it myself.

I follow my nose. It picks a mountain and I start heading towards it. I have no idea how much time is passing. The stars don't move and the constellations are unknown to me. If it wasn't for the moon I'd wonder if I was on an imaginary Earth at all. Come to think of it, the moon hasn't moved either. Its full face beams down at me, dumb, smug and benign. I look back and can't make out the cave I crawled from. The mountain is just as far away. It's like walking through a painting. I don't feel tired. I don't feel thirsty. More than anything I'm plain bored of stubbing my toes on rocks and my legs being stabbed by the thorny bushes. I sit down just to have a break from the act of walking. Closing my eyes, I try to wake up in the real world, in my tent. When I open them again I'm still in the desert, and nothing has changed. I feel angry. This is so stupid. I'm trapped in my head – hidden in a dream.

A dream. My dream. Who's in charge here? I've dreamed I'm naked at school. I've flown. Sometimes I'm naked then too. Dreams are never this…concrete, but it's all in my head.

I rise up into the air. Just an inch, then two. I move forward in the air, a millimetre, an inch, a foot, a metre. And then back again. I levitate higher. If I fall I'll either die or wake.

I conjure a ball of fire in my left hand, a sword in my right. I keep my clothes on. You never know who you'll meet.

Corbie said something about a hairy bridge. It sounds unpleasant – a matted nest of grease and lice, rather than shampoo ad silky.

Rising up into the air, higher and higher, my horizon recedes away. There is a cleft far off, almost beyond my sight. So far off that I can't be certain it isn't just a fault in the landscape.

Flying towards it, slower than walking, I feel slightly sick, like I used to in the backseat of the car when dad was driving. It passes and I try moving faster and faster. I'm at running speed, sprinting, and then flat out cycling. No bugs here to fly into my eyes and mouth.

The cleft broadens as I get closer. And deeper. It isn't a cleft. It's the wall on the far side of a canyon. A Grand Canyon. The far side is several miles away.

I fly over the edge. Then my support is kicked out from under me. I fall.

The edge slips past.

A long, thick root rushes toward me.

I hit it, hard. I slide off, and fall again.

My hands grasp it and hold.

My shoulders creak and my back muscles strain. But I hold on.

My heart is racing, my breathing heavy.

Looking down would be a bad idea. I know there is a clear mile or more to the bottom. My arms send me messages in pain. I ask more of them as I pull myself up onto the root. I straddle it and lie flat, resting for a moment.

The root tears grey soil from the canyon wall.

Slithering along it, I get up onto my feet as it comes away. Smaller roots stick out and I grab hold of them, pulling myself up towards the edge of the cliff bit by bit. My hands slip. My feet scramble for purchase. My grip is strained. I haul myself over the lip and stay there face down in the dust.

Eventually the pains in my arms, my chest, my back, all fade into the background. My breathing returns to normal. I sit up and try to wipe the dirt from my face using a hand caked in earth.

"What took you so long?" Corbie is perched on a large stake beaten into the ground.

I throw a clod of earth at him. It misses by miles and falls into the abyss.

"You need some anger management lessons," Corbie says.

"Where the fuck have you been?"

"Right here, at the hair bridge."

"I can't see any bridge."

"Look closer."

I look around, but the only object here is the stake. A thread is wound around the top, and then a single fine fibre stretches out from the stake and across the chasm. "What the hell kind of creature has a hair long enough to cross over a canyon?"

Corbie just gives his Gallic shrug.

"Since I can't fly over, I'm guessing I have to do some kind of high wire act on the hair." It can't be done. A hair that fine will snap as soon as I put my weight on it.

The bird just looks at me.

I get up, feeling stiff and raw. There's about two metres of hair before it passes over the edge and out across the wide canyon. Lifting my left foot onto the hair, I push down with some of my weight. Any moment I expect it to break and Corbie to rawk with laughter at his practical joke. The hair shifts a little but takes the weight I put on it. I increase my weight and to my surprise it appears to support me. Lifting my right foot I try to balance on the slender thread. I put my right foot down onto the hair and shift my weight forward. So far, so good. But I can still fall off onto dry earth. Moving my left in front of my right, my leg quivers as it tries to keep me upright. I put my arms out into a T-shape. I cross another foot over and come near to the cliff edge. The hair starts to give a little as it stretches under my weight.

While I want to jump off right now, I want to reach the other side and I know that it will be easier if I keep moving. Corbie jumps up onto my shoulder. I rock from side to side as I compensate for his weight and the surprise of him jumping on me. "Don't look down," he says. His thorns pass close to my ear, scratching the air beside it.

"I'll do my best not to." I would have batted him off, but I know it would only lead to me falling. Moving forward again, one foot is over the air. My breathing quickens. Sweat breaks out on my forehead. My back and armpits are wet and my shirt sticks to my body. I struggle to regain control.

Slowly my breathing returns to normal. My legs feel weak already. There's still a long way to go. I've haven't done anything like this since PE in primary school. It's fair to say I was more interested in PCs.

I put another foot in front of the other, leaving the safety of the earth behind. I put another in front, and another. I start to gain confidence as I get some rhythm to my movement. Another foot and another. Another foot and another.

"Eyes front soldier." Corbie seems to sense my desire to turn my head to see how far I've gone. "Don't look down. Don't look left. Just look ahead."

"Yes, sir!" I keep on shuffling forward, feeling the empty space around me. It's like when I was flying, except I don't feel in control. I laugh. Is this a lesson or am I just seeing parallels?

"What's so funny?" says Corbie.

"I realised just how much we depend on things we can't see, we forget they're there. Like this bridge." I keep putting one foot in front of another. The soles of my feet are starting to hurt. The trembling in my legs is almost uncontrollable. I feel like I've been walking for an hour. "How much further?"

"I think you're about halfway."

"Great." A drop of sweat drips down off my nose. I can't help it. My eyes follow it. I look down. Just for a moment. There's no bottom to the canyon. It really is an abyss. It stretches down forever. No end, just darkness. Are there stars? It pulls me down.

A savage pain rips across my ear. I snap back. And lose my balance.

I stagger forward and back trying to right myself. I sway to the left and the right.

Corbie swings out like bullion in the back of a bus, before hopping across me to help me correct myself. I finally regain control but my legs are stiff rubber. Blood trickles down my ear onto my shoulder where Corbie slashed me.

Slowly I put one foot in front of another. My arms are heavy. My shoulders ache. Moving forward is the only way. One more step brings me one more step closer to the far side. The long line across my sight nears.

I try to lift my foot, but it won't come up. My legs are tired but not that worn down. I pull as hard as I can risk without overcompensating. It's like my shoes are stuck to the hair. The other one is the same. I risk a quick glance down. The hair is like a fine cheese wire. It has cut into the soles of my shoes. Turning my feet slightly helps me move forward, but makes balancing harder. Only a few more steps and the hair cuts through the soles again.

I reckon I'm about three quarters of the way there. The fine wire starts to slice into the soles of my feet. Each step is slippery, each foot-step tricky, as I negotiate the lattice of existing incisions on the soles of my shoes, bearing the pain as I shift my weight, and then must try and get the ruins of my shoe loose again.

The far side is clear to me now. I can make out the stake the hair is suspended from on this side. It looks hauntingly familiar. For a moment it feels like I have gotten turned around and returned to where I came from. I almost let myself fall out of despair. But a small red ribbon whips out from around the stake.

I wish I could run the last few steps, but reaching the far side soon resembles Xeno's Paradox as I weakly make smaller and smaller forward movements. As it causes the hair to slip deeper into my calloused soles, I try not to slide my feet.

My final step is onto land which takes my whole weight. The dry dust sucks up the blood drips. I pitch forward as my leg collapses under me. Corbie flaps off. I don't even have the strength to turn over. Once more I just lie there breathing dirt.

Something jabs at my face and I bat it away lazily with my hand. Scorpion! I turn over and shuffle back. Only it's Corbie standing next to where I was lying. "I'd strangle you if I could hold onto your neck."

"We need to go," Corbie says. "You're dyin, remember? No time for lyin around nappin."

"Okay, okay. Just give me a minute." My shoes are cut to pieces. I try to take them off, but what's left of the inner soles is stuck to my feet. I strip away what I can and leave the rest. It's like opening a lobster. Habit makes me want to eat, but I have no hunger or thirst. My muscles feel okay again. However, every step lights up my feet with new agonies. "What is the point of that bridge? Couldn't they at least put a wider rope in?"

"Too much pressure would cut right through someone heavy. Your spirit is light enough that you could cross."

"Because I'm dying?"

"Because you aren't weighed down by your life."

"Isn't that the same thing?"

"Not at all."

"Where are we going now?"

"We still need to find a lost part of your soul."

"Shame we don't have a GPS tag on it." It feels like I'm in a shower of light. I'm beginning to recognise this as a Eureka moment. I don't think I'm in my imagination anymore – the bridge was the crossing point I expect. Surely I'm still connected to this lost part of myself? Would it have made much difference if I'd thought of this earlier? "Computer, locate my lost soul and provide directions." There is no reply.

"That was a good idea." Corbie lands on my shoulder again. "This is the Underworld, you're a shaman. Things don't work like that."

"If only there was a bird whose entrails I could consult instead."

A window opens up. In the top right is a bird's eye view of the local rocky terrain with a blue line across it showing a route. The main part of the window is see-through, but shows an arrow that appears to be a few metres ahead of us. An arrow pointing the way.

I blow a raspberry at Corbie. "Looks like augmented reality just saved your gizzard."

"If I had a hat I would take it off to you." Corbie bobs down in a way that seems like a bow. "I tell you, that's the first time I've been surprised in quite some time."

I start following the route, each step hot and sharp, leaving a trail of blooded footsteps behind us. The ground begins to change, turning from dry earth to slabs of warm stone, as though it retained the heat of the day from a scorching sun. Then the dark stone looks organic, rippled and folded – thick cream that petrified.

After a while we come to a round hole. Perhaps this was an old volcano cone. The GPS indicates we should go down. I can't see how to do that. This does remind me a little of the cave where I came into this place. Walking round the rim I think I see a pool of rich cobalt blue water at the bottom. A wisp of steam moves across its flat surface, I'm sure of it. If I'm wrong, if I'm actually looking at volcanic glass, the drop will shatter my legs, and the shards will slice up what's left of me.

I find a loose rock and drop it down. There's a small splash. Risky.

Hesitating won't get me anywhere. I slide over the lip where I think there is most water, lowering myself down until I'm hanging by my arms. I close my eyes, and let go.

After a brief moment of weightlessness I'm wrapped in a warm wet cocoon. Then I burst out of the water. Corbie glides down towards me. My eyes adjust to the gloom. Stalactites and stalagmites look ready to chew on anything between them. The water has a light whiff of bad eggs. A very polite entrance to Hell.

The GPS points me to the back of the cave where there's a wide tunnel of ribbed stone like a giant's calcified intestine. I follow the tunnel until I hear a shuffling, snuffling sound. Something breathes heavily and moves restlessly. Has it caught our scent? Surely we're masked by the sulphur from the pool? Around a curve the tunnel widens out and I guess it becomes a room. I peer into the darkness trying to see what is further round the bend.

Lying on the ground is a giant dog, a bit like a German Shepherd. Perhaps sensing my approach it lifts its head, then lifts it again, then lifts it a third time. It's hard to understand what I'm seeing. It stands up the same way. It's at least my height. Watching it gives me motion sickness. It's like there is future movement, the actual movement and then a trailing movement. I remember early pop videos from the 1970s with dancers surrounded by pre and post motion ghosting.

I sneak back up the tunnel. "There's a guardian," I say.

"Couldn't let any old riff-raff into the Underworld." Corbie's whispers, like mine, echo up the tunnel. "Think of it as your final challenge."

"So this is a test?"

"We've had a perfect pass rate, so far."

"Death is a strong incentive." I sit down on the tunnel floor. It feels warm. "I guess that's the Cerberus of legend. Three headed dog. Guards the way to Hades."

Corbie studies me, like he is waiting for something. I remember my driving test. The last one. The look on my instructor's face not knowing if I'd passed or failed again. I wasn't sure even with the paper in my hand.

Hercules wrestled it into submission, like everything else. Orpheus played his music. I doubt I have the strength or the musical talent, but without some drugged meat those are my options.

I stand and walk back down the tunnel, starting to whistle a tune, but I can't remember the notes. I try to make something up, but it's got no melody. All the songs I've ever known flee my mind. There's a snarl as the dog hears me coming. "In the town where I was born, lived a man who sailed to sea," I sing, my voice thin and trembling with nerves.

Walking into the hound's lair, it's immediately on its feet, growling. There is another tunnel beyond it and as casually as possible I head towards it, still singing. When I get to the chorus it is infected with the changes from childhood. "We all live in a tub of margarine, a tub of margarine, a tub of margarine."

The dog's lips are peeled back from teeth as big as my fingers, but it doesn't move.

Halfway across, I forget the next verse. It's just gone. My mouth starts another round of the chorus. Cerberus must like it as he hasn't pounced on me yet. Down the tunnel out of this chamber, blocking the whole passage is a heavy wooden gate, separated into two halves. The left half is slightly open.

The dog takes a few steps forward and I freeze, my song falters. It looks like it's going to leap. I remember singing my kids to sleep. "Twinkle, twinkle, little star, how I wonder what you are." Then, in a gravelly bass, Corbie joins me. "Up above the world so high, like a diamond in the sky."

Cerberus sits down on its haunches, watching me cross his cave. I back into the tunnel that leads into the Underworld. Passing through the gate, Corbie skips in behind me. I slam the gate shut and swing down the bar. My song ends and Cerberus barks. It hurts my ears, but it sounds like a demand for more.

Neither of us cares for an encore. I realise my heart is racing hard. Turning around, I see that we are now in an impossibly large cave. We stand at the top of a path that winds down to the cave floor like a Swiss Alpine road. The cave itself has an entire city within it – a true Necropolis. There's a Downtown of cave scraping towers straight out of Manhattan or LA. Thousands of cathedrals of all styles mingle with parks in which henges compete with barrow mounds for space. I see all sorts of hanging trees ripe with strange fruit. There are not so much roads as motorways of the Dead. Pyramids, mausoleums, mountains of bones sit beside the architecture of every civilisation.

Silver light diffuses through the city from the far side of the cave, as though a giant moon is reflecting off wet walls. It is bright and hurts my eyes.

"What are those?" I point to tall thin spires with platforms on top of them.

"Excarnation towers." Corbie waddles along beside me. "Put a body on top and in minutes vultures would have stripped the flesh."

There is a huge thud and I nearly jump out of my skin as the hinges on the gate squeal. The wood strains, but the gate holds. A number of angry barks drown out any thought. A moment later another impact rocks the gate.

"Don't worry. He can't enter the Underworld. The best he can do is open the gate again," Corbie says.

"He sounds pretty pissed off." I walk backwards keeping a close eye on the gate. "You'd think they'd change the situation. Breed a dog that's immune to a showtune."

"I guess they don't get enough visitors to make it a problem. Besides, we've still got to get back out again. It's like escapin from Alcatraz."

"Where are you from, Corbie? You seem to know a hell of a lot about the modern world."

"You thought that I was from some primitive tribe who lived in the dark ages or somethin? I died in the early seventies. The nineteen seventies. I was shamanizin in California and Nevada during the Hippie days. I got turned on at the New York World Fair in 64, before heading West. To be honest, I don't think I fully realised it at the time. I just helped people take their first acid trips in teepees. They saw new worlds and I still can't believe they grew up so square, denying the opportunity to everyone else. I died thinkin I could fly." Corbie flaps his wings. "Is this ironic or poetic? I reckon I was spiked by the CIA, their MK-ULTRA program. It wasn't just me, you know. So it wasn't that long ago, and I keep an eye on what's going on."

"The CIA tried to kill you?"

"They didn't try. They succeeded."

"Right."

We wind our way down towards the cave floor.

"Have you trained anyone else to become a shaman?"

"You got me there, bud. I'm earning my wings with you." Corbie laughs his phlegmy laugh. "One thing you need to know – gettin here with drugs ain't the way. You're here now in a kind of exhaustion induced ecstasy, that's the way to go. It's harder but it's all you. No filters. The shamans started using drugs and drink to get to the spirit worlds because the powers that be made the walls thicker. They decided man wasn't worthy anymore. They've changed their minds. Takin away the spirit worlds has only made things worse."

"The Great Spirits decided that we weren't getting into the club because we didn't have the right trainers on?"

"Smart casual only. We'll get back to the right sneakers later."

We enter the Necropolis itself. The streets are packed with people. Up high I couldn't see them for the buildings, but down here – I've never seen so many. Not in London on a sunny Saturday afternoon, not in New York on Black Friday, not in Edinburgh at Hogmanay. It seems like Mardi Gras, there's a troubadour with a mandolin, a Duchess from Versailles with elaborately stitched wide skirts scraping the tarmacadam, someone in a bright orange space suit emblazoned with a red hammer and sickle flag under the letters CCCP, any number of people in suits carrying briefcases and umbrellas, Roman legionnaires struggling to keep in formation, large shields locked, spears raised. People from every time and place. All intact. No wounds, no grave worms. In death as they were in life.

"This is the opposite problem to before," I say. "Now we have too much civilisation when before we had just desolation."

Corbie flaps up onto my shoulder. "Is your map still workin?"

I've been looking through it rather than at it. The arrow points the way. The overhead view shows a staggered route through the city heading Downtown. A flashing dot indicates our destination. "Not far to go. But this could still take some time."

Despite the crush, the crowd makes room for us.

I turn to speak to a cowboy, but he looks away. The thank you dies on my lips. Time and again no one will engage with me. "Guess they're not in a chatty mood." It's deadly silent here. So used to the desert above and the endless emptiness, I'd not noticed before. No murmur of a crowd, no traffic noise. Even our footfalls are quiet. Our words sound harsh and unwelcome like farts in a lift.

"What's that?" says Corbie.

"Nothing." No wresting any secrets from the dead. "It's like they don't want to see us, or touch us."

"Would you want to be reminded of heat and life?"

"I would be desperate, hungry for it. I'd expect to be beating them off like some kind of zombie apocalypse. Not parting the Dead sea."

Even with the crowd accommodating me, it takes a long time to follow the route to its end. In front of us is the highest scraper in the city. The plaza is clear of the dead. Even the steps leading up to it are free from the crowd.

A long queue leads up towards the building entrance. The area is roped off, but there's no red carpet, just a concierge with a frown and a lectern, like these people are waiting for their table at a high-class restaurant. While the concierge is dead, the people in the queue are more vibrant. They each have something or someone with them – cats, birds, wolves, a Native American tribesman, someone wearing a stag's head with antlers or a live version of what I saw on the cave wall. Shamans, like me.

"Don't think they were expecting a rush," I say.

"The Great Spirits must have given their gift to many. But if you think about it, this is still only a handful."

Over near the door I see something that looks like me. It's see through, like a ghost, a shade of pale, milky green. It is trying to walk through the glass – a bee buzzing against a window. "What do we do with it, now we've found it?"

"Reintegrate it."

"Don't we need to cure it or something?"

"No. It is the loss that is causing the sickness, not anythin in the shade itself."

"Why does it look so green? It doesn't look too healthy."

"This particular piece has that colour, that's all. It could just as easily have been blue or red or somethin else."

"I guess I just merge with it then?" I walk up to the velvet rope and get a twitchy look from the concierge. I cross a leg over and she is over to us in an instant.

"What do you think you are doing?"

One of the dead talks. She looks straight at me instead of out of the corners of her eyes. "Retrieving my lost soul." I nod towards the doors. "Let me just get it and I'll be gone."

"There's a line."

"Whatever it is they're here for, I'm not," I say.

"You're here to see the Chairman."

"No, I'm here for the soul over there."

"You're a shaman. You need to see the Chairman. You need to sign a contract with him."

"To get my own soul back?" This is stupid. It's right there.

"To leave."

"Can I get my lost piece first? I'm dying."

"You'll get it when you see the Chairman. If you want it back you need to agree to his terms." She speaks to me like I'm an idiot. I look up and see the damned soul piece has made it into the building lobby.

"Corbie?"

"I don't see we have much choice," Corbie says. "The Chairman is the boss, this is all his. Looks like we need to show him due respect, you know."

"Shit." More delay. I look at the line. It stretches across the plaza and down around the block. "Ok." I walk to the end of the line and stand next to a woman with a pyjama monkey clinging round her neck. "Hi. How are you?" She looks at me like I'm a bit slow or a foreigner who can't be trusted. The pyjama monkey stares at me with cold button eyes. Makes me glad I've got a raven made of thorns.

Time passes. The queue doesn't move. More people join – a teenager from Malaysia with a disturbing puma-shaped shadow that has yellow eyes and a large American woman with a reddish grey squirrel. The queue doesn't move. Time passes.

"I think the bureaucracy is broken," I say.

Corbie pauses his preening. "Perhaps it's workin exactly the way it's meant to."

I think I understand him. Leaving the queue, I walk round the side of the building. It's smooth concrete with windows starting a few feet above my reach. I follow it around to the rear. Corbie skips over the paving stones to catch up. "A-ha." In the middle of the wall is a fire exit, propped open with a fire extinguisher. Who could be nipping out for a fag-break?

Opening the door, there's a concrete corridor that makes a left turn ahead. No one is about. I creep in, just in case. Corbie catches up and I close the door after him. The corridor makes another left and ends in a wooden door. I open it a crack. The lobby is in the distance and four lifts are nearby, two on either side of the door. No guards patrol inside. There's only the concierge outside. I suppress a laugh.

We enter the lobby and I push the button to summon a lift. We wait. Time passes. "What the hell is it with this place? Does nothing work properly?" And the lift goes ding. I look around. It sounded loud enough to hear from outside. The doors open and I stride in, Corbie following. What floor do we want? I stab at the penthouse and the circle round the button lights up. There's a lurching tug as the lift moves off.

Standing in silence, I watch the digital numbers rise. "Why did we not see anyone before Cerberus? How did they all get here, and how often must that dog get tricked before someone suggests they need better security systems?"

"Maybe they got here through a different route. I only know this way, other shamans, other cultures, may have other challenges. It could all be different next time. Don't be too hard on Cerby; he's there to keep the livin out. You're borderline and you carry a tune better than you think."

The numbers keep rising and the lift keeps going up with them. After an age the lift stops, the doors open and we emerge into a grey marble lined hall. My footsteps echo as I walk. Corbie skitters across the highly polished floor so I lift him onto my shoulder.

Ahead of us are two doors made from a wood I don't recognise. I'm reminded of the dense knots in walnut but the colour is deep red like mahogany. Split across the two doors, engraved into the surface, is the image of a tree, gnarled and twisted. As I approach there appears to be a fruit suspended from a bough, but in front of the doors it is gone, just a trick of the light. There is no handle, so I push. The doors swing open smoothly.

Inside is a modern boardroom. Dark glass table, chrome and leather chairs. A man stands with his back to the door looking through the panoramic window at the city below. The Chairman surveys his domain.

He turns at our intrusion. "I wasn't expecting anyone today."

"We got that impression," I say. "Your staff kept us waiting a long time. But if my friend here is correct, I don't have time to wait."

His grey hair is short, similar in style to that seen on statues of Roman generals, Julius Caesar or Marcus Crassus. The deep set no-nonsense eyes, hard mouth and slight frown add to this impression. Careful, Kol'ka, careful.

"We better conclude our negotiations promptly then." The Chairman smiles.

"What is there to determine?" I say. The Chairman looks at me. I can almost hear Corbie slapping his forehead.

"Tribute. Compensation." The Chairman seems to be having difficulty getting what he wants out. "Rent." He sneers. The words are beneath him and I have forced him to say them.

"I apologise for the rude intrusion." I blunder on. "I didn't expect to be here or I would have brought something. I just want my soul and I'll be going."

"What you want is mine to agree or deny."

Cold slides down my spine. I have nothing. What does the King of the Dead need anyway? I can't give too much away. "I will abstain from drinking caffeine for a year."

Corbie jumps on my shoulder. "Buddy, you got to do better than that. This is about more than your soul. You will come back here for other people. Why should he let you in? Why should he let you leave? You die topside where else are you going to go?"

"A hand. You choose which."

"I will abstain from caffeine, alcohol and tobacco for five years."

"Really?" Corbie nips my ear. "Man we're never getting out of here."

"Two fingers. Different hands."

"I will abstain for a decade."

"An index finger."

"An offering of grains, fruits and other crops."

The Chairman almost laughs. "The fat portion of the firstborn of your flocks." There's almost a twinkle in his eye.

This sounds familiar. What are the Halal and Kosher rules? "A small animal sacrifice one a year."

"A large animal, once a week."

I'm tired of this. I want what is mine back. It's like losing my ball in next door's garden and being charged to get it back. "No."

"What are you doing?" Corbie hisses in my ear.

"I owe you nothing but an apology for intruding on you without an appointment. I am not one of your subjects. If I visit again it will be to retrieve something else lost by the living. Nice try, pal, but no."

The Chairman smiles. A genuine one this time. He claps, a little sarcastically for my liking. "Well done, Mr Munro. You can't blame me for trying."

I give a slight nod. "I'll let you get back to work." I walk back to the doors which had closed behind me and push them open.

"Oh, and congratulations on becoming a shaman," the Chairman says. "I look forward to dealing with you again in the future."

We head back to the lifts. I didn't ask about getting my lost property back. Lead sinks in my stomach. I've played too clever and now have to go back again.

"Where you going?"

I turn to Corbie. "To get what we came for."

"You did well. It'll be downstairs."

The lift arrives and we travel down in silence. Physically I'm fine but mentally I'm knackered. Will I wake up in my tent embalmed in my own waste?

The doors open and the greenish misty version of myself walks into the lift. It walks into me. It feels like I'm showering in fine jelly and it tingles a little.

"Feel better?" says Corbie.

I don't feel any different. "No."

"I'm sure you will when we get back."

"Do we have to go back the same way we got here?"

"We can go into the light. Either you'll wake up or at least get to the Middle World."

"The Middle World. Where we started?"

"That was a memory. The Middle World is the spiritual mirror of the Living World. Next time we go on a journey that's where you'll start."

Walking across the building lobby, the bright silver light outside is masked by tinted glass. We go through the rotating doors and I hear a murmur as the queue of shamans sees us emerge. I approach the concierge. "The Chairman will see the next one now." I feel her eyes burning into my back as I head towards the light.

It's still a long way across the city. We pass pyramids of various sizes, great statues of heroes and kings, anonymous in death, strange egg-like capsules made of metal. The houses of the dead are open and empty. The crowd is still there, parting for us, but one or two of the dead risk a glance in my direction now, making eye contact for a moment before breaking. I see a plea, but I don't know how to help. Across the whole city there are too many.

We try to stay behind buildings as we get closer to the light. It is so bright it washes out what little colour is left – everything is turned to chrome or darkness. Finally, we reach the edge of the Necropolis and stand in front of this light with no shade between us. My eyes are closed and still the light blinds me. I turn away and walk backwards.

I see the shade of Albert on the fringe of the city, waving. I don't know what to do. "Should I speak to him before I return?"

"Who?" Corbie says.

"Albert," I say.

"I can't see him."

"He's right there." But he's gone.

Covering my eyes with my arm, I walk into the light until it engulfs me and there is no darkness anymore.

Chapter 6

Opening my eyes, there is no canvas above me. I see the white tiles of a suspended ceiling and hear the regular beep of a heart monitor. There is a needle stuck in the back of my left hand and the heart rate sensor is pegged onto a finger on my right. I tense. I've been in places like this before. My arm is heavy but unrestrained. I breathe, but remain unsure, uncertain.

Is this real or just what I would expect to see? The Underworld was just as vivid as anything in – what do I call it now? The real world? What did Corbie calling it? The Living world? Sounds like where you go to watch TV.

"Hey. How are you?" I recognise the voice, but I can't place it. Her face comes into view above me. Rachael, Albert's granddaughter. What's she doing here? Maybe it's a dream after all. "I'll tell a nurse you're awake," she says and walks out of the door.

There's no other bed in the room. Grey light comes through a window, but I can't see outside. There are flowers and a card on a table beside the bed, along with a plastic glass and a jug of water. My thirst is raging. I try so sit up, but I have no strength in my arms. The needle slides inside the back of my hand and I collapse back into the soft pillows. The room lurches and I feel like I'm going to be sick. It subsides and I watch fluid from the bag drip inside the tube that connects to my hand. I still don't know where I am, but this isn't an NHS ward.

Rachael returns with a nurse in crisp whites. "Let me have a look at your husband." Husband? Then I catch up. "How are you feeling Nicholas?" The nurse shines a torch in my eyes and puts a machine in my ear.

I try to speak but my throat is dry and sore. My chest feels like it has a boulder sitting on it. Dry swallowing, I try again. "Like crap."

The nurse examines the machine. "Your temperature is coming down. You're past the worst of it. I think we'll be keeping you here for a while longer though. We'll see what the doctor says this evening. Drink plenty of water." She leaves.

"Does the other Mrs Munro know I'm here?"

Rachael shrugs. "I'd be surprised. Your phone is locked and no-one has called while I've been around. I got the rest of your stuff too, for safekeeping." She smiles.

"Thank you. I'm sorry for just abandoning you."

"I should be the one apologising. You helped a total stranger and I dumped on you."

"What day is it?"

"I found you on Sunday evening. It's now Saturday morning. You were pretty far gone."

A week? I've been out a whole week. I reach out towards the plastic glass but it's too far away.

"You could just ask, you know." Rachael tops up the glass. She helps me sit up and holds the glass to my dry lips. A little water trickles in. It hurts as I swallow greedy for more. Another little trickle. She repeats this until the glass is empty.

"Thank you. You're a natural."

"My mother was in a place like this, before the end."

"I'm sorry." My playful smile fades fast.

"I better go. It's good to see you're back in the land of the living." She gathers her coat and bag and turns at the door. "I'll see you soon."

I lie back and look at the ceiling. Corbie is not about. Could it all have been an hallucination? My body was already fighting the bugs a few days ago when I met him. The bird was just part of that battle.

That doesn't explain my nightly torment ending at the same time. It had never paused for any illness before.

Opening the drawer in the bedside cabinet, I see my laptop in there with my mobile on top. I pick it up and see that it is switched to silent. I haven't missed any calls.

I wake in the night and shuffle into the en-suite. The catheter was removed earlier. This is gonna hurt. Fire shoots up my dick and into my bowels as water flows out. Instead of just getting it over with I keep stopping and starting.

Back in bed I lie and stare at the ceiling. Outside a cat yowls. I don't know where I am. I haven't even looked out the window. This could be just as much a phantasm as the Underworld.

Lines and shapes and faces appear in the shadows on the ceiling tile. Reflections of my mind. Cognitive illusions. What is real anyway? Philosophers have wrestled with it, yet here we are, whatever the theory. Assuming the existence of those philosophers is not just part a clever simulation. It all felt real even if some of it wasn't possible in the Living world – I could fly, there were strange creatures and weird objects. Yet they all responded to me in ways that felt...natural, there were rules even if the rules were different, rather than in a dream where it all seems random. I could control myself and what I did – I've never done that in a dream.

A stranger rescued me while there's no word from my wife. I understand she wants out because I've been selfish. I've been foolish, I recognise that, and yet I get no response at all? A day or two I could understand but not this long. We usually talk a couple of times a week. Why would she go silent now? Rachael's attractive, sure, but not a total fantasy. If I'm still deep inside my head, wouldn't I invent a voice mail from Kathryn, a more beautiful rescuer?

I have a talking raven, worlds to explore and a fucked up life.

Emptiness fills my chest and the back of my throat feels hollow. I want to cry but only dry tears will come. My sobs are just noise.

There's a footstep behind me, but nothing more comes of it.

After a while I stop feeling sorry for myself. I have my health after all.

When morning comes I feel raw and delicate. Soon the lights are on and the nurses bring breakfast. Just toast for me. The smell of bacon nearly drives me crazy. I try to remember my last proper meal. Does a fast food burger with the kids count? My stomach growls after my second slice. I feel stuffed and ravenous at the same time. The hospital tea tastes great, but I had to ask for a fresh cup without milk. With no fridge in my tent I gave up on it months ago. Spoons of lovely sugar are welcome too.

Someone asks me if I want a paper. I have to admit I've got no money. They laugh and tell me it's complimentary. No wonder, it's just a big advert. Even the articles are previews for those in magazines. Nothing much has changed, except I don't feel like I live on planet earth anymore. I feel like a visitor. Around me a small army starts cleaning my room and presumably the rest of the ward. This isn't like any hospital that I've ever heard of. Rachael must have some mighty fine insurance and unhealthy guilt issues.

Time passes without any sign except the coming and going of meals and nurses' shifts. I don't want to turn on the TV or even switch on my laptop, to which I'm usually wedded. Picking up my phone, I check it for calls. What am I waiting for? I should tell someone in my family that I'm sick. If my wife isn't interested that leaves my mum.

I'd do almost anything to avoid this call. She'll turn it all into a great drama. She'll nag me to move in with her. I can't do that. Maybe if I don't have to stay here any longer I could go home to my tent. I've found what was missing. My body will do all the rest. And I'll avoid running up a larger bill for Rachael.

Dragging the drip over to the closet I find all my stuff in there, mostly in my Bergan. Even my tent is here, packed up. My pitch has gone, I know it. It was a good spot and I'll not see it again. Maybe I can go where Albert was. I remember the empty yellow pitches. Maybe not. My legs are weak and I have to go back to the bed.

I should call Kathryn. What if something has happened to her? So busy wrapped up in myself here I'd not considered that. Was I due to see the kids today? She'd have been certain to call if I was late, so I guess not.

Picking up the phone, my fingers find the right contact. Before I realise what I'm doing it's ringing. If I hang up she'll only call me back. "Hi Mum, it's me."

"Nikolasha? Where have you been? Why do you never call? There must be some crisis."

"Mum, you know I hate being called that. There's nothing to worry about."

"Pfft. A mother will call her child what she likes. Are you still in that field?"

"I'm in a hospital."

"What? And you didn't tell me? I knew something was wrong. A black cat walked across my path yesterday." I hear her sound like she is spitting. "I will be there pronto. Which one are you in?"

"Sorry. I've been very ill. I didn't think to send a message to the spirits to tell you." It's easy to fall back into my usual disdain, but could I have?

"You've been in some kind of a coma that you couldn't call?"

"Actually, yes."

There is silence.

"Which one? I'll be right there."

"Which coma?"

"Which hospital are you in? Stop playing with me, Kolya."

"I don't know."

"How can you not know?"

"Mum, I just woke up for the first time in nearly a week. I didn't think to ask which hospital I was in."

"Well go find out and call me back."

Getting up on unsteady legs, I head for the door. I have no idea where the nurses' station is. Given my condition, it can't be far. I walk out the door and see it just to my left. There are a couple of nurses on duty there. On the right the corridor continues in a light yellow shade, doors leading off to other rooms. I feel nervous. Just what kind of hospital is this after all?

"Mr Morrison, what are you doing up? Come on. Let's get you back to bed."

"Could you tell me where I am?"

"In hospital, dear."

"Yeah, but which one?"

"The Niniane Institute." Perhaps I'm a little impatient – she makes it sound like this should be obvious.

"I thought that burnt to the ground."

"It was rebuilt."

I'm led back to my bed. After she stops fussing and leaves I text my Mum. I tell her to ask for Morrison. I lie back and wait for the thunder.

Barely an hour later, there's a commotion out in the corridor, and I know it must be my Mum. She storms into the room wearing leather jeans and leopard print top. Her hair and heels add a few inches. I grew up feeling like Gulliver in Lilliput. She hugs me to her tiny frame and kisses me three times, alternating cheeks. I start to rub at the lipstick smears that will be left behind.

She perches on the end of the bed. I wonder where Corbie is. Maybe now I'm better I won't see him again. "Nikolasha," she says. "What happened?"

"Mum."

"Kolya. Speak to me. I want to know."

"I got sick. Pneumonia. A friend found me and brought me here." I don't know Rachael, but only a friend would put me in a private hospital on their health insurance. A stranger would have left me in the doorway at A&E. Some people have committed murder that way.

"Yes. But there is more, yes? Come on, it's no hassle." Her Russian accent still lingers, but her *hassle* is pure Glasgow. "I can see there's something you're not telling me."

Oh, God. "The nightmare is gone."

She looks at me like she doesn't believe me. Then it clicks. "Blya! I knew it. Your father was all psychiatrist this and ECT that. I'm so sorry, Kolya. I should have been stronger for you."

"He thought he was doing the right thing, mum."

"The road to Hell is paved with good intention."

"What's done is done. I turned out alright. Mostly."

She smiles. "Lovely wife, two kids. I made the right offerings on your behalf. It kept the spirits off your back."

"Hate to think what life would have been like if you hadn't." I smile to take the edge off. "By the way, Kathryn is divorcing me."

" 'By the way'. It's that easy for you? Is it this Morrison 'friend' of yours?"

I laugh. "This is ridiculous. I'm barely keeping things together and you take my wife's side. I'm not seeing anyone. Kathryn told me, asked me, last Saturday afternoon. I met Rachael over her grandfather's corpse that evening. I've pretty much been in the Underworld since then with a spiky parrot. It's pretty fucking far from easy."

She pales. I don't think I've seen her do that before. I imagine it happened when they told her about Dad, but I was at Uni. She holds my hand. "It'll be alright, Nikolasha." I let her have that one. "What's for you won't pass you by. Tell me about the Underworld. What is it like?"

I describe for her a moonlit cave, an empty quarter, my fall into the Abyss, the traversal of a hair-thin bridge, outsmarting Hell's hound with Lennon and McCartney, cutting through the eternal bureaucracy of the dead, and dealing with the First to die.

My mother weeps gentle tears. I have seen wonders she has dreamed about seeing and I never wanted to. "What now?"

"I have no idea," I say. "If I disobey the Great Spirits' wishes I get the feeling that they would make me sick again, give me back the nightmare. It's a real stick and stick approach they use." At least Abraham got a nation, those televangelists get their riches.

"I told yo–"

"Mum. Don't even start. I didn't want it then. I don't want it now."

I was dragged to institutions by my Dad and any number of psychics by my Mum. If I wasn't having my blood taken and my stool examined by a medical doctor then it was a voudoun priestess. Since neither could cure me I lost faith in both of them. And the spirits, they kept looking for that damn bone every god damn night.

"It's a gift, Son," she says. "A gift from the spirits themselves."

"A curse more like. Whom the gods seek to destroy they first make mad."

"I thought they first answered their prayers."

"You may have prayed for this. I certainly didn't." Old words, worn like comfortable shoes. "As soon as my teacher returns I guess I'll find out."

"They sent you a spirit guide?"

"Corbie, a bird made of thorns, looks like a rook or crow. It talks like a New York surfer dude."

"The spiky parrot."

I nod. My eyes are tired and it is hard to keep them open. Mum must see them flickering. "I'll let you get some sleep, Kolya." I feel her kiss my forehead as I slip away.

Chapter 7

I sleep for days. Not all the time, but most of it. Occasionally I eat, and I'm visited by Rachael, who tells me about her family and her job. Mum comes and tells me I've been chosen and it's a privilege and as soon as I can I'm going to stay with her.

"Listen, there's something you need to know," I say. I've got to tell her sooner or later.

Rachael looks concerned. "What is it?"

"I don't know quite how to describe it." I look at the sky through the window. "When you found me I wasn't just suffering from pneumonia. I was being press-ganged."

"Press-ganged? They still do that?"

"No. I mean I've had this dream. Since I was fourteen. Every night I was torn into pieces. These creatures were looking for something. They found it. The night before we met, they found it. And this talking bird appeared..."

"A talking bird? Are they still giving you morphine?"

"...and told me I had to train to be a shaman or I'd get sick and die. And that's why I got sick. While I was out of it I had to travel to the Underworld and find a piece of my soul. I know. It sounds crazy. I sound crazy. But trust me I know what crazy is like and this isn't it."

"You're a shaman? Like some kind of Native American? Isn't that a bit racist or something?"

"The word comes from Siberia so not really American at all. Shamanism is more like some hokey religion from ancient times. They intercede with spirits on behalf of the tribe. I think I just passed the entrance exam. I've still to get the induction video and the safety talk."

"So it's more table-tapping and ectoplasm then?"

"You're taking the piss now."

She smiles. "No, that's the nurse's job. So where's this talking bird?"

"Corbie's not here. I've not seen him since I woke up."

"That's handy. You're sure you didn't just hallucinate the whole thing?"

"You could be right. I'm sure I saw him the night we met though."

"Your own harbinger of doom. You should take it easy. Tell someone if you see this bird again."

It's good advice, except when it comes to tricks of the mind I've got used to keeping it to myself; saved myself another trip to a healer who couldn't help. I wasn't sure about saying anything to Rachael. I don't know why she's doing all this. She barely knows me. She might be able to laugh it off now, but sooner or later she'll realise I'm serious.

The dream may have gone, but I can still feel the hot lances piercing me. I remember being dismembered. It's an up-front no holds barred warning that the life of a shaman is one of pain, humiliation and death. What a privilege that is. If you can't handle it, get out now. Except, you have no choice once you're chosen. The spirits are gonna ride you til they're done. Or you put a bullet in your brain. So am I a horse or a corpse?

Feeling well enough to open my laptop, I check up on work. Horse or corpse? Everything is working fine without me. Horse or corpse? No email that was urgent. Horse or corpse? If I'm lucky no one will notice I was off sick and I'll get full pay. Horse or corpse? I catch up on some tech news. Horse or corpse?

I can be a horse. No one has to ride – a mustang roaming the prairie. Can't I?

Showing the Chairman of the Underworld I wasn't going to play his game means that I can show the rest of them I'll do it my way. Or I'll choose the corpse option. Better to die on my feet than live on my knees. I'm making too much of this, a melodrama out of a crisis.

Tap, tap, tap.

There's a hunched shadow behind the blind covering the window. I walk over, the drip no longer needed. Corbie is sitting on the sill outside. This is one of those environmentally controlled places. "Either walk through the wall or come in the door, the window doesn't open." I go back to the bed.

Corbie sits on the end of the bed, looking at my records upside down.

"That doesn't help me know if you're real or in my head."

"What's the difference?" Corbie says.

I shrug and laugh. "You know I've actually missed you. I didn't really have anyone to talk to. Mum is wrapped up in it all and I don't want to freak anyone else out and have them lock me up in a loony bin."

"You mean Rachael."

"I told Rachael about you. She thinks you're a morphine dream. I mean the nurses. I'm sure they could find a couple of doctors to agree with them pretty quickly."

"You've been here too long. You've got used to being fed like clock-work, lights out, lights on. You're institutionalised. Like a pet rat in a cage."

Or a horse in a corral. "Back to the Gardens then." It's cold outside. It'll snow soon.

"I still have a lot to teach you."

I get my rucksack out of the cupboard. It smells musty, as do my clothes. After putting them on I feel more normal. My prison robe I discard on the end of the bed. I pack the few things I'd got in the room, collect my toiletries and edge to the door. Away from the nurse's station, at the end of the corridor, is an emergency exit. It's my only way out without facing the Spanish Inquisition. I follow the nurses' movements and when I'm sure none of them are between me and the way out I go for it.

Walking in my boots feels weird and they make an annoying rubbery squeak on the polished floor. Everyone can hear me coming. My hand rests on the small lever over the lock. The metal is very cold and my arm breaks out in goose bumps. Where are my gloves?

"Go on." Corbie has waddled down the hall behind me.

I swallow and push down on the lever. The door swings open and the cold draught takes my breath away. I rush outside onto the fire escape, slam the door shut behind me, and clatter down to the foot of the stairs. There's miles of walking to get back to Glasgow. In front of me is an evergreen forest and behind the hospital building a hill rises up to a grey sky. Following the road is out of the question – I may be found and persuaded to return. I head into the dense conifers behind the small hospital.

Looking back I see that the hospital was once a castle, the typical Scottish solid box shape. Crenellation runs around the slate roof, small turrets occupy the top corners. To either side wings have been added in tasteful wood, glass and stone that matches the original building. My room was in one of these wings.

I smell damp pine and resin as I crunch over brown needles. The trees are tall, the boughs curling up at the ends like arthritic fingers. It's been a long time since I felt such fresh air on my face. I'm invigorated and cold.

Brushing aside prickly brambles and avoiding roots and branches I make slow progress through the forest. I stub my toe on a slab of stone and stumble into a clearing. The ground is littered with fallen tombstones. Only a couple remain standing to show this wasn't some loose crazy paving. The forest is encroaching though as little saplings emerge from the spaces between stones and moss is trying to cover everything. Beyond the ancient cemetery is a round building with a metal cross sticking from its roof. A church of some kind, but not one I've seen before. It's holding up better than the graveyard next to it.

It would be good to stay and look around, but I want to make decent progress before dark. They may look for me here as it's close to the hospital.

I text Rachael – Felt well enough to leave, thanks for your care and support. Hopefully she won't be too mad with me.

The easiest way back to Glasgow will be to go over the hill. I'm used to camping out, but not really hiking. Is this insane, should I go back now? What if this crazy idea to walk back is part of the illness or the drugs? I trudge on without an answer. Corbie has gone AWOL again. My pack is heavy. Absolutely everything I have is on my back. It isn't the end of civilisation, but this is what it would be like. A long walk in the forest, unless everything burns first.

Do I have enough change for the bus? I could get on and ride past my fare. Hope the search party doesn't notice me waiting in a bus shelter. Why am I so sure, so paranoid, that they'd send anyone anyway? I remember that they always did before.

I start walking up the hillside. The trees give me something to cling to until they find it too steep themselves. I have to zig zag back and forth. Just as I get to the brow of the hill I find it wasn't the top after all. There's a long flat bit ahead and another steep slope beyond. Trudging through the scabby grass is like the walk through the moonlit desert in the Underworld. I got past that by flying to the abyss. Can I fly to Glasgow? Land like Superman in the Botanic Gardens. I stop and give it a try. Closing my eyes, I will myself to rise. I open them again, one at a time. I'm right where I was, on terra firma. Just for a moment I felt lighter. I thought maybe…maybe I'm an idiot with some real problems. Fucking fly home. Who am I kidding?

I walk on, the wind making my eyes water.

The top of the slope isn't the highest point on the hill either. I walk round instead of over. Passing a rocky outcrop the Clyde valley opens out before me. Glasgow sprawls across it, some tall blocks still stand, but most of them have been levelled since I was small. Windmills turn lazily on the hills on the other side. I feel a fierce pride. It might be a crime-ridden grimy shithole, but it's where I live. My city, my home.

I sit down and give myself a break. Unlike the Underworld my legs ache with the exertion. My chest feels like it's under a rock. I don't know if I should have left. The familiar rumble of hunger rises in my belly. How quickly we adapt to luxury, take it as a given. This is the beginning of that near permanent sense of something missing – but also the satisfaction of being fed.

I can go back. I can eat. I don't need to do this. But I do. I have my doubts, my weaknesses. I don't want this, this life. But I need it. It calls to me. The comfy beds, the regular meals. It isn't me anymore. I think Kathryn knew this when she asked for the divorce. I could go back, but I'd not be happy. She knew I wasn't ever coming back. My place is in the tent city. I didn't know what it was before. I couldn't say that I've been fulfilling it up to now. The role of shaman is not one anyone there would recognise. Hell, I barely know what it is myself. But the *sense* of it, the *feel* of it – like running my hands over the body of a lover in the dark – it feels right.

It's downhill all the way from here to the West End, even on rubbery legs I should make it. Using the distant spires of Glasgow University I orientate myself. Half a dozen carefully tended golf courses, numerous farmed fields and then the streets of Maryhill if I'm not mistaken. I'm no expert but it must be about five miles across country.

It's after dark when I get back to the Botanic Gardens. I can almost feel frost growing on my brows and cheeks. My body is warm, wrapped in coat and jumpers, my head in a hat and the coat's hood. As soon as I slow down though the cold will seep in.

As I expected, my spot has been taken. I don't recognise the tent, so it could be someone new. But no one told them it was my spot.

The ground is hard. I don't think I'd put my tent up well in the dark either. I look over to where Albert's tent was only a couple of weeks ago. That space and those around it are taken too. Despite the winter really starting to bite the camp appears to be growing. I'll know better in daylight.

I wander over to the main gates where Byres Road and Great Western Road meet. The church on the other side lies derelict. The artwork inside its roof burned away with the rest of the interior. An insurance job was the implication in the press and on the street. Like the nightclub in the listed building that got torn down. The stones still stand here however. Maybe I can find a nook for the night and set up my pitch in the morning. I stash my pack in the bushes beside the gatehouse. It's good to get it off. I stretch my back like a cat.

On the other side of the ragged Keep Out tape whipping in the icy breeze is nothing but treachery and charcoal. Sodden beams, fallen masonry and the heavy smell of charred wood. I was married here, when it was an entertainment venue, beneath the constellations painted on the ceiling. Now the stars have fallen and there's no shelter here.

I retrieve my pack and look at the wall between the railings and the gatehouse. I've seen it, but not paid it any attention. It rises up to head height, made from sandstone blocks, with a slightly oval capstone sitting on the top. There's a short section at this end, and a longer section heading parallel to Great Western Road. I follow it round. It's like a tall isosceles triangle with the top part lopped off – the short end where I started. No doors, no roof. With difficulty I pull myself up onto it and catch myself from falling. On the other side it goes down below ground level. Four thick iron I-beams span the gap. The inside of the wall is lined with small rectangular ceramic tiles, which where once white or grey. It's too dark to make out, but there is something flat down there.

Of course. This is an air shaft. Someone once told me there used to be a railway line along here. The station must have been near here too, where the bushes and trees get thick beyond the airshaft wall. Perhaps it too burned down in suspicious circumstances. I must be looking down onto the platform.

It looks too far to drop without twisting an ankle or falling onto my back. Although maybe from one of the crossbeams it might be okay. If they left this open and exposed what about the remains of the station. Along the road there's a wall breaking up the perimeter railings. Now I come to think of it, a relatively new one too.

Getting off the wall, I go to where the bushes and trees look impassable. Crawling under a well-developed rhododendron, I can just about see that most of the area has been reclaimed by nature, but there are two spaces around which is a low fence made of rotting wooden posts and wire. Inside are iron stairs, leading down.

I straddle the fence easily and go to where the steps start. The wooden treads are almost gone, showing a honeycomb of metal beneath. I'm not confident about the iron holding together. This must have been exposed for at least thirty years, probably more. I test it with my weight. It holds. Taking the next step down, I try to be as light as possible. The metal flexes and I rush down to the first landing which feels more secure. The final set of steps I take in another rush.

The platform heads into gloom towards the north, to the south light comes through from the air vents. There is a platform on either side of a wide ditch where the rails would have sat. This ditch is overgrown with bushes and thorns. In summer it must be a jungle. Pools of water lie scummed with ice, but my breath is no longer steaming. I rummage around in my pack for my torch, but I can't find it. This is what happens when someone else packs your stuff.

I head into the gloom of the south tunnel which leads towards Kelvingrove. It is lined with red bricks and my footsteps echo. I hadn't expected it to be dry in here, but the Victorians must have built in drainage when they made the railway line.

I follow the tunnel until I can barely see anything. The ground here is flat. There doesn't seem to be any rats. I take out my mat and my sleeping bag, remove my boots and climb in. It only took a fortnight, but I've forgotten what it was like sleeping like this. I can feel every brick under my back. I hear drips of water echoing down the tunnel. An ambulance siren brings me back just as I'd nearly nodded off.

I feel like I'm falling into the darkness of the tunnel above me like I was falling into the abyss.

Chapter 8

An ambulance breaks my sleep again. It must be returning from the callout. It's much lighter in here. I can see the roof of the tunnel. Snug and warm, I'm content to stay here. The light is bright and sharp though and won't let me get back to sleep. My phone is dead, so I have no clear idea what time it is. I'm pretty sure it's Friday, must be after nine to be this bright.

I look down toward the platform. It seems unnatural. Clean and fresh compared to how it seemed last night. After crawling out of my bag, I walk towards the stairs. Nature calls. The sight is beautiful and terrifying. Jack Frost has been hard at work. The whole platform area beneath the air vents is covered in a fine white down, from the hard surface of the platform itself to the spindly limbs of the trees growing in the centre.

If I had been outside last night I would have died for sure.

I take even more care going up the rusty steps to the surface. The orange corrosion is quite clear against the stark white. I emerge into a crisp fantasy world. Every bush and tree is heavy under snow with a thin hard film on the surface. My breath is heavy in front of me. It feels like the moisture is freezing before it hits my face. I clear the fence and duck through the bushes. The tent city looks like a number of strange hillocks. I would never have been able to walk through this if I'd left today. The men's facilities are more Baltic than ever. I don't want to touch the seat in case my flesh bonds to the plastic.

My stomach feels like an empty pit. Getting up has woken it. I've not eaten since yesterday lunchtime. Only a few weeks ago this was hardly unusual, but I also walked five miles too over countryside. My legs are stiff and heavy. I'll need something to keep me going in the cold.

On my way back to the station I see Janice struggling out of her tent. I start to move some snow out of the way. Janice starts and Brutus begins yapping. "Jesus, Nik you scared the shit out of me. We all thought you was dead. Got whatever Albie had. I thought you was a ghost. Thing is you look less like a skeleton now."

"Soft living in the hospital."

"You shoulda stayed there. Jesus, Nik, if you can afford hospital what the fuck are you doing back here?"

"I wasn't footing the bill."

Janice has a knowing look on her face. I expect her to wink saucily at me. "You shoulda stayed there," she says. "I'm sorry, someone took your pitch. No one ever comes back, you know. We thought you was dead."

"That's okay. I understand."

"Where did you stay last night?"

"In the railway tunnel. It's so much better there than here, Janice. You should join me there. Everyone should. We'll freeze to death up here. It's snug down there, and with more of us it'll be warmer."

"What railway tunnel? Nearest station is Partick."

"The Victorians built a line that runs under the Gardens. Plenty of tunnel, and out of the elements."

"How'd you get in?"

"The old station is gone, but the stairs leading down are still there. Look I can show you."

"Aye. Maybe later, Nik. I need to walk Brutus here."

"Ok. I'll be about." I expected more enthusiasm, even from Janice.

I head back to my stuff to get ready for work. I really ought to check in. If I'm lucky I may even have been paid. There's a grating scream and the step gives way beneath my weight. I'm suspended in space, then fall through the gap, landing hard on my left leg. It is rammed into my hip socket. My knee is bright blue pain.

The demon tugs my leg off. My skin rips like thin paper.

Flakes of rust and snow fall onto my body. My arm feels wet. Have I slashed it open on the metal?

Feeling something jabbing at my cheek, I swat it away. It comes back.

"Get up," Corbie says.

Slowly I come up to sit. My head is throbbing. My arm is cold and wet where it had broken through puddle ice. Pain flares in my hip when I shift my weight. "Fuck."

"Dude, why are you always in some mess when I come and look in on you?"

"Maybe you're the cause?"

"I see your humour hasn't broken." Corbie stands beside me, head tilted up.

Carefully I come up to stand. It feels like a lump the size of an egg has grown on the back of my head. My stomach growls. I laugh. I can't keep it in. It's almost hysterical. I just can't seem to get an even break. "Let me guess. Playtime is over and it's time to go to school?"

"Yeah. If you're well enough to throw yourself down some stairs…"

"Can I get something to eat first?" I hobble along the platform to the tunnel, careful not to slip on any black ice. "Then I really have to check in at work."

"What were you plannin?" Corbie glides along behind me.

"I know a great place to get a bacon roll and tea. You got twenty quid you can loan me. It'll be my treat."

"Sure I got it right here." I look up from stowing my toothpaste and brush. If the raven can get us money then things might not be so bad. "Aw crap. Looks like I left my wallet in my other pants. Tell you what I'll get the check next time."

I am such an eejit. I grin despite my pain.

The café is warm and welcome as ever.

"Who's been feeding you up?" Sindi takes out her pad and comes over.

I smile. "I was in the hospital. Pneumonia."

"Sure, we nearly went out of business without you."

"I'll have the usual, please."

"Breakfast of kings it is then." She waits.

"Sorry." I wave my phone at her terminal, but it's dead. "Shit. I forgot to charge it."

"Hey, don't worry about it," Sindi says.

"Gimme a second." I remember I still have some change from the hard currency that Kathryn gave me and dig the crumpled notes out of the pocket I'd thrust them in.

"I think she digs you," Corbie says, after Sindi's gone. His talons dent the fake leather upholstery on the couch opposite.

"Yeah. She's a waitress. She digs me until I've paid the bill, then the smile slips. I used to like the old indifference more. It was at least real. Once someone brought the great American customer service over, everyone had to do it."

"No, I get that. I think she really digs you, man."

"So what's the plan?"

"You should ask her out on a date."

"I'm not divorced yet. That's not what I meant anyway."

"You got work. Then I guess you learn."

"How do we start?"

"We'll take it as it comes. You seem to be with the programme now, but I think an element of surprise would do you good. Keep you on your toes. You just sort out your work life and we'll get into it later."

"Who you talking to?" Sindi places a plate with a bacon and egg roll and a mug of tea in front of me.

"Oh, just myself. Just planning my day."

"You know what they say about people who talk to themselves?" she says, with a playful look.

"No. What do they say?"

"They have a great conversation." She laughs.

I laugh too. It sounds fake to me.

"I'll see you later."

The tea is scalding hot, the bacon crisp, the egg just runny enough. It's Friday and I've earned it.

There's no rush getting to work. The office is quiet. Checking the servers, everything is green. I should be grateful that nothing went wrong while I was ill, but I'm peeved that I'm really not needed. I'm proud of the code I've hacked out, it works well. It's what I was paid to implement. I'm worried that someone will notice and terminate my job. I manually set up some stress tests and go through the server logs while they are running just to be sure the software hasn't missed something and should have alerted me. It's not long before my stomach is crying out for food again. Eating is a habit that I'd successfully gotten out of.

I chew on a pen and sip water from the cooler in the corridor. It reminds me of quitting fags all over again. At least there's no one here to get grumpy at. Even Corbie has buggered off. I think he's allergic to technology.

When I leave to go home I see Corbie through the glass in the lobby. Looks like it's time to go to school.

"It's not easy voluntarily enterin the Otherworld." Corbie sits on my shoulder and talks into my ear. "If it was, everyone would do it, and there'd be no need for shaman. You need to reach a state of ecstasy, an altered state of consciousness. Sure some drugs will take you through the door, but like bouncers they'll throw you back out again and sooner or later the landin will be rough. In my case, literally."

I walk up Woodlands Road, close to where Corbie first introduced himself a fortnight ago. It seems much longer. I guess the Sleeping Beauty act didn't help.

"You got dancin, jumpin, runnin, fuckin, almost any kind of physical exertion, until exhaustion. You got meditation, but that's real hard. You can use music and drummin for all of them. Breathin right is helpful."

"That sounds tough. I can't imagine the sexual technique is easy without an understanding partner."

Corbie's laugh sounds like he's bringing up phlegm. "It helps if you're both tryin to get there. Boy that brings back some memories. Free love, man. A whole tent of people tryin to get to Heaven. It's all gone so borin."

"Sounds kind of icky to me. You don't know where anyone else's been. Who knows who's sticking what where… "

"That's what I'm sayin. Borin, dry, caged in your ways. Don't knock it til you tried it. It's about trust, about love. People you trust and love ain't stickin anythin anywhere you don't want it."

"So entering an ecstatic state… "

"Yeah. I'd recommend we go the exhaustion route first. Then if the meditation route don't work you got somethin to fall back on. Either way, you gonna need a drum."

"I can't afford to buy a drum."

"Who said anythin about buyin one? You can make one."

"So I need some plastic for a skin, a bucket or something for the body and something to tie them together."

Corbie laughs. "You need skin for a skin."

I turn up towards Great Western Road. "Some Hannibal Lecter thing? I don't think so."

"Hannibal Lecter?"

"A serial killer cannibal."

"Why did you go straight to human skin? A deer would be fine."

I shrug. Corbie has to keep his balance. Digging his thorned talons deep into my skin makes me gasp, but an electric thrill runs through me too. It's like playing with a milk tooth before it falls out. "Why an animal skin?"

"Dude, you're a shaman. There's no power in plastic. No life lived through it. When are you going to get it? This is about blood and pain."

"You're wrong. It's about minds and symbols. We do that rather well these days. Even if it means wearing out the meaning."

"You may be right. On one level. But nothin works so well as the real thing. You'll know it's not real. Even if the drum makes a sound it won't be the heartbeat of the animal itself."

"What about the rhythm of the city? The almost imperceptible flicker of fluorescent tubes, the underground trains moving in perfect time from station to station, the morning inhale and evening exhale of commuters?"

"That's not life itself, that's an abstraction."

"Ha. An abstraction is just a symbol. A symbol is a state of mind. I think therefore I am. Symbolically, there's no difference between the simulacrum and the simulated. If there was, the Otherworld would not be meaningfully real."

"Okay. We'll try it your way for now." I feel more than see Corbie lift a wing and dip down in some semblance of a bow. "We'll make the drum out of somethin symbolic. I still think it would be good for you to learn how to hunt an animal and tan a hide."

"Thank you. I'm sure I'm not supposed to take a life unless it's necessary or some flower power crap like that. But I'm willing to bet those streetlights have spirits too."

"Don't push your luck, buddy."

"Hey, I'm on a roll here." I feel a light buffet of a wing by my ear. "Hey."

"That was a symbolic knock upside your head. Let's get the materials together first."

We reach the gates into the Gardens. "I'll unpack my tent and get that setup. When I've found my torch we can go looking for what we need. Maybe get some food too."

Down in the tunnel I'm reassured that my stuff is still there. Not a word from Rachael. I thought she'd be mad with me for walking out. I take out my phone. Still as dead as it was this morning. Stupid Kol'ka didn't charge his phone up at work. The tent won't provide any power as it's not been set up for ages. I'm pretty sure I'm meant to see the kids tomorrow. It's amazing that Kathryn hasn't been in touch at all for two weeks. Either I've really freaked her out or something's wrong.

I set the tent up and unpack my things. Corbie supervises when he's not nosing about in my pack. The brick floor is pretty uncomfortable, but I'll see if I can find some cardboard boxes to pad under the tent. Should I light a fire? There was an agreement between us and the city council that we wouldn't light anything other than gas stoves in the park. Down here is another matter. No doubt someone will see the smoke and I'll have the Fire Brigade giving me a good dousing.

Amongst the flotsam and detritus along the Kelvin River I find what I'm looking for – a wheel from a bicycle, about the size of a bodhran and a large piece of plastic sheet from an advertisement, a large eye is printed on it. Several cable ties I liberate from round a lamppost.

Back at my new home, I knock the spokes out of the wheel and use a couple of sticks to brace across its full diameter. The sheet I cut slightly larger than the wheel and secure it tightly using the cable ties. If the plastic slackens I hope I can tighten it further. My new drum makes a deep, dull sound. The resonance lasts for longer than I had expected and echoes in the tunnel.

Corbie doesn't appear too impressed. "What's so symbolic about this? An eye? Isn't that a bit obvious?"

"Don't you think that splashing around a riverbank in the dark of winter and we find a large enough piece of material, that just happens to have an eye on it just a little unexpected. Besides I like that it is made of tokens of the modern world; industry, invention, and advertising."

Corbie is just a dark smudge in the black tunnel. It is too dark to see his eyes. "You should get started on the first run through," he says. "If you're ready."

I've no idea what time it is and I have a nagging feeling about seeing the kids tomorrow. "What happens next?"

"Start trying to get a rhythm goin, keep it simple and sustainable. Your arms may start gettin tired but you gotta keep goin. When you feel it workin into your bones move about."

I start hitting the drum with the tips of my fingers. It sounds okay, but doesn't feel right. Instead I use the heel of my hand near the rim like I've seen bongo players doing on Buchanan Street. This is much better and I can move my hands faster and with less effort. I soon get the hang of keeping a rhythm going, although not a very fast one.

Every now and again I feel a little spasm. Like the jerks of my body as it starts to fall asleep. I try to control these until I remember Corbie's suggestion to move with the beat. I feel weird and distinctly self-conscious despite there being no one else around. Each twitch of movement takes me out of control of myself. My arms start to feel leaden and my wrists are aching but I if I stop I'll only have to start all over again with a bird nagging at me to do better. The judders begin to occur more regularly and I feel my feet and legs move, even my body twitches. This probably looks like the worst Dad-dance ever. I'd never get up at clubs, in the rare times that I went, unless I was very drunk. My face burns with embarrassment.

The spasms and jerks begin to feel less random and more in time with the beat that is harder to sustain. Soon I'm moving round in a circle and I feel taken up. My arms beat the rhythm out faster and heat begins to steam off me. I don't feel so tired as I get a second wind and my legs take up more of the strain.

Round and round I go, beginning to twist and whirl, like a planet in orbit around a dark sun. The pace quickens and I turn faster. Round. Twist. Beat. Turn. Round. Step. Beat. Turn.

I lose track of where I am and what I'm doing.

It is daytime. The tunnel is warm and golden. Beneath where the air shafts open to the blue sky is a thick copse of weeds, brambles bearing black fruit, tall thin saplings and long grass.

I walk out of the shade of the tunnel into the beautiful heat of the sun. I can't remember a summer so fine. If I knew I could go here before I don't think I would ever leave. No need for holidays in the Caribbean. Soaking in the rays, I have a huge grin on my face.

At the top of the stairs I expected a difficult tangle hindering me. Instead I climb up into a brick and tile building where the main exit leads to Great Western Road, past a turnstile and a ticket booth. It's like a London Underground station. Except there is an odd quality to the light. It is brighter in here that it should be and the light is grey.

My eyes adjust. The whole structure is a little translucent. Some light from outside is filtering through the station. Where it is most opaque burnt beams are visible. It is an old photograph film that was exposed at different moments before development. Now different layers of time are visible, the eldest fading out of sight. Outside, twin towers emerge from the station roof, with onion-style domes on the top that are eerily reminiscent of Moscow. Across the junction, the church is still standing. The BBC building further up Queen Margaret Drive is intact, still awaiting demolition. What would I see in a Roman ruin? Would it have faded away by now, or would there still be a ghost of its former glory?

In the park itself the Kibble Palace gleams like a newly made space-craft. The flower beds are filled with Pansies in a rainbow of colours. On the lawn normally occupied by the tent city are strange pyramids made from some kind of thick webbing. It's like huge spiders have been trying to create a replica of what is in the Living world. This place appears to shadow what's there, but it takes time to form and time to dissolve.

I go to where my tent used to be and see the dark brick tunnel arching over me. My legs kick as they try to keep walking. I sit up, cold and clammy with sweat fighting the disorientation.

Corbie looks at me blankly. "Where did you go?"

"I was here, but it was summer, sunny. I could see the station up above and other buildings that are now gone." Ducking into my tent I find a jumper and slip it on. My stomach groans. I'm hoping I can find an instant noodle packet and make dinner. Looking at my phone once again I'm reminded I haven't charged it up yet. I plug it into the tent's charger. There'll be almost no light down here to help the tent generate power, but it might be cold enough to make some juice from the heat pump. However, it's unlikely to charge it up much before morning.

"That's good. I didn't expect you to go over so easily," Corbie says.

"You mean you thought the drum wouldn't work."

"You weren't gone more than a minute or two. No point goin on the journey if you don't spend any time at the destination."

"Hey, it was my first time. I'm sure I'll get better with practice."

"You need the right tools for the job."

"You sound like my Dad. He was always fixing stuff." I laugh. "I can change a motherboard but don't ask me to change a tyre."

"We're goin to get a proper skin for your drum."

"Not tonight. I need food and I've got my kids tomorrow."

I put on the gas stove and heat some water. If I don't find noodles I can make tea.

Chapter 9

My alarm startles me awake. It comes from everywhere at once. My stomach has turned into a hollow ball with a leaden core. If I don't eat properly today I'm going to get sick again. Some fruit, some meat. That sounds good.

My phone is charged at least. I have several missed calls and messages from my Mum. Where are you? Why can't you come home? I can help you through this.

There's a single text message from Rachael – I think I understand. Let me know where you are.

I wish I understood. Maybe she's been speaking to Mum. Feeling bad walking out on her again, I reply – In Botanic Gardens Station. Got kids today. Maybe talk later?

Nothing, still, from Kathryn. It's too early to call, but I don't have a good feeling about this. I go to the toilet block, and then head to the shops to stock up on essentials. Good thing about this time of year is that food keeps well, but I'm still wary of buying too much fresh stuff. I've not had to buy anything for a few weeks, so I've some money in the bank. Putting some sausages for dinner in my basket, I also get a big bag of potatoes, dozens of packets of noodles, cheap tins of beans. It's like being a student all over again except that my teenage body could cope better with this diet. I buy apples, crisp and tart and also get some kale. It tastes green and a bit bitter, but full of vitamins and pretty cheap. I still hate it. I also need a big bottle of water.

Calling Kathryn, a friendly voice tells me her number is no longer available. I'm on the next bus to her mother's house. Fiona answers the door but doesn't open it. She leaves the chain on.

"You've a bloody cheek showing your face here," Fiona says. "Clear off before I call the police."

"What are you talking about?"

"Don't play innocent with me, you silly little man."

The ferocity of her anger shocks me. I thought I knew Fiona but clearly I was wrong. "I've been in hospital for the last fortnight," I say. "Unconscious for most it. Whatever you think I've done it is highly unlikely I did it."

Fiona frowns.

"I've dozens of witnesses."

"You can still make calls from hospital."

"Again, I was completely out of it, in a coma. Check my call log." I push my phone towards the crack in the door. Fiona takes it and slams the door shut. After brushing snow away, I sit on the step and shiver.

A couple of minutes later she opens the door again. "Would you like some tea?"

"If you agree to tell me what's going on." I follow her through to the kitchen.

"It started almost as soon as you left. Kathryn's phone rang. Caller ID said it was you. The line was silent and then you hung up." The kettle's whistle pierces the conversation. Fiona puts a splash of water into a china teapot. "Well, not you, apparently." She swirls it around and empties it into the sink, then scoops leaves into the pot and tops up with water when the kettle boils again. "Whoever it was called again and again and again. Nearly every hour until she switched the damned thing off. That Sunday we called the police who told Kathryn to change her number. There wasn't anything more they could do."

"Where is she now?"

Fiona stares at me. "On the Tuesday the calls started on the new phone. We thought you'd hacked into the phone company's records."

"I honestly wouldn't know how."

"You're good with computers." Fiona lifts the lid and stirs the contents of the teapot.

"If I had a dollar... Never mind my wife, where are my kids?"

"With their mother."

"Let me guess, since my hacking skills are so good that I could track her down anywhere she went, the police told Kathryn she should pack a bag and go somewhere with them."

Fiona pours tea into two old mugs.

"No one looked for any proof it was me beyond the caller ID in Kathryn's phone. I'm sure my number wasn't in her new phone, unless some helpful person transferred over her contacts too."

Fiona sips her tea and avoids my eyes.

"Nothing like being innocent until proven guilty. Can I expect a visit from the police? As a hardened computer hacker and wife harasser I must be high on the list of their priorities." I take a mouthful of my tea. It is too hot. I can't spit it out all over Fiona, as much as I might like to, so I burn my mouth and throat swallowing it down.

"Biscuit?" Fiona offers me a plate covered in foil wrapped domes.

I take one. Food is food. I peel off the cover and the chocolate dome collapses into gooey marshmallow beneath my teeth. "What do we do now?"

Fiona shrugs. "I didn't want to think ill of you. I've just been so pissed off with you after you went and hid in a field...I saw that you did make one call to Kathryn that Saturday."

"I left a message. I tried to tell her I'd changed my mind. That I was ready to come here if need be and start again. I was so sick that night I didn't know what I was doing. But that was the truth. I guess she never heard it."

"I will let her know. It may not be too late. But she's very shaken. Even with proof it wasn't you...I don't know. She took it hard. And the kids are seeing things from her perspective, you know. I'll tell the police too. You're right. I'm sorry. We should have gotten some proof before jumping to conclusions. I know you've never meant to do anything but the right thing for Kathryn."

"It isn't that you all felt I could really do this that pisses me off. It's that you never stopped to think about it, didn't question it once you decided it really was me. It's that it was so easy for you to believe it." I get up from the chair. I feel heavy, tired. "Ask her to call me. When she's ready."

The bus ride home takes forever. It gives me plenty of time to think about the calls. I could access the phone company records. I've never tried to do something like that, but I reckon I could do it if I wanted to. Someone has attacked my family. I can't just sit back and do nothing. What I don't understand, is why it would start when I got sick though. That's an odd coincidence. There's so much happening lately it's hard to keep it all in my head at once; learning to be a shaman, my impending divorce, work, getting sick, Rachael, Albert's death and now this. Are there patterns? Can I make some sense of it all? It's like a Rat King; many tails and many heads too intertwined to separate and you'd likely lose a finger doing so. I rest my head against the window, opaque with condensation. The cold and the vibration are soothing. I just can't believe how quick they were to accuse me on such little real evidence. Perhaps Kathryn and I truly have moved too far apart in the last year. I have no one to blame but myself.

The snow in the Gardens is starting to turn to slush. I nearly jump out of my skin when Corbie ambushes me. I was just thinking how weird it was to have a Saturday free when he swoops up behind me and lands on my shoulder.

"Jeezus. You scared the crap out of me."

"Sorry, Boss. Guess we got time to work on that drum now. You're also gonna need the right clothin."

"First a drum and now a new outfit. It's like it's my birthday. What do I need to kill to make that?"

"It will need to be made of skin and iron."

"Lucky for us the shops will still be open. We can walk down Byres Road and check out the charity shops. Bound to have plenty of suits. If we're lucky they'll have a skin and iron one in my size."

"Why are you always pushin back? You don't want this, fine. You don't wanna work with me, fine. I'll take it to the spirits and we'll see what they say. Maybe they'll figure you're just a pain in the ass who's not worth the effort. Maybe they'll decide to give you a real disease or kick you in the ass some other way til you get with the program."

"Fuck off. I've got other shit on my mind right now. Someone's been messing with my family. Do you get that? They're more important to me than finding a stupid fucking fancy dress costume."

"Important enough that you spent a year livin in a tent, so you could provide for them. Please spare me your bullshit, Dude. You're so full of crap you can't even smell it anymore. You wanna make a difference? You wanna help people? You wanna help your family? Then get through your trainin. That way the Powers That Be will leave you alone, and them."

"Wait, are you saying that spirits are behind these calls to my wife?"

"I'm sayin that they could be. And if you do what they want there'll be no reason for them to carry on."

"This is seriously fucked up. I swear to you now, sooner or later I'm taking this to them and I'm gonna fuck with them the way they're fucking with me. They want Mafia tactics fine, I'll play along, but one day I'll be the Godfather."

"Fuckin A, Buddy. Fuckin A."

We go to the heart health charity shop just past the supermarket and all I see there are cloth suits from the Seventies and Eighties, some hideous ties, a few floral shirts, and tea sets from the thirties like my Dad's parents used to have. Those on my Mum's side probably used jam jars or whittled cups out of wood with old nails the way she makes Soviet Siberia sound.

Further down the road we've been into a couple of cancer charity shops, seen some immense collections of VHS tapes and Stephen King paperbacks, but nothing I think would fit the bill. It's a long shot but I decide to go into the specialist vintage clothing shop. It has an interesting rack of elegant silk gowns from the early Nineteen Hundreds. You could get a uniform for almost any armed force in here too. Hiding in the back I see a short rack of biker jackets and a leather coat which, with its wide lapels, must be from the Seventies. I try them all on. It is skin after all, just like the doctor ordered. The Seventies car coat fits perfectly. Too well. I smile as I slide it on. I'm a bit embarrassed to wear something so old-fashioned, slightly cheesy. But it feels right and looks damned good. It feels weird not to be wrapped in my jacket made from man-made fibres, inner fleece and stow away storm hood. The car coat is heavy too.

"That, my friend, is far out." Corbie looks me up and down.

We walk further down Ruthven Lane to the market hidden alongside some expensive restaurants I once enjoyed meals in. They are mostly small units piled high with bric-a-brac; broken Apple IIs, Bakelite phones I doubt even work on the modern network, pieces of obscure furniture like a leather dentist's chair, a Betamax VCR, and boxes and boxes of vinyl records. It's like a technological elephant's graveyard here.

There's a heavy metallic clunk and white pain flashes from my foot. Several items rattle settling into a new position as I stub my toe on something under a table. I keep my curse to myself but do a little dance stamping my foot to shake out the pain in my toes.

"You should remember that for next time you go into the Otherworld," Corbie says.

I accidentally stamp my foot down on Corbie, but the prickly muppet steps aside. I see the stall holder looking my way with concern. I fake a smile and he goes back to smoking his roll up and reading the paper.

Underneath the table is a large red toolbox. I lift one flap and concertina out one side. Hammers with balls, claws and rubber heads, and spanners in a myriad of Imperial gauges mingle with screwdrivers of different sizes and cross sections. In the other half I don't recognise most of the tools. All of them are covered in liver spots of rust.

"Would this be good for the iron part of this outfit?"

The raven sticks his head in the box. "Could work."

"What do we need the iron for anyway?"

"Bones."

"So it needs to look like I've got an iron skeleton?" Corbie nods. "Then this should be perfect." I try to lift the toolbox, but can barely move it. "This could be a challenge." I see a skateboard and grab it. I just about get the box secured on top of the board. Inside the toolbox is a roll of waxed twine. I tie the box down and make a lead.

The stall holder looks at me through thick glasses and a cloud of smoke. "Twenty quid."

"For an ancient skateboard and a rusty box? I'll give you ten."

"The metal alone is worth more than that these days. How about fifteen?"

"If that were true you'd have scrapped it already. Twelve fifty."

"Deal."

I wave my phone at his and the deal is done. It pains me to pay so much, but I keep it to myself. The box trails behind me like a lost puppy as we continue on our trip down Byres Road looking for skin.

The charity shops for the aged, children, cancer, children with cancer, and sick animals, all turn out to be busy, but none of them have any leather clothes or any other replacements. Would anyone recognise a Nazi lampshade if they saw one?

Tired I sit down on my new mobile throne. It is too late today to go into the city centre and try there. Besides there's not so many places to look. I'm not buying anything new from the leather shops on Argyle Street. I turn round and head back up the road. It's starting to get dark.

There's a fancy dress vintage shop just along Great Western Road. Instead of crossing the road back to the Gardens, I go past the burnt out church towards Kelvinbridge Station. Super Trouper even has dummies dressed like Bjorn and Anna-Frid in the window. I have fifteen minutes before the shop shuts. The proprietor has long blonde hair, like Agnetha, that looks like it may be real, but something about her complexion makes me wonder if it is a wig. On the left is a long rack of women's clothes sorted by year, on the right is a shorter rack of men's which is unsorted.

On a hanger underneath a denim jacket with an Iron Maiden back patch sewn on it is a pair of leather biker trousers with thick reinforced knees. I try them on. They're a bit big for me, but with a belt I should be okay. I could afford them, but its steep, and I'd rather not.

"Hi. I'd like these please." The woman looks up from her laptop. "Thing is. I can't really afford them though."

"I can't give you credit."

"Perhaps you need something doing in exchange?"

"This isn't a porno, pal. And you're no ma type." The illusion of Swedish sophistication is easily shattered.

"I meant like a website or some IT stuff."

"Ah dunno. Ah dinnae need much."

"It's really important that I get these. It'll help me to help other people."

"Well, look, ah cannae connect this thing to the Wi-Fi in here. Almost useless without it. Maybe that would be worth half ae them."

"Okay, deal." I pay for half and spend ten minutes rooting through menus to find the problem. Agnetha locks the door and turns the sign to Closed. I can't find anything wrong. I check that the router in the staff room is working fine, everything blinking green and return to the laptop. I look through a number of other menus and prod and poke the machine. I turn it off and on again. Then I notice she has moved the Wi-Fi slider on the front of the laptop to off. "There you go, should be fine for now. But if you need anything else give me a ring." I hand her my card.

"Magick. What did you do?"

"One of your settings was switched off. I've fixed it now."

"Excellent, thanks, pal."

In the dark I'm wary of carrying the toolbox down into the tunnel in case I go through one of the steps again, so I leave it near the surface until morning. It survived sitting outside shops on a skateboard, it should be fine here.

"We still need to fix your drum." Corbie nudges the one I built yesterday with a talon.

"You mean I still need to kill and skin something."

He shrugs. "If you prefer."

While I'm thinking what to do, I hear the eerie woman-being-attacked yelp of a fox. No matter how often I hear it, it puts me on edge, makes me want to find and help. Looks like I'll just be having noodles for dinner tonight.

I find some plastic bags, shred them and weave them into a net. I use the waxed thread to loop over a branch and cover the bags with other rubbish in a spot near the water, well away from the tent city. No one with any sense will be out walking down here after dark.

The newly bought sausages sit in the middle of my trap and I wait patiently feeling sick in my stomach knowing what I'm going to do. I'm sure any sensible fox would smell me and stay well away. While I wait I prepare a rough square frame from large twigs that I collected and piece of smooth wood that is a perfect fit.

I hear rustling and tense up, when a small dog comes out from under a bush. It goes straight for the meat and I throw beer cans at it until it takes the hint and returns to its master on the path. Will the scent of the dog and the beer cans have soured the site? I wait for a long time. At least half an hour. There's no snow here, but it's still damp and cold. The cold seeps into my joints. I wait a little longer.

Again I hear rustling. I hold my breath. A large fox, probably a male, bursts out into the middle of the trap. It sniffs at the ground and in the direction of the sausages. It turns to go then decides to leap on the food. I pull hard on the twine. The bag-net surrounds the fox, which yelps and kicks out ripping the thin plastic. The twine snaps unable to hold under the weight of the fox. Before it can escape, I grab a rock and dive into the trap. I bring the rock down on its head. Blood sprays across my face, warm and wet. The head caves in too easily. The body kicks out beneath me, then lies still. Blood seeps from the head wound. The fox's tongue flops obscenely out the side of its mouth.

I stare at the rock in my hand, bits of fur and bone smushed into its surface. My stomach flips and I'm dry retching. I hate myself and I hate Corbie for getting me to do this. I retch until my throat and chest is aching. Nothing but thin water comes out. I feel dizzy.

"Hurry." Corbie stands near my head. "It's better to skin it while the body's still warm."

I have no idea what I'm doing. Fumbling for my pen knife, my hand slips pulling out a blade.

"The easiest option is to cut off the paws and head," Corbie says. "Then gently and not too deeply cut from throat to anus, circle around the anus, and then cut along the inside of each limb to the central cut."

"Cut off the head and paws, with this little knife?"

"Then cut around them."

I can't quite bring myself to do it. Knife in hand, I freeze up. Fuck's sake, Kol'ka, you've already killed it. Now get the job done. I turn the fox onto its back and slip the blade in above the back left paw. It slices easily through the rough russet fur. I repeat with the other paws and around the neck.

"Now be careful. Too deep and you'll go through into organs and intestines. You do that and you'll have a real mess on your hands and we'll have to do this again."

I hesitate again. Come on. Enough with this crap. I carefully nick into the skin in the circle around the neck and work my way down. I cut round the anus. As it turns out I have some luck. This is a vixen, giving me one less thing to worry about, as anyone who's changed a baby boy will know. Then I cut along the inside of each leg down to the cut in the middle.

"All you have to do now is take it off like a coat."

My nose itches but with my hands covered in God knows what I resist the urge to touch it. I grasp the flap near the bottom left leg and tug it. It peels back with a light tearing sound. It is like taking skin off a pack of chicken legs, but easier. Every now and then I have to use the knife to separate some tissue. Before long I have peeled the fox.

"Let's leave the body for the spirits, but there's one more thing you'll need. Crack open the head a little more and get the brain."

"Jeezus, Corbie. What next? We put another brain in there and spark it to life with electrickery?"

"You'll be fine. We need it to tan the hide. It'll keep longer."

I find an empty tin and go back to the fox's head. The grey gelatinous mess I scoop into the can with my hands. I go down to the dirty river and wash my hands in the water. It is aching cold and my fingers feel numb.

"Now take your knife and scrape away the fat and any tissue left inside the skin."

I follow my instructions, after tying the skin to the frame I'd built. My knees and back ache from kneeling too long while I do it. This is slow and hard to do in the darkness.

Turning the frame over, I start to strip the fur away too. I use an old razor blade at first, but it goes dull fairly quickly. My knife is okay but I can't seem to get a good angle on it. I use the lid from the tin the brain is in and although it has a ragged edge from an opener, it works well. Bending it over makes working easier.

When I'm done I wash the defleshed and defurred hide in the river using some washing up liquid. I'm tired, but I know that my night is not yet over. My hands feel frozen into claws.

I'm wary of crossing the Gardens too openly. Even at night there'll be people about. I'm carrying a fox's hide on a crude frame and can of brains. It's like the opening to a joke. A man walks into a bar, and says "Ow!" Corbie creeps along beside me. Leaving the body out in the open feels wrong. The scene of my crime should be covered over. All traces erased. What if someone finds it and they get back to me? Don't worry. The Great Spirit Mafia will make it disappear for you. Would they disappear my wife, or my kids? Was that the purpose of those calls?

Down in the tunnel Corbie tells me that I need to simmer the brawn in water. I refuse to use one of my cooking pots so I sit the can I collected it in on the gas. It forms a thick porridge that blurps out a whiff of sulphur every now and then.

Taking it off the burner, I let it cool a little before being instructed to rub it deep into the skin side of the fox hide. It takes some time to cover both sides of the whole skin and when I think I'm done, the smell of cooked brain finally no longer nauseating me, I have to put a second coat on. I take the hide from the frame and wrap it up tight and put it in a plastic bag for the night.

My stomach doesn't know what to do. I want to hurl, but have nothing left, and at the same time I'm ravenous. I clean my hands with the undisturbed snow lying beneath the air shafts and crack through the ice on a pool of water to rinse them off.

Whether I want to eat or not, my arms start to shake and feel weak. I boil up some water and add two packs of cheap noodles. I'm done in. With food in my stomach I go to sleep.

Chapter 10

It's cold when I wake. It must be much worse on the surface. I'm content to lie here for a while. My hands are stiff and my shoulders ache. Corbie climbs on top of me, his feet just pricking my skin through the sleeping bag.

"Rise and shine, camper."

"Go away. I want some rest. I was up all night skinning a fox and tanning its hide."

"It's light already. Long past lie in time."

I sigh. "What do we do today? Build a tepee from a herd of wildebeest now that I've got my skinning skills?"

"You still need to finish the skin and make the drum," Corbie says. "Then we can try again taking you to the Lower World."

"We already did that."

"No. Think again."

"That was the Underworld." I crawl out of my sleeping bag, pull on my trousers. "We've got my outfit to do as well."

"Then there's no time to waste."

"You remind me of my Dad – he never let me have a lie in either."

I'm about to make porridge when I recall the brains cooking. Beans are off the menu too. I make noodles again before going to the toilet block.

When I get back I lug down the toolbox from the surface and take out the hide. Corbie tells me to twist it and rope it up to squeeze out as much moisture as I can. The brain stuff seems to have been absorbed into the skin like moisturiser. There are a couple of tufts of red still left. This will make a good drum head, not that I'm an expert. Not bad for something done in the dark.

Removing the stray hairs, I also get rid of any bits of fat that got missed last night. Stretching the skin and rubbing it with a large stone softens it. Soon it is supple and dry.

"You'll need to smoke it before it's done," Corbie says.

"I doubt we'll get anything to burn," I say. "Any twigs will be wet and I don't want the police to be called because of the smoke."

"If you set it up deep in the tunnel then maybe the smoke won't come out this side."

I explore the tunnel heading south to Kelvinbridge. There are pockets of water on the floor further in and what looks like the start of stalagmites forming on the ceiling. Here and there is a blackened circle of an old fire and a few bits of left over wood. Timber liberated from building sites by the look of it. I go back for the skin and set it up so that it envelopes the fire, like a chimney. The wood is damp and takes a while to catch, but when it does a lazy smoke comes off it and rises up to meet the skin.

"How long will it take?"

"Half an hour should do it."

Back at my camp I look at the leather jeans and car coat and root through the toolbox taking out spanners or screwdrivers and holding them against the sections between joints seeing what fits well, iron ulnas and steel tibia.

Returning to the smoked skin, I put out the fire. Back in the daylight the skin has gone a dark golden colour. With reluctance I remove the skin from my drum and start measuring the right sized cut from my fox hide. Having done this once I'm less hesitant, but wary of tearing the newly tanned hide. Once I've stretched out the new skin onto the bicycle wheel and secured it in place I have to concede that it sounds like a real bodhran. There's a deeper timbre to each beat which also lasts longer. It resonates in my head and in my torso. I don't know if it is a matter of there being more life in the fox skin so much as it just being a more effective material. I smile, satisfied with a job well done.

Using the waxed twine from the toolbox and a small screwdriver to punch tiny holes I secure metal bones onto the outside of the jeans and along the arms of the car coat. "Do I need ribs and a spine too?"

Corbie cocks his head to one side. "A coupla ribs won't do you any harm."

I fix a series of spanners in descending size across the front of the coat. They look more like the ornate braids on Hussar's uniforms in the Napoleonic era than a skeletal ribcage. Once done there's only one thing for it – time to strut my stuff on the shaman catwalk.

The leather jeans pull on without a problem and I tie them tightly in place with a belt. The jacket already weighed a lot, with the additional iron it feels like lifting weights at the gym. I tug it on, the metal clanking. It isn't as bad as I thought, but my shoulders feel the strain.

"Not bad. Not bad at all," Corbie says. "Not what I was expecting, but it'll work. Now pick up your drum and let's go to work."

I get my new drum and without any further edicts from the thorny emperor I begin to find a rhythm I can keep too. Raising the pace, the beat starts to infect my limbs, resonating in my chest and loins. It is hard to move in the leather and the added extras don't help. I expect the trousers to fall down any minute.

The pace of the beat increases and my feet begin to shuffle, my arms spasm and I feel an even bigger tit than before. I'm praying no one suddenly decides to visit while I'm doing this. But this is keeping me from concentrating on what I'm doing. I absorb myself in the beat and nothing else. I'm twirling around stamping my feet beating my drum sweating clanking moonlight.

Moonlight on my face, as I lie on the ground. I was in the tunnel when I started. Once more summer is in full bloom and it is a warm night. Butterflies flit between flowers. Bats dart overhead. Small white clouds drift across the midnight sky.

"No time to be lying about." Corbie nudges me with his head, piercing me with a thorn as my coat lies on the platform beneath me.

I explore my side underneath my shirt and t-shirt, it feels sore, but there's no blood. I stand up and follow the bird up to the Gardens. "Where are we going?"

"We need to find a tree," Corbie says.

"There are plenty of those around."

"Not like this."

We head toward the back of the Gardens where there are more trees.

"Anything in particular we're looking for?" I say.

"You'll know it when you see it. We're lookin for a way down into the ground."

"We could have stayed in the tunnel." There's a particularly old and wide tree ahead. It resembles an oak, but is a lot taller. Near the base there is a dark hole. The closer I get, the larger the tree appears to be. On the lower trunk there is something clinging to it and around its base is a pool.

I've not seen anything in the Gardens like this before. The tree is growing breasts. All shapes and sizes – some have long nipples like tubes, some are colossal mammaries suitable for a porn star, many are ordinary shapely breasts. There are all shades of skin; dark red-brown, white as porcelain with blue veins, green dusky olive. All of them are swollen with a thin white fluid which oozes out of the nipples, glistens on the skin as it dribbles down to congregate in the pool at the base of the tree. A pool of translucent, opalescent white, liquid silver in the moonlight.

I remember Kathryn's breasts when she was feeding Lucas and then Samantha, and the warm sweet nutty taste of her milk. Nothing like what is packaged in bottles. The whole thing is slightly arousing and gross.

The hole I saw is down in the base of the tree, nestled between roots and breasts. It looks more human than tree, more ovoid than round. It's like a sheela-na-gig I saw in Ireland with the whole doorway being parted between her legs.

"Down the rabbit hole, eh?" I say.

"Aye," Corbie says.

There's no other way to get there than to walk through the milky pool. I can't tell how deep it is and sink up to my knees in the fluid. It's not far to wade and the milk is slightly warm. It soaks into my socks and clings to my legs beneath the leather trousers.

When I clamber out at the base of the tree I'm on my knees which seems the easiest way to enter the hole. I crawl forward into the narrow tunnel beyond. The fluid oozes down my legs. The grass turns to a dark black soil. Roots hang down from the top of the tunnel, poke out of the sides and floor. It's a real challenge to make my way round and through them. This is like potholing. As I go deeper thick sticky earthworms appear writhing through the soil, and a faint green glow emerges from the tunnel walls. The tunnel gets narrower and I've no idea where I'm going or how far I need to go. I don't normally think twice about enclosed spaces, but I can't turn around now. The roots are pushing down on me squeezing me forward. I start to panic, my breathing gets faster, my heart working hard, and the pit of my stomach is hollow. What have I done? Why did I blindly crawl into here?

The only way is forward, with less and less space to move. Then my arm misses the ground and I tumble out of the tunnel into a riot of animals and plants. It's like a jungle gone mad.

A hazy light, filtered through green leaves, dapples everything. Brightly coloured flies swarm, the light on their wings iridescent. Birds swoop past me chasing dragon flies. Any of them could fall foul of the insects with webs, the lizards with long sticky tongues, or the plants able to snap shut and drown them in digestive pools. Furred animals with arms and tails run along branches snatching at the passing buffet. The trees are wide with large heavy roots and thick branches garlanded in orchids, ivies and other climbing plants. The ground is a sea with moving waves of soil, insect armies carrying their spoils home, small rodents carrying out guerrilla attacks on their supply lines and snakes ready to strike. Further into the jungle I see yellow eyes that look suspended in the air like a Cheshire cat before their owner blends into the background. Something roars deeper in the madness of an ecosystem in overdrive. The air smells heavy and green, tinged with vegetal and fleshly decay. Thick scents from flowers dripping nectar mingle with the copper of fresh blood.

I'm scared. Something, whether flying, crawling or creeping, will eat me up.

Corbie emerges from the tunnel behind me. "It's a lot to take in, isn't it? Come on." He flaps his wings and heads into the jungle a few feet off the ground.

Following, I step over branches and rows of insects. Many just crawl over my feet and carry on their business. Fanning my hand to bat away things flying too close to my face, I also duck in reaction to something coming too close. I have that back of the neck tingling of something watching me. No doubt sizing me up for dinner.

After walking deeper into the jungle for ten minutes I'm sweating profusely. We emerge into a clearing in which a small waterfall forms a pool and a stream empties out of it. Kneeling beside the clear cool water, I cup some in my hands.

Corbie tries to interrupt me as I lift it up. "I wouldn't do that if I were," I splash it over my head, "you." The water patters onto the surface of the pool.

I can think more clearly. The humid atmosphere releases its push down on my skull for a little while.

There is movement beside me in the pool. I roll back out of the way, heart suddenly fast, expecting a piranha or crocodile to leap at me. Instead a figure emerges gracefully from the water. Hair of fine grasses and reeds, a face mask of dark polished mahogany, almond eyes looking through the holes, the shoulders and then the rest of a body composed of branches, leaves and flowers. A rivulet runs from the plant woman's shoulder, around her breast, like milk on the Tree, and down her waist and slender legs.

My embarrassment must be plain to see. I get up out of the dirt and brush myself down trying to get back some level of dignity.

Corbie flaps up onto my shoulder. His voice is a whisper. It is hard to hear over the noise of the rainforest. "Be on your guard, Nik. Treat this one like royalty."

"Hello, my lady." This sounds like nonsense and is clumsy on my tongue. "I am Nikolai Munro and this is my mentor Corbie. Please accept my apologies for disturbing you." I hold out my hand.

The plant person steps out of the pool. Her feet have rose thorns for nails. When she grips my hand I find that it does too. They scratch my skin, drawing thin lines of blood. "Shaman?" Her voice is the soughing of barley. Her grip strengthens and the thorns dig deeper.

I don't cry out with the pain or snatch my hand back. "Corbie is. I'm learning."

The plant person's eyes, all white and expressionless, appear blind, but they follow my movement. "Why have you come here?"

Did we disturb her sleep? Is she angry with me? Her tone is neutral but I still detect an undercurrent of menace. "Er, well, to visit the Lower World. It's my first time here. I really am sorry. I didn't mean to wake you."

"Do not worry. You can make amends," she says.

"Careful, Nik," Corbie says.

"I doubt I have anything of value to you."

"I would like a kiss."

No harm in that. It wouldn't be cheating on my soon to be ex-wife. A simple peck on the cheek.

"Nik, don't do this," Corbie says.

"It's okay. It's just a kiss. I thought you were all for free love."

"It ain't ever just a kiss, and this one's love ain't free." Corbie jumps off my shoulder and lands on the grass.

Stepping in closer to the plant woman, I tilt my head to come in close to her cheek. She releases my hand and pushes her body close to mine. It feels like flesh. She wraps her arms behind me and I try to pull back. Branches and vines wrap around me and pull me in closer. Her breath smells of nuts and nectar. One hand holds the back of my neck scratching it with the thorns. She tilts her head. Our lips touch. I expected solid wood, but it is soft and yielding. Despite my entrapment I find myself aroused kissing an essentially naked woman. Something darts quickly between my lips. Did she just slip me some tongue? I break the kiss and try not to cough. My tongue feels numb where it was jabbed. The vines and branches release me, her arms let me go. I am light headed and feel the need to sit down.

The woman sits cross-legged in front of me. "I am Midori. I am pleased to meet you." The menace has gone, but like a cat that has sheathed its claws, the threat is still there. "Welcome to the Green World. This is where you will find the animal and plant spirits. Many come here to find animal guides."

Corbie walks over and stands just in front of me. "We're pleased to meet you too."

The words are thick as I try to get my mouth to work. "I have Corbie, so I doubt I'll need any animal spirits."

Midori chuckles. "The greater the shaman, the more spirits he commands."

The feeling of numbness passes. "I'm no great shaman, madam. I'm just trying to get the Great Spirits off my back."

"I could make you a great shaman, if you wished." Midori smiles. It is the smile of a tiger. "How else will you counteract the Great Spirits' influence?"

It's tempting. All this could be so much easier. But I've gone down the easy road before. This is the Devil's deal. How to get out of this while keeping face for everyone? "That is a wonderful offer. I'm sure you are a powerful supporter of many shamans greater than those the Great Spirits patronise. I need to find my talents and strengths in order to be worthy of your interest. I'm sure your advice here would be invaluable, however I have no currency and 'neither a borrower or lender be' as my Dad used to say."

She laughs again. "You flatter me, sir. I think you have talents you don't recognise within yourself. If not a protégé, perhaps you would be my ally?"

"It would be an uneven alliance. I wouldn't wish you to feel our relationship was one sided. Besides, why would you want to ally with a shaman who has nothing?"

"I've not heard anyone speak out so bravely against the Great Spirits. Perhaps we have mutual goals."

"I wouldn't want to find later that we did not. My enemy's enemy is not necessarily my friend. It already sounds like shamans and spirits work in some kind of feudal system. I don't think that would rest comfortably with me."

"There are some who feel enslaved. Some are happy with their yokes."

"I would have preferred a choice in being a shaman. I might have accepted, if anyone asked. Instead my family and I have been subjected to thuggery and intimidation that I would expect from a street gang."

"You have a family?"

Why should Midori be interested in this? "Two kids and a wife, technically."

"You either you do or you don't."

"With the greatest of respect we haven't even agreed to be allies and this is rather personal."

"I am disappointed. We seem to agree on so much. I thought we were comrades in arms. Should be draw up a contract?" Midori says.

"Lady, I mean no offence. I just got here. You're the first spirit I've spoken to. We appear to have common aims, it remains to be seen if we have common purpose."

"Very well, Nikolai Munro. Perhaps we will meet again." Midori stands and walks away, submerging smoothly into the water. I thought I was doing okay, yet somehow I offended her.

"Dude, that was well played. I thought she'd eat you for breakfast. Let's go home before you start a diplomatic incident."

I turn and head back the way I think we came.

"You don't need to walk," Corbie says. "Just think yourself back the way we came."

I imagine myself speeding along like a bullet through the jungle, along the tunnel, out into the pool beneath the breasted tree and back down beneath the station to where I started underneath the air vent.

My body is covered in a fine layer of snow. I feel stiff and cold. And ravenous. It is getting dark. Standing up, I try to shake some life into my limbs, my metal bones clanging. I try to come back to this world, to feel grounded here.

There are small footprints in the snow. They lead to my tent, inside there's the warm glow of a lamp. Who would walk past me lying out in the open, but stay instead of robbing me? "Hello?" I say.

"Hi. Are you okay?" Rachael unzips the tent and comes out. She is wrapped in a thick woollen coat with a tailored waist and long skirt – it has a Victorian military great coat look to it. "I could tell you were still alive," she says. "But wasn't sure if it was part of being a shaman or if you'd had a seizure. I didn't realise you were serious."

Why do I suddenly feel guilty about a kiss with a plant spirit? "Not that I had much choice." I pick up my drum and brush the snow off it. I'm sure getting the new skin damp will not be good for it. "It must be a bit disturbing to keep finding me delirious every time you visit."

"Given your outfit, I figured it was more likely you were in a trance."

My face goes hot. "Yeah. It weighs a ton." Moving towards the tent, I smell my own sweat soaked into the clothes underneath. "You'll have to excuse me. I'm a bit fragrant."

"You're forgetting I deal with hordes of pre-pubescent kids. I'm used to all sorts of smells."

"What brings you to town?"

"I came in to do some shopping and found myself in the West End," Rachael says. "Since I saved your life, and presumed the authority of the gods, I'm now responsible for you. Seemed a good opportunity to check in on my responsibility."

"So many seem to want my soul these days. I should feel privileged. I hope I didn't cause you too many problems."

Rachael frowns. "I had to explain to a senior nurse over the phone that my husband had decided to come home. Caused a few raised eyebrows at work."

"Sorry about that. I really appreciate all you did for me. I had to follow my calling."

"When you told me about it, it seemed kind of wishy washy. Like all you did was have a vivid dream."

"I'm getting real cold and I need to eat something," I say. "Would you mind if we go back to my flat?"

"Why don't you get changed and I'll buy you some dinner?"

"Are you sure?" She looks at me as if to say *If I wasn't sure why would I ask*? "Okay, that would be great." It's weird feeling that I owe someone enough to accept their invitation to dinner. Besides I still couldn't face beans and I'm sick of noodles. I get changed, emerging in a small cloud of deodorant. Without the coat and the leather jeans on I feel like I'm walking on air. We carefully climb the steps, cross the fence and crunch our way over the freezing layer of snow to the nearest path.

Rachael hooks her arm around mine. "There's a nice gourmet burger place I'd like to try."

"Sounds good to me, but how on earth can you afford it?" From Corbie's absence I take it that I've got the night off for good behaviour.

"I don't go out very often."

I push my last chip into the pool of mayonnaise and even though I'm stuffed full I'm still wondering about dessert. The downside of not eating big meals is that you feel full quickly. Rachael is still picking at hers, the bun discarded. "Everything okay?" I say. I don't think I looked up from my food until now.

"Yeah. It's weird." She pushes some hair behind her ear. "Meeting you. I mean I could have picked nearly anyone in the crowd."

"You did. It just happened it was me."

"But you helped," Rachael says. "Someone else could have left me to it. Like you said, the Tent City really makes for a lousy community if my grandfather is one of the few who really gave a shit."

"That was a weird day alright. Things keep getting weirder. I had to make that drum. From scratch."

"What do you mean? I thought it was an old bicycle wheel."

"The skin is new."

"Oh." She bites a chip in half. "Best I don't ask about the donor."

"Yeah, not unless you want to see your dinner again."

Rachael drinks her wine. "That's not really where I was going."

"Sorry."

"I was lucky to meet you." I recognise the look on her face, even if it's been years since I've seen it.

"And now you're responsible for my life." I smile. "I'm not sure its luck you should thank." Rachael frowns. I recall Midori's similar expression. Where women are concerned, luck seems to be deserting me today.

She puts her glass on the table. "You shouldn't put yourself down so much."

"I'm a failed, near bankrupt, businessman. I live in a tent. In an old railway tunnel. My wife will soon serve me with divorce papers. I'm learning to be a shaman with all the blood, shit and other fluids that come with it. I can't pay my share of this meal and without your health insurance would be dead. Thank you for helping me. Thank you for feeding me. But I'm beyond rescue."

She laughs. "I'm not trying to rescue you. This is exactly it. You're all living in your little tents but you've thicker walls between you than anyone else. You're so fucking wrapped up in your own self-pity. You can go anywhere you like, leave anytime you want."

"I would have agreed with you once," I say. "Maybe other people can, but I can't."

"Bullshit."

"No. I tried to leave. Just before I got really sick I offered to move back in with Kathryn and the kids. She was harassed for days. Someone kept calling her phone with my Caller ID coming up. I'm getting so stressed about all this I'm tempted to book an appointment with my shrink."

"You're seeing a psychiatrist?"

"I was. I watched my colleagues impact one after another. As part of my severance package they included trauma counselling. But in the interest of full disclosure you should know that I was in and out of mental institutions in my youth as my Dad tried to cure me. You already know I now see an invisible talking thorn bird and travel to spirit worlds, so good that that worked out so well."

"I don't even know where to start unravelling all of that. Some shit happened to you in the past. Shit happened to us all in the past. Time to saddle up and move on. You're so obsessed with what you have, even if it's nothing. It's just stuff, you say, but you don't seem to mean it. You have other things. Relationships with people. Your kids for a start. Hell, you even have a new career."

The chip is cold and stiff, the mayo eggy. "Okay. Thanks for dinner." I stand up.

"Oh no you don't, Mister. You're not walking out on me a third time." I squeeze along the booth. "There's nothing you can do about it."

"I own your ass, remember." She grabs my hand with a strength I didn't think she could have. I can't pull away without dragging her over the table. She exits the booth and standing on tiptoes pulls me in to her and kisses me. She smells musky and sweet. I can taste her Pinot Noir.

Someone cheers and there a few sarcastic claps from the other side of the room.

"Look, I…" Where do I start? "I'm still married. After your pep-talk in the morgue I decided to move back home. I've not yet heard Kathryn's response to that. I like you but we still barely know each other and I'm not about to give Kathryn more grounds for divorce."

"I know. I heard you." She smiles. "I just wanted you to know. You don't need to protect me. I know what I want and what I'm doing."

After Rachael pays the bill I walk her back to the underground station. "Thanks again for dinner."

"I probably shouldn't say this, but if Kathryn wanted you back, she wouldn't have let you go in the first place."

"She was just supporting my decision."

"For who's benefit?" She pecks me on the cheek. "Take care of yourself, Nik." She goes through the turnstile.

I have a lot to think about on my walk back to the park.

Chapter 11

It's a struggle to get up for my first Monday at work in several weeks. My limbs are tired and heavy. My head feels woolly even though I didn't drink last night.

Still no word from Kathryn. I wonder if Fiona has even spoken to her. Perhaps Rachael is right – she isn't interested in carrying on our marriage and was happy to see the back of me.

Work is quiet. Everything is in the green. I spend most of the day surfing, catching up on news of various sorts, mainly tech related.

Back in the Gardens, Corbie is waiting for me. "Free love, man. You can't beat it," he says.

"Are you spying on me?"

"I have eyes. I see things you can't see. Only because you're not lookin. Besides Florence Nightingale was waitin for you."

"I'm married."

"You can wave that bit of paper around like it will stop you from having feelings," Corbie says. "It's just a contract, not a shield. Love is free. You just have to accept it and give some away."

"What are we doing today?"

"One day you'll learn to be free." Corbie laughs. "I thought we could try for the Upper World. Could be tough to get in, but it's worth the journey."

"The right tie again. This spirit world seems full of little cliques and clubs. I hope you're going to teach me all the secret handshakes."

"You seem to be opening doors with your lips. Way more fun than a handshake."

"You tried kissing my arse?"

Corbie laughs again. "Ass, man. Ass."

I climb into my shaman suit and take up my drum. It all appears to be holding together well. I start to find my rhythm, but every time I think I have it, it moves away from me. Feeling it would be better than thinking about it. I stop and try again. More slowly this time I count out the beat. As soon as I think I have it I raise the tempo and keep it simple. Beat after beat. I feel it in my chest and in my groin. My limbs begin their jerky spasms which graduate into a smooth dance. Round and round I whirl on the spot and around in a circle. Around and around. Beat after beat. It is night time, but late, the moon is going down and I think I see the first hints of dawn in the sky. The calendar of the Otherworld isn't so much a reflection of the Living World as its opposite.

Out on the grass there are no webby pyramid tents like I saw on my first trip here. I didn't notice their absence yesterday. I used a different drum that time.

"Come on," Corbie says. "We need to find the Tree of Life again."

"The one with the big boobies?" Corbie just looks at me.

We head off toward the back of the Gardens, Corbie gliding along behind me with the occasional lazy flap of his wings. The fertile breasts on the Tree of Life ooze a metallic strawberry milk as the dawn rises in the Otherworld. I watch as the pool changes to red then yellow. The shadows of the trees lengthen and the stars clear from the sky as it turns light blue.

"Where do we go?" I say.

"For the Upper World?" Corbie says. He looks up.

Scrabbling up over rows of fat lactating breasts will be awkward. I like the feel of a breast beneath my hands, but this will be like fondling a number of different women in succession and I've no idea if they will be too slippery to gain a decent purchase. I see the hole down into the Lower World, the wooden lips around it. There is a space there amongst the breasts and from the top of the hole I think I could reach one of the lower branches and pull myself up.

Getting onto the top edge of the hole is no mean feat. There aren't many footholds and it is far too high to just step up onto it. My feet keep slipping on the bark and soon my hands are sore from all the abrasion.

There's no choice but to try the mammary route. The bottom ones are taught enough and obscenely large enough for me to step on to them. It's like stepping on to a ball without enough air in it. They depress beneath my weight. Great fountains of milk spurt forth and splash into the pool and beyond. Where the milk drops fall on the grass it quickly grows thicker and flowers spring up.

I try grasping at breasts above me in a way that would get me slapped in the Living World. My hands can't get a grip as they are so slick with the milk of Yggdrassil. I slide off the tree, a damp smear down the front of my clothes. Wiping my hands on the grass causes small green shoots to emerge from the earth. I half expect grass to start growing on my palms this stuff is so powerful.

Corbie sounds like he is being strangled or has something caught in his throat. His laugh is humiliating at first then I join in.

"So how do I get up there? I've tried everything except use a rope or a ladder."

"Imagine yourself floating like smoke from a fire on a still day," Corbie says. "Not dissimilar to how you moved in the desert to get to the Underworld."

I picture a fire. A circle of stones with a cone of twigs crackling and burning. Warm orange, flecks of wavering yellow, black carbon and white ash. Over it a thin grey tendril of smoke is tentatively joining the fire to the air. There is no breeze so it rises steadily and without effort up towards the sky. Opening my eyes, my stomach lurches as I'm six feet off the ground. I land heavily, but only my ego is bruised. Last time had been a laugh, this time I was unprepared. I'd not sensed any movement.

I try again. The fire is a vivid image in my mind. The smoke curls as it starts to dissipate out of sight. I open my eyes, prepared this time. I am several metres off the ground, almost to the height of some of the other trees. The Tree of Life has gotten larger. I look down and it is like an office block. I look up and the tree now goes on and on up into the sky. The branches are huge and could support houses and shops. This change in perspective makes me dizzy. I have to close my eyes again. When I open them I'm higher still. About the height of the church steeple on the corner of Byres Road, which I have to remind myself isn't there in the Living World.

Corbie is flying up alongside me. "You should get onto a branch and climb the rest of the way up."

As soon as I float close enough I step over onto a branch as thick as my body. Not as titanic as the lower ones but still as big as many normal trees. The branches are much denser here too.

I haven't climbed a tree since I was a kid. It takes a while before I get into the rhythm of movement that leads to good progress; my eye looking for a route, my hands reaching for a branch without any thought, my feet finding knots to stand on. As ever my costume holds me back. The weight of the coat draws me down to earth and I have to exert twice the effort to get where I'm going.

Looking down is a bad idea. You'd think I'd have learned from crossing the hair bridge. I feel dizzy and my balls retract. This must be the height of the flats still dotted across the city, like in Castlemilk and the Gorbals. Beyond, Glasgow stretches out along the Clyde and up the sides of the valley, windmills on the crests.

Corbie lands on a branch next to me. "C'mon, no time for slackin off." He takes off again, beating his wings to hover near my head.

Rolling my shoulders and stretching my back I prepare to start again. My hands feel rough. The bark of the Tree of Life is a patchwork of other trees; the dry papery bark of Birch, the rough cracked diamonds of old Redwoods, the smooth skin of Oak. It makes it harder to climb as I can't be certain of my grip in advance.

After a while the air starts to feel damp and I notice the trunk of the tree has narrowed, the branches are not so thick. Around me is just white mist.

I hear something scratching against the bark. It gets louder, accompanied by a tremor in the tree. It must be big. A dark shape above me gets closer. Do I hold on tight or get out of the way? Corbie is not far away. If I shout to him will it draw too much attention to me? I hold still and tight to the trunk.

I can make out reddish fur, a bit like the fox I had to kill. Warm blood on my face. Cracking of bone. I shake my head. Focus.

It's a squirrel. About the size of a large van. The huge brush of tail moves to balance it as it climbs downward head first. It sniffs – it must have my scent. It pauses on the branch above me. Its dark eyes look me over and it sniffs again. Maybe I'll be considered a bad nut. It could easily knock me off if it wanted to. Instead it climbs past me and continues on down the tree. I stay still until the tremors pass.

"I see you met Ratatoskr." Corbie swoops in close.

"Sounds like a villain in an Opera. It wasn't very chatty."

"How's your Old Norse?"

"I take your point. Does it guard the Tree?"

"Ratatoskr delivers messages between the eagle at the top and the wyrm Níðhöggr at the bottom."

"I must have missed the snake at the base of the tree. I was preoccupied with the breasts."

"He's down in the roots," Corbie says. "Gnawing his way to Niflheim."

"I guess his success would not be a good thing."

"A dragon might warm the place up a bit."

I look up. The Tree stretches away. "Are we nearly there yet?"

"I'm sure you'll bump into it sooner or later."

Putting one hand after the other, hauling myself up onto another branch, I continue my climb. Once I'm back into the flow it gets easier. The tree narrows to the point where I'm sure my weight is making it sway slightly from one side to the other. My hands are covered in bark and sticky with sap. I go from one branch to another as I plot my course, but my head hits something. I look up and can't see anything above me. Did something strike me back in the Living World? I've been pretty confident in my body's safety without me. Nothing is stopping some bored neds robbing me while I'm away. But this wasn't a hard hit. It was like heading a Space Hopper or a bouncy castle. It was firm, but yielding.

Rather than cramp my neck I go back down a branch and reach up. Sure enough there's a see-through surface. It's resilient but flexible. The Tree's trunk passes through it no problem. This must be what Corbie was referring to. It's no coincidence that he has buggered off.

Maybe I can just poke through. It can't be like a balloon and the whole spirit world will burst as the Tree sticks through no problem. Unless this membrane, or whatever it is, grew around the Tree and it's all sealed up. I sit peering into the white mist hoping for some insight. None comes.

Stand up on the next branch, I push with my head and feel the barrier doming up over me. It puts a huge strain on my neck and shoulders, but also my legs on the branch. I feel the bough dip down and the Tree swing to one side. It could move out from under me and I'd fall until I hit a branch on the way down.

I give one more push as I try to climb a little higher bracing both feet on branches either side of the trunk. My neck hurts.

Then there is a pop and a sighing sound. The pressure is gone and the film flops on my face as it slides down and around my torso. I haul myself up through the tear into what looks like a stereotype for Heaven.

I'm looking out at a surface of white cloud. Bright blue skies surround me. More clouds are floating in the air. Golden sunshine warms me. The Tree continues up into the sky beside me.

In the air fly a variety of birds; eagles, sparrows, even what looks like an ostrich. Is that a horse with wings in the distance? Passing between clouds a Chinese dragon undulates by.

A black dot plummets towards me, before resolving into Corbie. He lands in the cloud, raising puffs of steam around him. "How do you like the Upper World?" Corbie says.

"It seems vast and empty, compared to the Lower World. It's not really Heaven is it?"

"You've seen the Underworld. That's all I know about after death. Maybe there's somethin after that." Corbie gives his Gallic shrug. "This is the land of ideas and abstraction, Gods and math, Platonic Ideals and beings of light."

"Angels?"

Corbie laughs. "Apply your natural scepticism here as much as anywhere else. You may find teachers as easily as torturers. Who knows what skin they'll be in? This isn't Heaven, as you say."

I imagine myself rising up into the air. Surely I can fly here? Opening my eyes, I'm still stuck on top of this cloud. Do I need to grow wings, flap my arms? "Why can't I fly? Everything else seems to be able to."

"You need to think yourself somewhere."

"Which is a great way of doing things if this is your first visit."

"How about you give it a try?" Corbie says. "Think yourself forward a few feet."

Moving forward is without any effort. Instead of thinking myself in flight, I just think of being at the height I wanted to go to. I pick up the knack of moving around the cloud and avoiding birds. Quite soon I feel really tired and have to supress a yawn.

"Yeah, really takes it out of you, doesn't it?"

What purpose is there really to this part of the spirit world? "Do these Great Spirits live here?" I'll go over there and give them a piece of my mind right now. Hopefully not literally.

"Dude, I honestly don't know. Maybe they have their own spirit world."

I take that as a yes. It's not his fault. He has a job to do. I only get told what I need to know to do mine. Give it time though. Knowledge is power. "There anything here you want to show me?"

"We can come back another time, unless you fancy going to school? We can find you some teachers. I'm just tryin to get you used to comin over and findin your way about."

I've more than enough to cope with from the teacher I've got, but I'll be back alright. "I'm alright for now, thanks. How do we get back down? Squirrel ride?"

"I'm sure he wouldn't mind if you asked real nice," Corbie says. "But it's as easy as before, just think your way back down the path you came on."

I speed down through the branches like a skydiver whose parachute hasn't opened. Then I crash into my body and wake up damp and sore.

Chapter 12

Crossing the Gardens on my morning business, I pass through the Tent City. Why weren't they there, in the Otherworld, like they were the first time? Did the different drum skin make that much of a difference? Was it just that it was my first trip? I still have the material with the eye printed in the middle. I could find another shell and have another go now I've got some practice under my belt.

My phone rings. Kathryn. A bolt of adrenaline runs through me. Rachael kisses me. I like it. Midori kisses me. I am laughing with my kids on Christmas Day, only a few weeks ago. Kathryn asks me for a divorce. Fox blood splashes my face. My arm feels weak as I lift the phone to my ear. "Hi. Good to hear from you."

"Mum got in touch. Not easy when you've taken a hammer to your mobile."

"I had nothing to do with that. I was out of it with pneumonia."

"Mum said. It's hard to believe."

"I understand. Proof is no use when it's faith that's lost. How are Lucas and Sam?"

"They're okay. A few days off school, it's almost a holiday. I may have said a few negative things about you in front of them."

"Are you back now?"

"Mum said you wanted to move back in."

Do I really? That was a long time ago. Would moving back be running away from this? "That was essence of the message I left. A lot has happened since then."

"I don't know, Niki. Before it would have been easy to change my mind. I was still hoping you'd say that when I last saw you."

I sigh. "I'm becoming a shaman. Not exactly willingly. I got sick because I refused to do as they wanted."

"A shaman? That crap your mum was always going on about? I remember she made us put those skulls up all around the house to keep some spirits out. Didn't do anything but scare the kids."

"Yeah. Just like that. This is exactly what the calls were designed to do. Keep us apart. Keep me on this path. I don't know what would happen now if I did move home."

Kathryn's laugh is bitter. "So you're seriously telling me that you're being blackmailed by spirits? It's one thing to live in a tent instead of our home, but as excuses go that's low. You know what? Forget about it. This is inane."

"Inane? How many nights did I keep you awake with my so-called Night Terrors? Huh? Bet you can't even count them. We practically had to sleep apart to get any rest. They're gone, Kathryn. Completely. This is a whole new life now. I'm visiting places you wouldn't believe."

"I don't know what's happened to you, Nik. You should listen to yourself. You're so full of your own shit. I have to go to work. You can see the kids this weekend and next, then we're back to normal."

"Kathryn, c'mon. Let's talk about this –" She has gone. "Properly."

It doesn't matter what I want. What little I had left I didn't hold on to. It isn't the Great Spirits' fault I'm here, but they did set fire to my last bridge. I'm angry and in despair.

After work I scour the river side looking for something to finish my drum. Another wheel or something like that. I find a large plastic tub which once contained tile grout. I'm not sure what the solid bottom will do to the sound. It could be like a snare drum and add some resonance. I don't need a skin, just beat on the bottom, but something is nagging at me to use the material I found. In my tunnel I tie the eye-skin in place and beat the drum a few times to get a feel for the sound. It is deep and louder than I expected, my head and chest fill with each beat. Even more than my fox hide bodhran the booms echo back from the tunnel. Corbie isn't here but I'm tempted to have a go at passing into the Otherworld at least. I give in and start the beat, banging the drum and dancing to my own rhythm. I'm beating and dancing for a long time. Have I forgotten something? Maybe this is a poor skin to use after all. If I doubt it then it certainly won't work. I keep on dancing and beating the drum. My shoulders ache and my calves are burning. Then evening is early morning. Darkness is turned to day. Winter turns to Summer. I hadn't taken the time to put on the coat and leather jeans. Nonetheless I am in the Otherworld.

I climb up the stairs into the ghost of the Botanic Gardens station and walk out onto the lawn. Once again the Tent City is replaced by a series of pyramidal cocoons glowing golden in the morning sun. Why aren't they here when I use the fox hide drum? Am I in the same place at all? It looks identical, except for the webbing. Since the tents are recent, if fairly permanent, structures maybe I'd see the same where something else is being built. I can't think where though – the building trade has almost dried up. No one is moving house, so no one needs new houses. Many apartment blocks are empty shells. Once it was the rundown estates with steel over the doors and windows. Still the Riverside museum and the apartment blocks down there may be empty but they are only a few years old.

It's a fair walk down to the Clyde, but nothing like my trip across the desert to the Underworld. I could fly, but Shanks' Pony serves me fine. I've not really left the Gardens in this World. I have a peek and see that the Salon is still a working cinema.

Near the bottom of Byres Road I can already see the tops of some of the flats near the river. I was right. They are replicated here as towers of webbing. What kind of spider could build a block of flats? I'm intrigued and scared to find out. I didn't see any by the tents though, and they're newer than these flats.

Maybe there's no spiders, no actual agents as such, and these objects form spontaneously out of spirit material, ectoplasm say. Like an accretion of mucus around sand forms a pearl. The longer these objects exist, the more solid their spiritual counterparts become. Conversely, when they no longer exist in the Living World, they are not reinforced and fade away, worn down by time.

This doesn't explain how I have ended up in a version of the Otherworld in which these constructions are obvious. Is this a better reflection of the Living World? The natural drum opens a door to a natural spirit world. The artificial drum opens a door to a more constructed spirit world. Where would I end up if I used my laptop to play a digital synthetic drum rhythm? Unless I danced my socks off I suspect it would be very hard to cross over.

I open my eyes and feel the prickly sensation on the back of my neck that I am being watched. Rachael had gone discretely to my tent and waited there. This is different.

"You can come out now." I stand up, stiff and cold. I shake life back into my limbs.

Something shuffles in the dark of the tunnel. Corbie would have no qualms coming out and pestering me. A figure emerges. Even in this poor light I can make out dark stained trousers and a padded jacket with gaffer tape over rips in the soft shell. The face is buried beneath long hair, a heavy beard and the shadow of a hood. Two eyes, though, burn. Perhaps because they're the only human thing I can see. "Who you to go ordering me about?" The voice is old. It sounds unused to being used.

"I'm not giving orders. I just wanted to know who was lurking about. My name is Nik. What's yours?"

"Lurking? Lurking?" he says. "This is my place. You've no right to be here. To take my spot."

I move slowly towards the man. Maybe he does stay here occasionally. "There was no one here when I came down. There's plenty of room. We could share."

"You're in my spot," he says. "You have to go."

I'm not going anywhere, but I don't want to antagonise this guy. There's no one here to look after my stuff when I'm gone. The guy has material bound around his hand like a crude bandage. I can also smell him. Despite the difficulties doing so I've kept myself fairly well. This guy has a unique feral stench. Sweat mainly, but there's something else. Almost sweet, like meat that's gone off. Is his hand infected? "I'm not leaving. I'm not in your spot. Would you like some food?" I say. "I'm hungry. Fancy some noodles?"

"You're gonna poison me. Take my things."

"I'll make some noodles. I'll eat some and you can eat some too, if you want. You'll see there's no poison."

He just watches while I boil water and add the noodles. In the weak light from the stove his skin looks tea stained. I put some food in a mess tin and put it on the ground for him. I eat some from the tin before eating from my own portion.

The guy seems lost. He sways forward, the savoury smell drawing him in, and then he backs away as his distrust pulls him out.

"It's going to get cold." I point at the mess tin with my fork.

He lurches forward. Squats down and practically empties the whole tin into his mouth. Noodles sprout from his lips like fine tentacles. To my surprise, he doesn't appear to burn his mouth. He slurps and chews.

This guy must have been on the hard end of the economic downturn for much longer than the rest of us and been kicked so hard so often he doesn't trust anyone.

"Stevie." He tips up the mess tin and drains the rest. "I'm Stevie."

"I can make some more, if you like."

"No. No more poison." His eyes beg me for more.

I start boiling up some more water and get another pack from my tent. Stevie has settled down, sitting cross legged on the ground. Newspaper sticks out the bottom of his trousers. "What happened to your hand, Stevie?"

He cradles it to his chest with his other hand in front.

"It's okay. Maybe I can help. I'm training to be a shaman. A healer."

"Kid with a knife. Hostel. Wanted my bed and my stuff."

"Did someone at the hostel look at it?"

Stevie laughs. "Kid got my bed. Didn't stay long enough."

"I've got a first aid kid. At least we could clean it and put a proper bandage on it." It's not like I have any real healing skills. I doubt a trip to the Underworld is going to help heal a wound in his flesh. I wonder about his head, though. I haven't seen Corbie all day, now I think about it. Maybe he only does half-days on Wednesdays.

Again, Stevie appears to contradict himself. He shelters his hand, even turns away slightly. But his eyes plead for help. I rummage around in my pack for my first-aid kit. I think there's even some iodine in there. I also grab a lamp. When I return to the stove Stevie's done a good job of making his own instant ramen. Glad to see he can help himself.

When I push the button on the LED lamp bright white light stabs my eyes and casts deep shadows into the tunnel and along the platforms. Stevie looks like a rabbit caught in the beams of an oncoming truck. He shovels more noodles into his mouth, barely chewing before swallowing them down.

I offer to look at his hand again and tentatively he lets me take his arm. I put on gloves from the kit and unwrap the t-shirt bandage. The blood is still sticky. Either the wound isn't closing or this happened only a short while ago. Cleaning away the blood I see a long wound on his palm. "You really need to get stitches. We should go to A&E."

"No. They'll take me in. Take my stuff."

"Okay. But I can't put stitches in so I'm going to use this glue." I show him the small bottle in the first-aid box. I wash the wound and use some iodine. Stevie doesn't flinch. Pulling the skin together, I dribble a line of adhesive along it. For good measure I use the little I-shaped plasters then cover the whole wound with a large section of sticky bandage which will stay there for weeks. Stevie just stares at me the whole time.

When I finish a few flakes of snow catch the light from the LED lamp as they fall in through the air vent onto the platforms below. They look like ultraviolet shards falling to earth. Soon more flakes tumble down onto the platforms and everything is covered in bright neon.

I feel weary and cold. I want to offer Stevie space in my tent, but there isn't any, and I'd suffocate in such close proximity to him. Some humanitarian I am. "Do you need a sleeping bag or something?"

"No. I have my stuff. You're in my spot."

"I'm not moving. You can sleep next to the tent. Might give you some shelter." Stevie just stares at me. I shrug. "I'm going to bed." I take the pots and go to clean them. I give everything a wash and brush my teeth. Will Stevie occupy the tent? He's so protective of his own things I doubt he'd take someone else's. Unless what's mine is his if he thinks it's in his space. No sign of Stevie when I get back, but I hear him in the tunnel.

I put out the LED lamp and pack it away. Stevie sounds like he is shuffling about beside the tent now. Native American Medicine Men used to sleep next to their patients and extract the sickness from them. Through dreaming I guess. I'm not so worried about Stevie's hand getting infected, but I'm convinced he's not mentally well. Gut instinct as I've no real proof or qualification to say this.

I try something. An extension of the evening's experiment. I flip open the laptop. Bathed in the cool glow of the screen, I program a fairly simple drum loop in a music application. Putting on my headphones, I hit play. The rhythm is familiar. The headphones add bass and depth. Not quite as good as either of my drums. The sound is in my ears, but not in my head or heart.

Listening I drift off to sleep. Everything is made of fine webbing. Everything man made. My tent, the bricks, the steel beams overhead. The computer is a bright overlay of several geometric shapes, pulsing, glowing. Tiny shards dart away from the laptop into the air. Others arrive, dock, and are absorbed into the geometric matrix, changing colour and shape.

Stevie lies beside me. His body wrapped in a fine web. I see through his flesh and bone, like a CT scan. A web is moulded to his kneecap. There are tiny webs in his mouth covering some of his teeth. He rolls in his sleep and I see a large web replacing part of his skull. I examine him more closely. I see webs shaped like pins in his hip and an area of his lower jaw is all webbed too.

Then I see an area deep inside his brain. It's the size of a walnut and it's red.

Corbie appears, with red laser beam eyes. Instead of thorns he is made from steel nails. He swoops out of the dark. I think he is going to land on my shoulder, but his talons tear at my face. Trying to grab him, I impale my hands on his body. I cry out in agony.

I wake myself up.

I've not had a dream like this in a few weeks. Maybe it isn't all over after all. I lie awake staring into the dark before I find sleep again.

Chapter 13

Stevie is still there in the morning, sound asleep. Kathryn and I rarely ended the night in the same room.

I flinch when I see Corbie standing outside the tent, but he is his normal self.

He cocks his head to one side, blinking. "What's wrong with you?" he says.

"I had a dream last night. You ripped my face off."

"I'd be lyin if I said that the thought hadn't crossed my mind once or twice."

"I'm serious." Corbie just looks at me. "Ok."

"Sorry I wasn't around yesterday. I hope you enjoyed your day off."

Should I tell him what I discovered? Knowledge is power. I don't really know if I can trust him. I'm sure he knows more than he is telling me about the Great Spirits. I don't know if he's teaching me out of service, self-interest or the goodness of his heart. On the other hand I've no one else to turn to for advice. No one outside the King of the Underworld's offices was interested in making friends.

"I worked on my own actually. Tried an experiment. I made a completely artificial drum."

"How'd that work out for you?"

"I went to another Otherworld."

"Sure you did," he says.

Who needs to lie when you won't be believed? "It was different to the one I went to with the fox skin drum."

"How can that be? There's only one." Do I detect an element of doubt in Corbie's voice?

"This one has webbing where new buildings and objects are in the Living World," I say. I'm sure there's more to it than just that. I tried using electronic beats last night and entered a weird dream with more webbing. I could see the artificial parts of this guy."

"I'm sure it was just an ordinary dream."

"I don't think so. I had a visitor last night. He's still here." I whisper in case he's awake. "I think he has a brain tumour."

"Saw it in your dream did you?" Corbie tries to pour scorn on my analysis.

I nod. "You can go and have a look yourself. Let me know. He also has a ceramic knee cap, pins in his hip and a ceramic plate in his head. Or it was all just a dream."

Corbie looks at me. Maybe he's trying to see if I'm bullshitting him. He turns and walks behind my tent to where Stevie is sleeping. I grab my washbag and go to freshen up. When I'm finished Corbie is gliding over the Tent City towards me, a dark shadow over the snow. I cover my face when he swoops up to land on my shoulder.

"Still worried I'd ruin your pretty features?"

"What did you find out?" I say.

"I hate to admit it, but I think you're right," Corbie says. "About the tumour in his head anyway. I could smell cancer on his breath. I'm not able to detect the prosthetic parts."

"Can we do anything about it?"

"We're healers. Shaman. We can't guarantee a result. Sometimes it's just someone's time. We can try though. If he wants us to."

"That's going to be an interesting chat. He's difficult enough to talk to as it is. Sometimes he looks at me like a man trapped inside a prison. Like he knows he's saying things he doesn't mean but there's nothing he can do about it."

"It's all part of the job. You gotta learn some time."

"You talking to yourself again?" Janice's breath steams out from her tent before I see her face peeking out.

"No. My invisible crow familiar," I say.

"No need to be sarcastic." She climbs out of the tent. "God it's cold this morning."

"It's pretty snug in the tunnel."

"I bet your WiFi access sucks though."

"Seems alright to me, but it probably tails off deeper inside. I'm sure we could set up a solar powered relay box."

"There's people here to look out for my stuff too."

"I'm just saying."

"I bet you've got to get off to work," Janice says. "And Brutus needs his walk."

"See you later."

I continue back to my tent, following my original trail through the snow. Janice is right it is freezing today.

"How do I cure him?" I say.

"Of cancer, in his head? Jeez Niki, start with an easy one, why don't you?"

"Well how do I cure anything? I'm not a doctor."

"No, but you can visit the spirit world. Maybe someone there knows somethin?"

"Are there particular healing spirits?"

"I wouldn't have said so. Plants know some of the effect they can have. Animals may know a few tricks, but they mainly help with your work, improve its effectiveness. There are teachers in the upper world you can ask. And obviously if it's somethin missin that's causin the problem, you kinda know what to do."

"I better get started then."

"Need a hand?"

"Of course. I still barely know what I'm doing."

Half way up the Tree of Life, I stop for a rest. Stevie wasn't in the tunnel when I got back, but a bag of things was still there, so I'm confident he'll return. At least this way I might have options for him, when

I tell him. Should I even bother? I don't know if I'd want to know. But the headaches, nausea, loss of muscle control, or whatever would tell me something was wrong eventually. I keep seeing his eyes pleading at me for help.

I start climbing again moving from branch to branch. Corbie swoops past flapping himself higher along with me. No sign of the giant squirrel so far. "It would be so much simpler if we could just get the lift or something," I say. "I'm all for the scenic entrance for first time visitors, but isn't there a back door we can use?"

"Exercise is good for you," Corbie says. "Think of it as a meditation, a physical preparation for enterin the hallowed Upper World."

"You don't sound like you believe that yourself."

"Don't get me wrong, some of these guys are alright, but many of them are so far up their own asses they can see daylight."

I laugh. "Tell me what you really think."

"You could try risin up higher as smoke, if you like. It's a long way down though."

So if I overcome my own instincts I can move up more easily. Otherwise I have to do it the hard way. I make the mistake of looking down. The hard way it is.

My head butts up against the membrane and this time I keep pushing upward. It's like trying to burst a thick rubber sheet. The strain on my neck and shoulders is almost too much, then it breaks and I feel the membrane slide over my face like spider silk.

Pulling myself into the Upper World I feel the air change. It is light, fresh, and slightly damp, like being on top of a Munro on a spring morning. The sun is warming. It seems to shine all the time here. Two hawks circle each other. I don't know if they're fighting or courting.

The servers at work will be fine without me. Everything was green when I checked online. No one missed me when I was sick. They'll be fine. This is important.

Corbie comes at me from out of the sun like a Kamikaze heading for an aircraft carrier. He pulls up at the last minute leaving me his phlegmy laugh. I shouldn't have told him about my dream. He comes in for another pass and I grab him out of the air, his thorns prick my skin.

"What the hell?"

"You thought I was going to let you keep doing that?" I let him go like I'm freeing a pigeon. He flaps away and circles round. "Where do we go from here? You said before that I would need to think myself to places in the Upper World. Is there somewhere the great medical minds hang out?"

Corbie shrugs. "You seem to be good at findin things for yourself."

Of course. "Computer, where will I find teachers for curing medical problems?"

A window appears in front of me. Like before there's a list of search engine results. This search must scrape the bottom of my memories. There's Stanford, John Hopkins, medical courses at Bristol, a book, links to entries about Hippocrates and Asclepius, and the image of a single snake wrapped around a stick. Asclepius was a mythical healer, the snake and stick his symbol. Maybe I need to speak to a snake. But they would be in the Lower World, surely? Unless this snake is more than an animal spirit.

"Where would I find a snake who could teach me?" I say. "Is that someone from Lower World or the Upper?"

"Good idea, and a good question. I still woulda said the Upper World is the place."

"So I need the Well of Souls."

"Never heard of it."

"It's in Tanis, in a film. Raiders of the Lost Ark. Lots of snakes."

"You're overthinkin this."

"Okay so let's go to a temple of healing or something. The Platonic ideal of a hospital."

"Why didn't you say so in the first place?"

"Because it was too obvious. I couldn't see it for looking at it. I still don't know how to get there."

"Just think yourself there. How many times do I have to tell you?"

I sigh and control the urge to throttle the bird. I close my eyes and imagine a cool marble Parthenon. Fluted columns and a triangular apex. Briefly I see the folly on Carlton Hill. Great minds are discussing perplexing ailments. Complex drawings of anatomy made on blackboards are indicated by wooden pointers.

Hearing the scuff of feet on stone I'm distracted. I open my eyes. I'm there. I can't believe it. I stand in a colonnade, a series of steps leads down to a large square where groups of people are in conversation. All of this is perched on the summit of a hill. More hills rise up in the distance, rocky and unforgiving. Turning round I see empty doorways leading deeper into the massive temple. I've never been to the actual Parthenon, which was a temple to Athena anyway, but this is much larger.

"Well that's the first step. I guess we need to find a consultant oncologist now."

Corbie looks around. "Take your pick."

"I'm going to go inside. Maybe someone there knows who the right person to speak to is. Otherwise we could be here a while."

I turn to head inside the temple and a figure emerges from the doorway nearest us. It has a male body, with a white skirt, and leather sandals, but the head is that of a bird. It is still proportional to a human head, but it has a long curving beak. It looks like an Egyptian god or something out of a nightmare.

It notices me and starts walking over. I don't know what to do. My instinct is to avoid it. I might be used to birds made of thorns now, but this is actually unnerving. Looking at hieroglyphs and pictures in books when you're a kid is one thing. This is approaching and unsettles me. Why this is wrong, but a naked woman made from plants is okay, I'll have to think about later.

"Hello." The bird-headed monster offers me its hand. "I don't think we've met before." Its voice is deep and resonant, not how a bird should sound. I hesitate too long. "All still new to you, isn't it? I'm Djuha."

"Sorry. I'm Nik."

"Are you just on the grand tour or are you looking for someone?"

"Corbie brought me here before." I indicate the raven which is shrinking out of sight behind my legs. "I'm hoping to cure someone of brain cancer."

"Corbie? Ah, Corbin McLean," Djuha says. "I didn't recognise you like that."

"Corbin? Corbin McLean?" I laugh. "You sound like a serial killer or a thriller writer."

Corbie edges back round from behind me, now his cover has been blown. "Screw the both of you." Corbie stretches and stretches, growing taller and his wings become arms, his legs more human. Blonde hair sprouts from his head down to his shoulders. A man stands in Corbie's place. He is still formed from a tangle of sharp thorns. His feathers have become a dark kaftan. He looks forty years old with the start of a beer belly.

"That looks more like you." Djuha shakes hands with Corbie. He doesn't seem to notice his palm pressing against the prickles. "How have you been?"

"I'm doin' alright," Corbie says. "Yourself?"

"I'm well. So this is your protégé?"

"I'm showin him the ropes. He's a good kid."

Djuha turns back to me. "Brain tumour? You didn't want to start with something easy, like a yeast infection or a weeping sore."

"A man comes to me for help – he maybe doesn't know that's why he's come to me – but who am I to turn him away? It's what I'm supposed to do, right? I don't get to choose my clients."

The bird-man seems to smile. Not easy to do with a beak. His expression turns serious. "We can only teach you medicine for the spirit, not the body. It isn't a matter of saying 'here take this pill' or doing surgery on a limb. Herbs may help the spirit and the body, but we cure the soul and hope that the body follows."

"I need to understand why, or how, his spirit is injured. Then look to fix that."

"Indeed. Each ailment will not be the same, as each patient is differ-ent. Each time you treat the same patient they too will be different," Djuha says. "How did you get on with Abel?"

"Abel?" Killed by Cain. The first person to die. "Ah. The President and CEO of the Underworld. We got on fine."

"So you understand that often there needs to be a sacrifice by the shaman to help heal the patient?"

Corbie laughs.

"What is so funny?"

"Nik didn't give him anythin. Told him he was there for what was his and walked out without payin any tribute."

"Really?" Djuha tilts his head at me the way Corbie does in his usual form. "It must have been his birthday." He claps me on the shoulder. "How extraordinary. Nevertheless sometimes we make sacrifices on behalf of those who seek us, whether it is to spirits or the gods."

That doesn't sound good. If I have no currency I need to trade with something. Favours, tasks, services, in advance or owed. Abel cer-tainly wanted prohibitions, taboos or some kind of sacrifice. Too many clients and I would have nothing to give. Midori talked about power structures, building up a network. Being a successful shaman starts to sound like being a Mafia Don more and more.

"I have two questions then. How do I avoid giving myself away in bans, taboos and promises? And how much do I owe you for this ad-vice?"

"Don't worry about owing me anything. As in the Living World, not everyone wants something for information. Some of us help out for the greater benefit that comes from it. I was taught by Chiron and all that was asked from me was to do the housework."

That name is familiar. "The Centaur who taught Theseus, Achilles and just about anyone else who was a demigod worth knowing?"

"The one and the same. It was a great honour. Perhaps one day you may meet him. The only away to avoid giving away too much is to be frugal with what you have, and only barter it in desperate need. But if you can escape without owing Abel your arm then I think you drive a hard bargain and have nothing to worry about. Besides, I can teach you some things, and I'm sure Corbin hasn't begun to show you what he knows. A brain tumour though." Djuha shakes his head. "I don't know. That is a lot to ask of a shaman. You could try spirit surgery. But we should find you that expert."

"Spirit surgery? I thought that was for cult leaders and charlatans."

Djuha shrugs. "In the wrong hands, used to manipulate people, all of a shaman's tools can be discredited and mocked. Faith and belief help the spirit. The mind is the master of all it surveys. Usually this is forgotten."

"Maybe I should focus on finding the root of the problem. Perhaps he's mentally ill and this has become physical? Maybe his spirit has been affected by some adversity in his life."

"These are all possibilities. It is rather rare that mental illness becomes physical. A mental illness is also not always a spiritual one. It doesn't always come down to shamanism and psychology. Sometimes people are just sick, and sometimes, many times, we can't help."

"You know I think it's like being a psychic plumber." Corbie says. "It's our job to unblock the toilet and sometimes it means gettin up to our elbows in other people's shit. And sometimes we have to go into the sewer and fix the problem there."

I have the image of my hands gripping a plunger sucking someone's exposed brain. "Maybe we can meet up again tomorrow, later though." I'm feeling guilty about not being in the office. "If Stevie comes back tonight I'll see what I can find from him."

"Later?" Djuha looks confused.

"I have work to go to. I shouldn't be there now…"

"Work? Other than shamanism?" His tone conveys such dismay, like how can I not be one hundred and ten per cent twenty four seven committed to my calling.

"Some of us need to eat. The High Heed Yuns may have taken away my family life, but they're not taking my income. Of course if they rain down manna every day, and a cup that never empties, then I might be able to change that."

"I understand. I will be here, later, tomorrow."

We shake hands and Djuha heads off to greet a nearby discussion group.

"How long have you known him?" I say.

"Only a few years, I guess," Corbie says. "He's an alright guy. Can be a bit stuffy."

When we get back to the Living World, Corbie has returned to being a raven, Stevie is still gone, but it's only ten o'clock. I know it'll bug me all day if I don't do it, so I head off to work.

I'm surprised that Stevie is still gone when I return. I am not my brother's keeper, but for some reason I do feel some responsibility for him. I'm even more surprised when Janice comes to visit with Brutus. The dog starts yapping until Janice threatens to kick him. Perhaps it would be better if she didn't move down here after all. They both have a good sniff around the platform and a nosy in the tunnels. The snow beneath the air vent slowly builds up while I brew us a cup of tea.

"What the fuck do you do down here? I keep hearing dull booming sounds for a few minutes each night and now in the morning too." Janice takes her cup.

"I'm practising to be a shaman."

"You're what? A shaman? Mr C an all that. I remember them when I was a student."

"No, not dance music. Although there is some dancing. I'm sure that's not the correct term anymore, but it's what my mum called it. Someone who travels to the spirit world and returns with knowledge and power to help their people. I'm sure hunting and planting was once as important a part of the job as healing."

"Right." Janice says. "How did you start learning that?"

"I've had terrible dreams since my childhood." I sip my tea. "My mum thought I was being called by the spirits. My dad had other ideas. Anyway, you know I was sick and that sickness, and curing it, was part of the hazing process after being chosen to be a shaman. Now

I'm being taught to travel to the spirit worlds. The booming is me drumming away until I fall into a trance."

"You really was talking to an invisible crow this morning?" Suspicion still clouds Janice's eyes.

I nod. "How are you keeping? One downside of being down here is I don't see people about so much."

"I think you're a wee bit mental, pal, but who isn't round here?" She shrugs. "My chest feels tight when I breathe. I can't cough although I want too. It's just stuck in there."

"I'm not a doctor, please bear that in mind."

She smiles. "Half the time they can't fucking help anyway."

"I'll see what I can do for you, but you're probably as well getting some expectorant from the chemist. Have you tried giving up the fags?"

"Aw, Nik. Smoking's all I've got."

I can't help but sympathise. "I don't know how you can afford it."

"I know a guy who sees me right."

I hold the mug between both my hands to warm them. "Isn't that dangerous? You could be inhaling floor sweepings and rat droppings."

"That's my problem no yours."

"It becomes mine if you're asking me to help you."

"I didn't fucking ask you for anything. Come on Brutus." She puts down the mug and marches along the platform. She scrapes a fag out of a packet and lights up before climbing the steps.

I shake my head. You can't help those who won't help themselves.

Corbie is still absent. I guess I've done my homework already. I'm intrigued by the difference in the Otherworld I experience through man-made or technological materials and the one where I use more natural resources. How can a drum skin make so much difference? I want to learn more, and my guide is not so much sceptical as in denial. It appears to be easier to pass over on an empty stomach, so I finish my tea and collect my bucket drum then put on my leather jeans and iron coat.

I quite quickly settle into a fast rhythm of movement and sound. The booming echoes off the walls and resonates in my trunk and my head. I increase the speed and then I'm in the Otherworld. Are the Lower and Upper Worlds also affected by these areas of webbing? There's only one way to find out. I climb up out of the station, grateful for the early morning sun starting to creep into the sky, and head towards the Tree.

It smells strange. Normally the Tree is an area of sickly sweetness, all the flowers blooming. Instead it's more like ozone with a touch of petrol, the scent of fresh plastic.

The tree looks grey. Like it's been petrified. As I get closer it seems less like a fossil and more like it is made from crystal silicon.

Where the variety of human breasts oozed milk, the lower part of this Tree is a mass of data ports. Sockets and slots of all types from large tape drives to Thunderbolt ports and plenty, probably obsolete, that I don't recognise. All of them are emitting streams of data; geometric shapes and beams of light passing out of sight. Nearer to the Tree I can make out pulses beneath the bark conveying information down into the ground and up into the sky.

Walking round the outside of the Tree, there's no pool of human fluid. No vulval passageway to an animal world. But there is a round glass plate on the ground, with a series of concentric blue rings getting closer together as they approach the middle. It looks familiar and is large enough for one person to comfortably stand on. I've seen enough TV to know the score. Without hesitating I stand on the glass. One to beam up.

There is an increase in white light and then it fades in a shower of silver. I feel like I'm crumbling into dust, and then this feeling runs backwards.

I expected to appear on the deck of the mother ship. Instead I'm somewhere far more abstract. It reminds me of both the stark emptiness of the Upper World and the riot of life in the Lower World.

Objects of different sides and colours pulse like jellyfish, moving slowly through the air. Smaller, more nimble sparks of light, or simple shapes, dart around, moving amongst the slower polygons like bees amongst flowers. Beams of light rush past.

Amongst the clouds of colour and polygons are tall, organic-looking structures which continually morph into complex geometries. It's like they are physical abaci that change form as they compute. Hidden beneath the structures are presences I can barely discern, shadowy and sinister. Almost everything is filled with energy which either radiates out or pulses beneath the surface – these things which are cold and dark.

The landscape is metallic, copper, silver, gold, titanium and steel. Crystalline clusters emerge from the ground like bushes and trees, but they are rare.

What sort of place is this? It must be completely different to those that Corbie has shown me. I feel that this is a technological space, but there are no obvious circuits or wires. There seems to be computation, mathematics, going on here. But is it as simple as that? Some of this must be related to the Upper World's abstractions and ideas. Is this a world of information and communication, or rather its spiritual equivalent? Would that make this is a world of subtext, of implication, of back-channel data transmission? An Exformatic World.

How long has it been here? It could have come about as soon as we started drawing things and speaking, but it would have been small, barely noticeable, and it would have grown as our means and methods of interacting through symbols and codes proliferated.

Is it all mine? Surely I can't be the first to find this place? If I am this is like finding oil or vast reserves of gold. Not that I know how to interact with the spirits here. Not yet.

I barely know what I'm doing in the rest of the Other World. Here I could be Captain Cook exploring new territory – territory that will keep growing and expanding. Hopefully with less fatal disputes with the natives.

Looking at the furious exchanges going on, and the predators lurking in the wilderness, I am truly in awe, and completely terrified.

I turn to go and a mothership appears after all. A massive flying saucer arrayed with bright lights comes down out of the solid blue sky. True to the stereotype I am enveloped in a beam of white light. I don't know if I'm scanned and studied. I'm certainly not staying around to get probed.

As I've been taught to do, I think myself back along the route I took. But I stay stuck where I am. I start to walk back the short distance to where I teleported in and either the UFO stays over me as I walk or I'm just moving but not travelling. While this is slightly better than being held down on a slab amongst a sea of fire and having my limbs torn off, my heart rates rises and I start to feel the familiar panic within me.

The beam switches off and the saucer moves away. It extends legs and lands in a large space amongst the computating fronds. I'm free to move again.

In a hurry I try to find a plate to beam back to the Other World. I can't see one. There just isn't one here. How am I supposed to return?

In the side of the UFO a door irises open. Three figures emerge from the saucer. They are about half my size, bipedal and come towards me.

I think about running away, but I have nowhere to run to on this infinite plane. Their ship could catch me again with ease. Looking about for a weapon, I find that all I have are the spanners and wrenches tied to my car coat. There are no rocks or branches on the floor. Acting like a threat is probably a stupid idea, but it's good to know I have something to hand.

The figures may be wearing suits. As they approach there is a shimmer around them that is hard for my eyes to focus on. They seem to sparkle too, like they're wearing diamonds on the surface of their clothing.

I can make out more clearly their heads and arms. The shimmer and sparkle are because their bodies keep changing, like they are made from fractals – Mandelbrot sets that are zooming in on deeper levels of identical detail. It makes me dizzy and nauseous to look, yet I'm also drawn in to the hypnotic effect. Their heads are more constant, but they too are three dimensional fractal objects which continually reveal their detail. They simply change at a slower rate.

The closest one's head resembles a rose or chrysanthemum and appears to constantly unfold its petals. It is strangely erotic and raises the expectation that something will be eventually revealed, but it never does.

The one on my left looks architectural. It's head is like a labyrinth inscribed into the side of the Grand Canyon and an ever deeper more complicated arrangement of pathways are shown to me.

The entity on the right resembles bone being wind-eroded into weaponry. An array of long savage thin edges display intricately detailed long serrations which are in turn serrated. I feel like I'm bleeding just by looking at it.

Opening Flower steps closer. "Hello. We are interested to meet you." Its voice is similar to the neutral female voice my phone uses.

"Hi. I'm interested to meet you too." I look out the corner of my eyes to see if I can spot the beam plate back to the Other World.

"May we ask your purpose in being here?" Opening Flower says.

Looks like I've been caught in a stop and search. What is the nature of your business here? Could you turn out your pockets for us? Handy how we're all speaking the same language. "I'm just exploring. I'm a shaman, spirit worker, whatever you want to call it."

"It is unexpected to meet an organic originating being here." Opening Flower sounds genuinely perplexed rather than finding a bloke in the changing room offended.

"I'm a bit lost to be honest."

"Perhaps we can help transport you home?" Eroding Blade's voice is dry and masculine like sand rasping on stone.

We suggest you go home. Please just get into the car. "If you could just show me the way, I'm happy to find my own way back."

"That would be no way to help a lost stranger." Amazing Mesa also sounds masculine but like wind whipping cables in a gale.

How do I get out of this trap? If I refuse their hospitality I could insult them, also I have no other means to get home. They've said nothing hostile, yet I'm finding their manner intimidating.

"We have not met an organic being here before," Opening Flower says. She is studying me intensely. I get that eerie feeling on the back of my neck.

"I didn't mean to intrude into your space. I was just exploring."

Opening Flower giggles, dissipating some of the tension. "We do not own this place. We genuinely wish to help. Perhaps we can show you more?"

"Indeed." Eroding Blade beckons and turns to go. "Come with us, please?"

I nod and follow, but keep on my guard. Perhaps they're friendly after all. Then again there's three of them and one of me and I'm lost and trapped. Do I really have a choice?

The surface of their craft shimmers and reflects everything around it. If the ramp was withdrawn and the lights turned off it would look like a heat haze. Walking up the ramp, Amazing Mesa behind me, I nearly change my mind and make a run for it, but I control myself.

"Have you been in a craft like this?" says Amazing Mesa.

Can he sense my fear and reluctance? "No. I went to Kennedy Space Centre once on holiday."

"What is there?"

"Space craft. Large vessels for leaving my planet and going into the vacuum around it. Nothing like this."

I step inside the craft. It is made of a material that looks like flowing mercury. Light emanates from it to help us see our way but I can't see any direct sources like LEDs. Down a narrow corridor we walk single file towards the centre of the craft. In the middle are four chairs, like those a dentist would use. Opening Flower gestures to one and I sit down carefully before leaning back. I expect restraints to sprout out at any moment followed by an intense experience with sharp lances.

"Are you alright?" Opening Flower again gives me the feeling of intense scrutiny. Without eyes or a face I only have my gut instinct to go on.

"I'm not a good flyer."

"We are sure you will be fine." Was that a smile deep inside the unfolding petals?

The others lie down on their chairs and there is the smooth sense of extra weight being added, like going up in a lift. Around us appears a 360 degree view of the world outside. At first this makes me dizzy, like being in an IMAX cinema film of a rollercoaster, but I look away for a moment and it passes. So long as the craft moves smoothly or not too fast I'll be alright. I wouldn't be a good guest if I threw up, although I'm sure some kind of robot would appear promptly to clean it up.

We fly through this technological spirit world and I quickly realise that I had arrived in the desert. The craft goes past great buildings, alive and alight, made of metallic and crystalline parts yet moving with an organic grace. These become more frequent as we enter an area that must be a city. Amongst the buildings fly craft, none of them like this one, and on the ground beings too small to identify go about their business.

"You are not from here either," I say out loud.

"That is correct," Eroding Blade says. "We have our own world. We came here looking for answers. We found you."

"What was the question?"

"Our question is somewhat delicate," Amazing Mesa says. "We would not wish to give offence."

"I have thick skin." There is a long pause. Maybe whatever it is that translates for us is working hard. "I'm not easily offended," I say, but I still sense tension, hesitation.

"We do not believe that animals, organics, possess any higher functions like we do," Amazing Mesa says.

Animals? Organics? Either these guys are not made from carbon, or they mean that they're more like computers. "I don't represent all organic forms, but I am talking to you now. I'm skilled in mathematics and its use in programming computers. What sort of higher functions were you thinking of?" Maybe I'm a little annoyed after all.

"Do you have a soul?"

Ah. I understand now. I laugh. This is ridiculous – machines are asking *me* if *I* have a soul. "I believe so. Many intelligent people in my world think that there is no such thing as a soul, that our thoughts are just complex biochemical reactions. They point to inorganic things, mere machines, computers running software, and say we are like them, just made from meat."

Opening Flower giggles again. "We deserved that."

"I've always thought that was too simple an explanation," I say.

The craft takes us over something that resembles a cathedral made of light. The detail is astonishing and I wonder of it is truly made from trapped photons or if it is a clever illusion.

"You know, you're in the wrong place, if you're looking to see if organics have souls. In the spiritual worlds I've seen so far, everything organic has a spiritual essence. If you can really take me home then you will see far more that you want there."

The craft veers away from the city of technology and light and vibrates. The scene outside shimmers and fades, before being replaced with the Tree of Life, albeit the one with the metallic skin and the data ports in its bark.

The three beings speak in a low murmur. I can't quite make out what they're saying.

The craft hovers near the Tree and there is a slight jolt as we land. I get off my couch and am ready to leave before someone finds the probe collection.

"We are grateful for you bringing us here," Eroding Blade says. He directs me back down the narrow corridor to the ramp. "It would not have been possible to find it without you."

They follow me down the ramp. I am glad to be on grass again. The sun is past noon, which means I have been in this trance a long time. What has happened to my body? I'm barely over pneumonia without getting hypothermia too.

Suddenly I feel like a host wanting his last guests to leave so he can tidy up and go to bed. I don't want to leave these people here by themselves – on some level they are inside my imagination – but I need to wake up. "Perhaps next time I can show you around properly?"

"Yes, we would like that," Amazing Mesa says. He reaches into his suit and pulls out a flat crystal, about the size of a fifty pence piece. "Use this to contact us and we can find you."

I watch as they walk back into their craft and after a few minutes it fades from sight.

Above me is taut plastic, not curved brick. I am under my sleeping bag. Someone has moved me into my tent.

My hands are tingling and cold. There is a numb and yet sharp pain at the tips of my fingers. They feel itchy too. I think I have a touch of frostbite.

Someone moved me back here, and not too late either. Could it be Janice? I'm hungry and have a deep need to urinate. I put on another jumper and some gloves and leave the tent. There are even drag marks in the snow outside the tunnel. Beside the tent there is a deep snoring noise. Stevie's in his sleeping bag packed in with newspaper.

I trudge through the deepening snow between the tents. It hits me like a sledgehammer and I almost fall on my knees. I've shown alien intelligence how to find Earth.

Chapter 14

Stevie is sitting on cardboard looking out at the falling snow when I get back to the tunnel after work and shake off the small mounds that have formed on my shoulders.

"Thank you for putting me in my tent yesterday."

"It's in my spot, you know."

"So you say. I'm not moving it though."

"My stuff is still here."

I can't go through this every conversation. "Stevie, listen. I have something I need to tell you." I look in his eyes and the trapped intelligence peers out at me. "I think you have a tumour in your brain." His eyes widen. He nods slightly. "Is there anything you can tell me about this? I'm going to try and help you. I stole your spot so we could work on curing this together."

"It's my spot."

I change into my shaman suit and enter the Upper World. It's as empty and spacious as I remember it. Birds fly high and the clouds are cool even under the sun's warmth.

The bird headed man is waiting for me beside a pillar outside the Temple of Asclepius. If I'm late, or he's been waiting long, he gives no sign.

"How are you, Nik?" Djuha says.

"I'm okay. Yourself?"

"I am fine. I think I have found someone who can help. They understand the brain and know some surgical techniques."

"Great. Thank you very much." I hope I can learn these things but surgeons dedicate their life to their discipline and I've been at this five minutes. "Where do we find them?"

"She's a colleague of mine and she's waiting inside." Djuha leads me towards a doorway in the marble wall of the temple.

Inside I'm surprised how light it is. Windows high up on the walls let the golden sun in, but there are still patches of gloom. Djuha takes me along a corridor and into a large room with rows of marble slabs along each side – part hospital ward and part mortuary. A slender woman, naked to the waist, has her back to us. She is wearing a similar white skirt to Djuha. When she turns around, a shaft of sunlight highlights her bared breasts and the head of a black jackal with tall pointed ears. She's a female version of the Egyptian god Anubis.

"This is Anput," Djuha says. "She has some experience of examining the brain."

"Hopefully not by pulling it out through the nose. Pleased to meet you. I'm Nik."

"Usually I just crack the skull open and scoop it out," Anput says, taking my hand in both of hers.

"Thanks for agreeing to meet me, maybe teach me."

"Tumours are not usually something we can fix," Anput says. "Even if you take out the core there is a good chance that some of the surrounding area will turn bad before long. You need to treat that too."

"With herbs or something like that."

"Modern medicine would use chemotherapy. Alternatively beams of energy, gamma rays or X-rays could be used."

"Unless we sneak into a well-equipped hospital I think that's unlikely," I say. "But then if that were an option an expert surgeon would be doing the operation not a novice shaman."

Anput's nostrils flare, like she's smelling me. An ear moves hearing something I can't. "Djuha, you didn't tell me he was a freshly weaned pup."

Djuha shrugs. "I thought it was obvious."

"The surgery you will use back in the Living World will be very different to a hospital's techniques," Anput says. "You will be working on his soul. It might be easier if you could bring the patient into the Other World and work directly on the problem here. Djuha and I will show you what to do and we will practice here for a few days."

"Okay." Something isn't right, I can't put my finger on it just yet.

"Lie down on this bed and we'll begin."

The stone is cold, unyielding. I've felt emotions in the Otherworld, but sensation has been muted, dampened, absent even. Fear, but not thirst, or cold. Talking of fear, my Spidey-sense is tingling. I try to lift my head up from the slab, but I feel weak and my limbs heavy. Djuha and Anput stand over me. "This won't hurt much," Anput says as she slides her hand straight into my abdomen.

(A metal lance pierces through my torso, chipping the slab below.)

I scream, but no sound comes out, as my skin caves in under her fingers before tearing eases the pressure. I feel her tickle my liver. A huge ball of heat builds just below my ribcage. It's going to burst, it feels so enlarged. But if I let it go I know it will be the end of me. My sight is dark except for bursts of blue pain, and the glow from my chest like someone has put a lightbulb in there. I hold on, like a child in a long-distance car journey needing a wee, praying it passes before I embarrass myself.

Anput pulls out her hand. A long stringy substance dangles from it with lumps of unidentifiable meat clinging on.

(– Is it there?)

"There. That wasn't too bad, was it?" Djuha says.

The lethargy is gone. I examine the wound with my hands but feel nothing there. I sit up and look down, lifting up my shirt and t-shirt. No scar, no blemish, nothing to show for my pains.

"We just need to teach you the same technique," Anput says.

I can't speak, but it is supressed rage. Are these two my demon torturers? Or am I just transferring onto them what happened? This is all too familiar.

My legs can barely hold me, when I stand. My thoughts are flashing between now and all those endless nights of agony.

"Where are you going?" Djuha says. He sounds like he is mocking me.

I fall heavily onto my knees. I crawl out into the corridor. I feel sick. This dream body has nothing to throw up. No cathartic up-chuck.

I don't notice where I am until someone puts their arm around me and lifts me up to stand. I'm outside the temple. I mutter my thanks and will myself home.

It's cold and hard on the tunnel floor. My stomach rumbles. I sit up. I wish I could light a proper fire down here.

Why was I so trusting? Did they really think they were helping me learn something like that? Perhaps it was all some elaborate joke. I'm angry with them, and even angrier with myself. It was stupid and naïve to think anyone could help me with a brain tumour. I shouldn't have said anything to Stevie, but I can't take it back now.

I lose myself in the mechanics of preparing dinner. I don't really want to eat but my body is crying out for something hot to fill my belly that isn't someone's hand. I know I'm losing even more weight and feel bone deep tired. Ecstatic experiences are not good for you.

I have the kids tomorrow. I feel nervous about that. I used to look forward to these Saturday's but I don't know how much Kathryn has turned them against me. I don't really want to see her either.

The snow has a crisp crust I keep breaking through on my way past the Tent City. With luck no more will fall on top of it tonight.

Chapter 15

She wasn't in when I arrived, but Kathryn's back home when I drop the kids off. I want to know where she spent the night. Who she spent it with. Asking won't get me an answer though. It would be like asking Corbie where he's been. Out on the wind. None of my business.

The kids were okay. Happy to see me. I love being with them, hearing their stories, hearing them bicker. But it feels hollow only having them for a few hours and I'm not sure I hide my sadness well. Not long ago I thought I'd be moving back in, becoming a family again.

The document is waiting for me, sitting on the table. Kathryn hovers nearby, coffee in hand. I turn to her with the pen in hand. She nods before I finish asking. "Are you sure we can't work this out?"

I sign away the years. I have no assets. I no longer need to provide for the kids, or her. I can probably afford a flat, somewhere where they could stay the weekend. Would this have happened without the phone calls? Possibly. Without the bird and the Otherworld? Probably not. Without the tent and whatever it was I was trying to prove? No.

This is not a comfortable bed.

We call the kids in and tell them together. Tell them we love them and that I'll always be around. Lucas pretends he's a man and just shrugs, but won't meet my eye. Sammy runs to her room. I wait for her to come out – I don't have the right to force myself into her space. After an hour Kathryn suggests I just go like it's all my fault, like leaving will make it all right again. I say goodbye to Sammy through the door. I think I see her curtain move as I walk down the street to the bus stop.

I haven't had time to think about Stevie and Djuha and tumours and saving other people from their own fucking messes. The vibration of the bus's engine rattles my teeth.

– Hey stranger, how are you? Rachael has perfect timing.

– Some kind of blue. You?

– Sorry to hear that. Fancy splitting some kind of red?

– Sure. My place or yours?

– Your place is a bit draughty.

– Where's yours?

She sends me an address and a time.

Crunching up the path in what passes for my best, I feel self-conscious without a gift. It's like meeting Sally McTaggart's family for the first time one Friday after school. I don't really know what to do with my arms or anything.

A yellow glow spills out from the doorway. Rachael has done something with her hair. Pulled it away from her neck. I panic. This feels wrong. I'm cheating on Kathryn. Kathryn who didn't come home last night. I hope none of this is on my face. I smile, pleased to see her. She leads me into the warmth.

It is a compact, tasteful, two-up two-down. Scandinavian flat-pack furniture and one or two antiques. Decent hi-fi, shelves bowed under books. It feels comfortable, right. Fiona's house was always going to be hers. We would always have been guests. I could never have lived there.

Something smells good. Rachael hands me a glass and curls onto the sofa beside me. She is wearing a nice green dress and tights. I don't think I've seen her in anything with a skirt before.

"How've you been?" Rachael says.

"Caught between two worlds."

"The dream within the dream?"

"More of a nightmare, really. I signed the papers. I guess I'll be free sometime early next week."

"Congratulations."

It doesn't seem like something to celebrate. The silence lengthens.

"It's Bolognese and linguine for dinner."

"I wondered what smells so good."

Rachael goes off to check the pasta. I feel awkward where before things have been easy between us. Corbie was right; a kiss isn't just a kiss. A kiss can change everything.

The food is good, but conversation is a little slower.

"How's your mum?" Rachael says.

"I haven't spoken to her."

"She worries about you, you know."

Have we said all there is to say to one another? I gaze into the candle flame as much as look into her eyes. Perhaps playing with the possibility was better than winning. Maybe it's just too soon and this has been a long day.

I want to tell her about the surgery, but where do you start on something like that? You'll never guess what happened to me yesterday. Gizzard talk is not good for dessert.

I think Rachael had a different plan for this evening, but she seems relieved when I go in time to get the last train back to Glasgow and the long walk home. I get a peck on the cheek and promise to call her. Am I relieved or have I screwed up something good? I look forward to my bed and a long lie.

Chapter 16

In the early hours the dam bursts. A recurring nightmare is one thing. Violation by people you trust...I still feel her hand inside me.

There is a knot of sickness and sadness inside and something primal I have no words for and I shudder thinking about it.

I can't contain it inside me. I howl like a wounded predator. It echoes down the tunnel. Stevie mutters in his sleep.

How did I keep it together yesterday? How did I sit with my kids, with this black filth tainting me? How did I have dinner with a beautiful woman and not corrupt the evening completely? How do I get it out?

I claw at my stomach. My ragged fingernails scratch at the skin. The blackness wells up, running free down into my crotch. I let it bleed out. But I know it isn't enough. I tear more strips away until the skins breaks along the line where she plunged in. I push a hand inside and scoop out darkness. It writhes like ink in water. I pull open the gash and tear out more. I keep ripping until it runs red. My hands are slick with gore. Then the pain kicks in. Fire prickles up and down the tear in my abdomen, runs along the lacerations in my belly. What the hell have I done to myself now?

The tent is melting.

I wake up again. It wasn't a dream. There are scratches, dried scars now, all across my stomach and chest, but no central one. It prickles every time my t-shirt brushes across the lines. Last time I felt like this I was a little kid with chicken pox, covered in Calamine lotion, hot and tender where I just had to use my nails.

Tea cures all ills. Walking through snow to get water probably causes many of them in the first place.

I feel a little better. A shower would be good, if agonising. Maybe calling Rachael to apologise and explain would be a good idea. Then like Kathryn she can move on because I'm never going to have 2.4 kids and a dog and live in a semi in a nice suburb. That was never part of the plan. I just didn't know it while I invented new ways to use other people's money. That was an island in time, a brief experience so I could understand how other people's lives were.

My mind has cracked, or worse, this is all real.

And I promised the bearded snoring creature next to me that I would help him. Not using this dubious technique I seem to have been infected with.

I'm waiting for the sun to come up when Corbie flies down the air shaft and lands on the ground in front of me. "How you been doin?" he says.

"That Djuha fellow is a very shady bloke. He took me to see a woman with a jackal's head. Egyptian god style, like him. I was held down while she put her hands inside me, pulled out gristle and left some black shit inside. He just stood there, watched, practically helped her."

"Sorry, man, I had no idea. Like I said, I thought he was a bit up himself, but that was all. Actually, I'd heard you'd been seen staggering out of the Temple."

"That was me trying to get away from them after they...invaded me."

"But why would they wanna do that?"

"Power. Why else does anything happen? Midori said that the spirit world was practically feudal. Little spirits need more powerful ones for patronage and protection. These guys were asserting who's boss, wanted fealty or something. Nothing's free, there's always a price, even if there's no payment."

"Hey some people really just wanna help with no ulterior motive."

"There are no true altruists."

"Jeez, you really woke up cynical today."

"Tell me, why would anyone want to be part of this? You get tortured to find out if you're chosen. If you're selected by the high and mighty spirits you're then thrown powerless into a system of grace and favour. Shamans need spirits to get things done, but why do the spirits need shamans? I just don't see how this works. Marx said you got to follow the money. The powerful spirits don't really need shamans to oppress the weaker ones, so what gives?"

"You got it all topsy turvy. The shamans are here for humanity's benefit. The spirits decide who they're gonna let in. Shamans bring back useful information, of course there's gonna be a price for that. This isn't about you. It's about what you do to improve the Living World with what you find in the spirit world.

"And I'll let you in on a secret. The spirits need the Living World; they need tribute but they also need change. Remember most everything there is an animal or a rock or a tree or some essence of something abstract. All the rest are former dead people. They've usually been dead a while too.

"It takes a long time for changes to happen there, and for a very long time there's been little connection between the two. There's been no industrial revolution there, never mind computers.

"You're a powerful person. They're scared because of what changes you can bring. Upsettin their little apple carts. I shouldn't have boasted about your meetin with Abel. Clearly Djuha felt his cock was too small and needed to find some way to win a pissin contest."

I laugh. "If the best he can do is get a girl to beat me up then he has a very small dick indeed."

"Exactly."

"So I'm expected to bring about a revolution?"

"Not you personally. Just the ideas you bring with you."

I'm probably going to regret this. "Remember I told you about the alternative Otherworld I went to?" Corbie nods. "I went back there. The Tree of Life was some kind of digital organic thing. And I went to some other place. Somewhere made of technology or information. I met aliens, spirits, I don't know what. It wasn't their digital spirit world. They had a spaceship and brought me back again."

"You what?"

"I found talkie toaster heaven and scary appliance angels."

"Shit. Really?" Corbie waddles up and down. "We can't tell anyone about this. Either they won't believe us or they'll try and cash in. It'll be like the Gold Rush."

"I think these guys know how to handle themselves. They've got flying saucers. Probably ray guns too. They asked me if organics had souls like they did. We're just primitive animals to them."

Corbie's laugh sounds like he's choking on a peanut. "Then we could be seriously fucked, Dude."

"I showed them how to get to our Otherworld. They gave me a lift home."

"You need to go back and first contact them properly. Get them onside. Revolution is nothin if there's gonna be an invasion."

"It's hard to believe that someone who goes out of their way to help you is going to invade earth from a spiritual reality."

"When did you become Neville Chamberlain?"

"Who's he?"

"Don't they teach you anythin in school. Mr 'peace in our time'. Next thing you know Poland is Blitzkrieged."

"Ah, the guy with the moustache waving the bit of paper outside the airplane. I'm not appeasing anyone. These guys are explorers like us. We should be natural allies."

"Like Cortez or Pizarro were explorers. Perfect example of a more advanced civilisation discovering a lesser one. That worked out well too. You sit here moanin about how everyone you meet in the Otherword tries to fuck you over. Why should these guys be any different?"

"They seem to know these other spiritual dimensions better. If there's something there that will give us an advantage they should know. You're the only one talking about revolution. The Otherworld may need to change but I'm not interested. You can all go hang so far as I'm concerned. I'll do the minimum to keep the Powers That Be off my back. I'll explore these other spaces because I'm interested."

Corbie turns his back to me. "You know, I don't know when you lost your balls. Maybe your wife has them in a jar or somethin. When you gonna start standin up for yourself? Are you not fuckin mad at all this?"

"I'm mad as Hell, but I'm not a revolutionary. I'm not much of a shaman. If I could I'd have this whole thing go away."

"And what? Go back to a mortgage, livin in a semi-detached in suburbia. You know that isn't your life. It never has been. Grasp the nettle, accept the chilli. Grow a new set of balls, or a backbone or something."

I laugh hard. "You're so full of shit yourself. Ok, sure, I know I can't go back to my old life. Doesn't mean I've not been programmed to desire that. It was in my grasp. But I don't want to join a different system of oppression either."

It's Corbie's turn to laugh. "Well, Che, that sounds like revolutionary talk to me."

"Fuck off." He does have a point though. I'm all mouth and no trousers.

"Stop denyin it, man. The path to inner peace is the one of least resistance."

"We'd meet a lot of resistance if we ran a guerrilla war in the Otherworld. Besides my inner peace is easily met by sitting on my ass doing nothing."

"Jeez, you're hard work. You wanna be a shaman your way? Give it a go. That may be revolution enough. Go talk to Midori, she liked you. I'm sure you could come to some kind of understandin."

I hear the insinuation and don't rise to the bait. Would a relationship with a spirit be easier than one in the Living World? I doubt there'd be a huge difference. Being a shaman would still complicate matters. I see now just how stuck in the middle this role is. I'm not part of either community. I'm a champion for both.

I leave it til later in the morning before I call Rachael. She still sounds sleepy. "Sorry for calling you so soon."

"That's okay. I needed to get up."

"I wanted to see if you were free this evening. I wasn't on good form last night. I wanted to leave work at the office but dragged it in with me anyway. I should have talked to you about."

"I would, but I have work to do myself. There's a pile of marking I need to do for tomorrow. I'll speak to you later in the week."

Although it is probably nothing other than what she says I still feel like I really missed a cue last night. It was too early, but I may also be too late. She needs to be more patient. I told her that already. It's going to be much better to leave this alone.

The cold water is good on my face, and it stings as it runs down my chest. I feel awake and clean – ready for the rest of the day. Janice is coming out of the Ladies as I head back to my tent. I nod.

"Sorry I lost my cool with you," Janice says.

"Don't worry about it. You didn't ask me for help. I should keep my nose to myself."

"You weren't interfering. You were just looking out for me."

Should I ask some plants in the Lower World for some advice for her cough after all? "Well we're a community. We should stick up for each other. No one else will."

"Aye. You're right there. I need to visit my sister and she's allergic to the dog. Would you look after Brutus for me?"

Me and my big mouth. I can't back out now. But maybe it will help bring the Tent City together, properly. Rachael was right. We are all isolated from each other. "When do you want me to get him?"

"He'll be okay in the tent. Just make sure he gets his walks, and some food. I'm leaving later today."

"I'll drop by before you go then."

I play it safe and use the fox drum, wade through mother's milk and emerge in the Lower World once more. I've not been here since my first proper trip. It feels weird. A bit like going home and a bit of an adventure at the same time.

The kaleidoscope of animals still whizzes, buzzes, zings and crashes past me and I'm always ready to duck out of the way. A large green wasp, the size of my hand, seems determined to fly into my head no matter how many times I try to gently bat it away until suddenly it's taken by something that passes with a whip of wings. There's an horrendous cat-howl that sounds like something in pain until it sounds like an answering call from the opposite direction.

The forest appears to be larger than before. I can't see any further into the chaos, but I sense a greater mass around me. Most likely I simply have the time to notice. It all seems so different too. Everything has changed. Foliage has fallen and been replaced. The light falls differently on the jungle floor. Almost nothing can have survived the constant cycle of predation, except some top of the heap cats or lizards. Finding Midori could be a challenge. Perhaps the river will lead me to the pool where we met. If I can find the river.

I climb over fallen trees, avoid the spores bursting out of fungi I fall on, crawl under giant leaves, swat away blood seeking flyers the size of humming birds and generally do a great job of getting myself lost. A swarm of millipedes, each the size of my arm, passes in front of me. In their wake I see what looks like a worn path through the writhing undergrowth.

This is highly unusual. Is it an elaborate trap? Some creature that lures in the lost with the hope of a passage to safety like an anglerfish in the depths of the ocean. In fairy tales the advice is usually to not step off the path rather than avoid it. Against my instincts I follow it.

The path tracks a random course, curving round trees and large rocks, obliging me to still duck under fallen branches or clamber over other obstacles, but never quite going back on itself. After some time I worry less about a crazed animal waiting in its lair and more that this is just a waste of time. I'm on the path to nowhere.

Sticking it out for just a little bit longer, it starts to feel like an hour or more has passed, when I hear rushing water and the path takes me to a huge tree that has fallen across a deep chasm through which a river crashes in a cascade of falls. I cross the tree, able to comfortably stand up on such a wide trunk. When I look downstream I think I recognise the pool where I met Midori. On the other bank the path heads off in the other direction and I have no idea if it will loop back down.

I wait for two bees the size of sparrows to pass before clambering down the steep slope alongside the river. Then the slope turns to a cliff. I remember hanging onto the roots on the edge of the Abyss and have no desire to try clambering down this. To my left the cliff face extends as far into the jungle. To my right the river cuts down into the rock. Perhaps I can follow the river, risk using the wet rocks and even jump from pool to pool.

I'd better be right about this pool.

Derr, there's always my in built GPS. "Computer trace a path to Midori." A familiar window opens and assures me this is the right place.

Slipping down the rocks, I splash into the river and am immediately pushed over by the current. I bob like an apple on Halloween, before finding my feet again and bracing myself against the flow. I'm soaked to the skin, but the water is refreshing in the heavy air of the forest. With care I edge my way to the nearest fall and balance on wet, sharp rocks until I reach the small turbid pool below. Two more later and it might have been better to climb down the cliff. One more to go and I'm finding it hard to concentrate. My foot slips and my shin is scraped raw by a sliver of rock which insinuates itself under the hem of my motorcycle leathers. Hot and cold at the same time, my leg is bleeding profusely, the red churns with the foam of the falls. I don't feel like I can put any weight on it and there's nowhere I can pull myself out of the rapids.

There's only one way out. I let myself go. I'm picked up and tossed over the edge of the fall before my stomach rises while the rest of me plummets down. Then I hit the water and the breath is taken from me. Fluid seeks to replace it and I surface choking for air and coughing up water. Behind me I hear a frenzied splashing and realise that this pool must be home to something carnivorous. My leather coat and the surfeit of spanners pulls me down and I struggle to swim.

I hear strange words and I'm sprawling on mud and wet rock as the river rapidly recedes from beneath me.

Midori strides out of long reeds on the banks beside the pool. She ducks down gracefully and supports me as we stand. I hesitate to give her my full weight, afraid I would crush her. She ends up dragging me out of the pool and laying me down in grass before the water floods back into the worn rock bowl. Without a word she pulls up the trouser leg and traces the gash with her finger. The flesh knits back together and the bleeding stops.

"Thank you." I try to sit up, but Midori pushes me back down.

She bends over me, her face close to mine. "Lie still, for a while." Her breath is sweet and heady like nectar.

My tongue aches slightly where she jabbed me when we kissed. "Thank you." I relax and drift off for a moment. When I come back I sit up. My head feels heavy and swollen.

Midori is kneeling just watching me. "It is good to see you again, Nikolai Munro. I wondered if you would be back. Where is your flying friend?"

"He had some other business to look after." I need to get my act together. Working with Midori might be good, but if every conversation is a duel it will get tiring.

"Have you come to accept my offer?"

"An alliance sounds very formal." Midori's scent is all around me, floral and yet musky too. Something stirs inside me.

"A partnership sounds very intimate, to me," Midori says, smiling.

It's like time stops. I have never seen anyone so beautiful. "As would a union, no doubt."

"You don't wish to be united with me?" She runs a hand up her leg, over her hip, round her waist and lifts her breast, mocking me.

The spell breaks. My lust subsides. "How about a coalition?"

"With just two of us?"

"We could invite more. All of us working together."

Midori strokes her chin. "Very well. Who would you like to invite?"

"Anyone can join. No one is anyone's owner. No vassals, no lords. Cooperation for mutual benefit."

"You want me to give up my obligations? Free the spirits indentured to me?"

"Your servants will also get the chance to be your allies. But through choice not obligation."

She laughs. Hard, brittle, like dry sticks. "Look around you, naïve fool. Do you see the lion lying down with the lamb? Cats and dogs living together? This is the jungle. Things get eaten."

"Of course they do. We all must do what we can to survive. But look beyond that. Not everything fights all the time. You protect your servants. You still will. But instead of some tired feudal struggle a new system will begin."

"It has sustained us well this long."

"If this world reflects the Living World then the change will happen anyway. Sooner or later the lords will ask too much of the servants. They will feel they do all the work and are taxed too much. Unearned taxes which are squandered on squabbles with other powers or plain indulgent excess, which is the rubbed in their face. The little people will rise up and cast the lords down alongside them. It won't be blood-less.

"You must have enforcers, knights, barons, who keep them in line. The workers will throw them down, or the barons will take your power from you. If you survive, instead of fighting with armies or trading witty jokes, you will have to work the land yourself."

"Your prophecy is empty," Midori says. "Nothing changes here. The spirits are too weak to revolt, that is why they serve. If they could pro-tect themselves and thrive they wouldn't need me. But let me indulge you, how will this new system of yours work? Will it not lead to the same situation? Servants will be workers, lords become…I don't know bankers, senators. People will always get fat on the efforts of others. You should leave. Before I get fat eating your carcass."

I see people falling past my window. I know that along one path she is right. But there are other paths. Socialism, communism. Dismissed as either failed or utopian ideals. I have no real answer for her, no response as I'm just against the way things work, and my alternative is just some woolly idea of a community working together. A vague New Lanark. I stand up and stride into the jungle while Midori stays kneeling beside the grass I flattened.

Perhaps the only way to know how it will work is to try and explore it. Find spirits who do want to work alongside me rather than for me. It doesn't have to be a world-wide movement.

I wish I knew what spirits ate. Something must sustain them, unless they actually eat one another. But the spirits at the bottom would need to feed on something, get energy from somewhere. The economics of the spirit world – bound to be a gripping bestseller.

I understand economics – I worked in a bank after all. I did the math on probabilities of making money from models. But I've come up against a more fundamental philosophy – how things should run. I'm so far out of my depth I wish I'd never started swimming.

Lost in thought I walk until I find that the jungle has started to become more familiar. The massive canopy trees are now heavy wide oaks and beeches. I can see sky. The business of insects, birds and beasts has calmed, to the point where the lack of movement made me realise the environment had changed. The soil is rich and red-dish, where it has been disturbed, otherwise a thick carpet of grass, moss and clover covers the ground. Cattle with shaggy coats and wide horns, graze in lazy herds. Swallows dart through clouds of midges and I hear the cooing of doves. It's like I've walked back in time to some British idyll.

I walk down a hard dirt avenue. Brambles and hawthorn bushes form a hedge at the top of the steep slopes on either side. Deciduous trees arch over the top. Ahead I see a strange figure in silhouette. The broad shoulders and legs of a man, but the antlered head of a stag. The cave-painting in the Underworld given life. I saw this figure in a TV show from my child hood; a silver arrow and Herne's son. Could this be Herne himself? The idea is exciting and I feel awed. The figure waits. For me? For the hunt to begin?

As I get closer I see that this is a giant of a man, wearing a Great Elk's head and draped in its skin. An array of bones and small animal skulls hang from threads sewn into the hide. His feet are bare, but he's wearing rough leather trousers beneath the skin. I'm almost knocked back by the stench of piss, sour sweat and excrement.

"Hello traveller." Herne's voice is deep, and touched with humour. "I saw you coming and thought it would be nice to have company, if you would have me."

"It's unusual for someone to be happy to see me. So I would be glad to join you."

"Then you should keep better friends," Herne says.

I finally reach him. This man is twice my height and twice as broad. "I can't fault your logic there. I'm Nik. Nik Munro."

Seeing my hand in his is like when I first held Lucas after he was born. "I am The Hunt."

"Pleased to meet you."

"You carry the world on your shoulders, shaman."

There is a subtle pressure in the presence of The Hunt. Not just the urge to stand upwind. A force of will. It's not being exerted, it's just there. "I'm no shaman," I say. "I don't know what I'm doing."

"You look like a shaman to me," The Hunt says. "At least you have the courage to admit your shortcomings to strangers." The Hunt walks slowly along the path and I, walking normally, just about keep up.

"Just one more example of my extreme stupidity."

"What is really at the heart of your trouble?"

"I'm lost here, in the spirit world. I can't see how the system works. What do spirits live off? How do they organise? Where does the money go to?"

"Money?"

"Energy, food, power. If I even knew that it would be a start."

"Why concern yourself with such things?" The Hunt says. "You are new. All this you will understand with time. What did Abel negotiate with you?"

"Why is that so important to everyone?"

"It is the first lesson." I look at him. "One of them anyway."

"I gave him nothing," I say. "I took back what was mine."

"And what did this tell you?"

"You sound like Corbie."

"Your teacher?"

"Yeah. It told me not to take any shit from you people. I should have paid more attention."

"Normally he extracts a gift, a promise, a prohibition, some tribute."

A light bulb flickers to life. "The tribute is the currency. It moves energy from the Living World to Otherworld. No one *needs* it, but it does raise power, to carry out the shaman's request, maybe with something left over after."

"Yes. It is like nectar or cream. And don't forget it binds you closer to that spirit. It remains a two way street as long as the agreement lasts."

"I've been looking at this all wrong." I feel embarrassment bloom. "Corbie hasn't helped. Socialist revolution. There are already contracts, binding oaths. Taboos, tattoos, offerings."

"Thank you for the fox."

"That went to you?"

"You hunted it, didn't you? You took some of me and it helped you. I took some of your kill for myself. Not everything is a conscious contract. Of course if you needed more concrete help we could come to some arrangement."

"I don't expect I'll be doing any more hunting in the near future. Thanks for the offer."

We walk along in silence for a while.

I was so easily caught up in the romance of creating a change in a system I didn't like, that I hadn't taken the time to understand it properly. I've also handled the situation with Midori very badly. There's still no excuse for how Djuha and his sidekick treated me. "Where does this road go?"

The Hunt shrugs his massive shoulders.

"There's someone I should apologise to. I've enjoyed walking with you, but I want to say sorry sooner rather than later. Maybe we can do this again sometime?"

"I would welcome the company from time to time. Don't be so hard on yourself. You *are* a shaman." I turn to go, but The Hunt's massive hand stops me. "Here. This will help you find me more easily." He passes me a flint arrowhead the size of my hand.

"Thank you."

I activate my GPS and sprint back through the Greenwood to the jungle, and eventually to Midori's pool. I could have tried thinking myself back home and seeing if I could interrupt it, but I didn't want to find I couldn't and be too knackered to get back in again today.

Kneeling beside the pool, I disturb the water, hoping this will encourage her to appear. I wait. And wait. It's risky I'll piss her off even more, but I splash the water, kicking it about. Mud clouds the pool, but still no sign of Midori.

It's hard to tell time here, but I reckon it's close to midnight. Round about lunchtime in the living world. I've been here about an hour. The longest I've been away from my body if I don't count my illness.

I hear a heavy sigh behind me. "You just don't know when you are not welcome." I turn and Midori is standing there, thorns catching the moonlight.

"I've come to apologise. I didn't take the time to understand things. I still don't. But I didn't listen to you properly. I rushed ahead with a crazy idea, assumed you and I were talking about the same thing."

"That is noble of you," Midori says. "It may take me a while to understand you too." The thorns retract.

Her perfume wafts towards me on the breeze. It is different to how it was before. It reminds me a bit of Kathryn, but also of expensive scents I have found enticing. My tongue tingles slightly.

"Perhaps we can go back to that alliance I offered before," I say.

I try not to stare at Midori as she moves. She is lithe like an athlete. I can feel heat from her body, she is that close.

She touches my arm and it feels right, like it completes a desire I've had for a long time. "Come, let us sit and discuss it." She sits down gracefully.

I feel a little dizzy and very hot. My heavy leather coat clanks when I drop it on the ground. I sit next to Midori. She touches my arm again and hesitantly I reach out to caress hers. The leaves of her arms are firm like flesh, with slightly raised veins. It's strange but heightens my sense of touch to feel them under my fingertips.

She reaches up and touches my face, rose thorns just scratching my stubble. I'm about to reflect her move when she shakes her head, her grass hair rustling. Midori takes the wooden face and begins to peel it off. I'm shocked and afraid, this is almost too weird and god knows what's beneath. She plays with the mask, like a burlesque dancer flashes glimpses under her fans. The skin is white and almost luminous in the moonlight. I see her eyes smiling when the mask holes let me. I think I see cherry lips. I know I want to kiss them. Then she snatches the mask away and her face is soft and oval, with the blind-looking almond eyes a creamy tint against the apple white of her face. A sharp nose is so cute I want to bite it. Her mahogany mask is a mask of war compared to the face beneath.

She breathes softly in my ear before nibbling it, her breasts pushing against me.

I kiss her warm cheek and then her rich lips. I'm hard and ready. I feel myself start to throb with my pulse. Her tongue worms its way inside and teases mine.

I want to touch all of her. I run my hand over her ass, her thighs, and lightly tickle up the inside of her legs. Eager but not yet invited to explore further.

We wrestle my clothes off and I'm pleased to be free of their weight and damp cling. She takes my cock in her hand and runs an exquisitely sharp finger along the underside. It jerks up and bobs back down. An electric pulse hits my brain.

I kiss her hard and find the damp stickiness between her legs. Complicated folds of soft leaves. A hard bud that she almost pulls away from when I first touch it. But she uses her own hand to encourage me to continue. Midori throws her head back and cries out. She folds a leg over my hip as we lie side by side and urgently guides me inside her. Hotter and much more thick and sticky than I expected. More like gel than human lubricant. She grinds against me and I thrust back. Each of us breaking the rhythm before relenting to the others pace.

I feel it building all along my cock and I just throw it all away, bucking and sliding, then she squeezes and I explode. I stay inside pulsing each time she squeezes. We lie together in a timeless space.

Eventually I come back, and she does too. We hug and kiss and regretfully separate. I find my clothes and peel them back on. Midori simply replaces her mask and yet she wears more than me.

We embrace and part without words.

I open my eyes in the tunnel feeling hollow and ravenously hungry. My limbs ache, deep down to the bone. My joints are stiff and cold. I feel like I could snap. There's a damp patch in my underwear. I get up and go to the supermarket.

Walking along aisles I stare at tins and dry packets. How can I sleep with a creature in the spirit world and yet shy away from a flesh and blood woman in the living world? Is one a pornographic fantasy image, just mental masturbation, while the other is complications, real emotions, baggage? I feel twinges of guilt, and perhaps Midori was making me open to suggestion with her perfume. Who am I kidding? I was a willing participant without being drugged.

Thinking of Rachael reminds me of what she said about my mother. I might not need to talk to her, but in the hospital I realised she might have a need to talk to me.

I carry my shopping back to the tent and give her a call. I'm almost glad when it goes through to the answer machine. I leave a short hello and hang up. Now she'll call me at some random moment.

Janice is just about packed when I drop by her tent. "All set?"

"Yeah. I've left it all in this note." She thrusts into my hand a small piece of paper torn from an envelope.

I see a fairly long description of Brutus' day. When he takes his meals, how to prepare them, when he takes his walks. It must have been hastily written with a very fine pencil. "This is a pretty tight schedule."

"He's a creature of habit. His food is all here. Just make sure he gets enough water with the dry stuff. I'll be back on Wednesday. Brutus you behave for Uncle Nik, you hear?" Brutus whines and lays his ears flat against his head which rests on the special blanket on the floor of Janice's tent.

"I'll see you Wednesday, then."

Janice walks off and I try to figure out when I next need to feed or walk the dog. I've got a couple of hours, so leave Brutus in the tent and make a late lunch.

Mum calls while I'm mixing the right amount of dry feed with canned meat. "Kolya, you called."

"Hi Mum, just give me a second. I'm feeding a dog."

"When did you get a dog? Don't you have enough to worry about?"

"It's a neighbour's. I agreed to look after it for a couple of days." Brutus is eating his food like it won't be there for long. He probably eats better and more regularly than I do. "I signed the papers. I guess I'll see the official document next time I see Kathryn. Nothing I could do would convince her otherwise."

"I'm sorry to hear that, Kolya. You tried your best."

I'm not sure I did. Maybe I wanted to be free. I just was too much of a coward to face it fully, too filled with shame to try and make it work. "Yeah. I even offered to move back, but it was too little too late."

"Have you seen that girl, Rachael?"

"We had dinner last night. That didn't go so well either. She wanted something I couldn't give her." Then I had sex with a plant woman.

"She knows it's still early days for you. She'll come around."

"Yeah. Maybe."

"You sound a bit down."

"I'm okay. Just bone deep tired. Got a lot on my mind. How are you keeping?"

"Usual aches and pains. Nothing I can't handle."

"You should go on holiday. Somewhere sunny and hot."

"Who would go with me?"

"Can't you go on a cruise? Meet some new friends that way."

"I'm too old for that. Besides, first sign of sun and I'll shrivel up."

"The mutt's finished its dinner, so I need to walk it now."

"Take care, Nikolasha."

"Night, Mum."

Picking up warm shit in a plastic bag is something everyone should do before they die. Sloshing through melting snow I see Silk and Malky lurking about. Practically joined at the hip those two. Are they eyeing up Janice's tent? Perhaps it's better I'm about to keep them away than just make sure the dog's looked after. Brutus barks at them.

"Away an shite wee man," Malky says, pointing in some vague direction. He nods to me.

"How are you two gentleman on a fine night like this?"

Silk looks at me like I'm speaking Swahili. "Whit you sayin'?"

"I was asking how you were."

"Aye. No bad. Yerself?"

"I'm carrying a bag of warm dog crap."

"A-hu. Malky wiz jist sayin he could smell somethin bad comin. Ah thought he wiz jist coverin for a fart."

I put the bag into the bin attached to the lamppost. "I'll see you later."

Back at Janice's tent I'm in time to meet one of her neighbours. "You drew the short straw," she says, nodding at the dog.

I smile and shrug. At least I don't have to live next to Janice. "I'm Nik. I used to be over there, but now I'm down in the tunnel."

"There's a tunnel?"

"Yeah. Ancient railway system. Even the station's gone."

"Is it no damp down there?"

"Better than up here."

She climbs into her tent and I put Brutus back in Janice's. Will he be warm enough tonight? With the snow melting he should be fine. He's got a fur coat after all.

Chapter 17

Walking home from work it's hard to keep my mind on track. I still need to help Stevie and I did promise Janice some herbs, but I want to see Midori again. I'm pretty sure that would be a bad idea.

Corbie swoops in to land on my shoulder. I move at the last moment so he over shoots and lands hard on the ground.

"What the fuck did you do that for?" Corbie says.

"That's how I felt yesterday wading in with the whole socialist spirit world thing with Midori. She nearly carved me up."

"What's that got to do with me?"

"You're the one that wound me up and sent me off in her direction."

"What are you talkin about?"

"All that revolution stuff you were feeding me."

"Jeezus. You're a big boy. I ain't responsible for you going off on one. I was just foolin around."

"Like you were when I got my insides carved up by some dog-headed bitch's hand?" "Hey, I was just tryin to help and you know that."

"Your help is getting me into trouble."

"Chill out, Dude. You're make too big a deal outta all this. Hey, listen. I tried to get to this technological Otherworld of yours. No can do. You sure it's real?"

"You mean unlike the imaginary places with the crazy plant ladies and the antlered huntsmen gods?"

"Okay. I take your point. Could you take me with you, next time you go?"

"No. I don't think so."

"After all I've done for you, this is how you repay me?"

"Chill out, Dude," I say. "It's not a big deal."

"Touché."

"I just don't know if I can trust you. Why should I help you get into somewhere you yourself said would be a huge source of power? I don't know who you're working for. One minute you're citing the Great Spirits, the next your inciting me to revolution against them. Don't get me wrong. I'm glad you're not following me around twenty four seven, but you do keep disappearing for long periods with no by your leave. Just what is your deal, Dude?"

"Okay, okay. I guess I had that comin. I was sent to teach you by the Great Spirits, that's true. But that doesn't mean I don't have my own thoughts, that I don't want to be free. I just wanted to get high. To break through the walls, man. Next thing I know, like you, I'm part of this crazy world and all the crazy shit that goes with it. My teacher was from Siberia. Only spoke Russian. I was called in the middle of the Cold War. How fucked up was that? Someone was having a serious joke at my expense."

At least I could've talked with him. "My mum is from Novosibirsk," I say.

"You sounded like you were on board," Corbie says. "Like you wanted a fight. I thought you wanted to change things. Why'd you chicken out?"

"I didn't understand how the spirit world worked. You managed to leave that bit out of my teaching. Let me carry on thinking it was some kind of feudal slavery system going on."

"I can't help it if you hear what you wanna hear. You've not exactly been the most cooperative student a guy could hope for. You do keep surprisin me, but not always for the right reasons."

I'm embarrassed. He's right. I've not helped, I've gotten by. Any cleverness on my part is more about getting round doing things the hard way. Maybe I haven't listened enough. I wanted to hear how horrible it all is to justify my own reticence to really get involved, give me something to rebel against. I really should be too old for this kind of crap.

When Kathryn first told me she was pregnant – we were pregnant – I thought that was the end of my life. No more parties, no spare income, no luxuries, just sleepless nights, more than usual anyway, a financial black hole and clinging on to the edge of terror that my kids would come to harm. She was ecstatic, I was faking it.

It was nothing like that. Well actually it was everything like that. I'm still terrified. But the fundamental basis changed. With only a wife, part of me could still be selfish, self-indulgent, but with Lucas and then Sam, I felt I'd moved across to another world. A whole new perspective of life opened up in a way you can't ever fully explain or share with anyone who hasn't crossed that Rubicon. It's a new state of being. Sure it was hard those first three or four years, especially when Lucas was two and Sam was just born.

I accepted my role, then I welcomed it, and then I owned it. Of course I had ten months to get used to the idea. I've had a lifetime to get used to the idea of being a shaman. No, I was teased with it for a lifetime. No wonder I've not yet truly accepted it. I've said the words. I've believed them to be true. But in my heart I've been faking it.

I stop and turn towards Corbie, disturbing the flow of people on the pavement. "Can we start again?"

"We don't need to do that," Corbie says. "We just need to find a way to trust one another."

"Isn't that the same thing?"

"I didn't get you sick. I didn't scare your family. Please believe me, you have my sympathy. To be honest, I'm not sure how much more I can teach you." Corbie sighs. "I did fail you though. I didn't give you the full tour. I could've made sure you knew how it all fitted together. But now you're goin to places I can't reach. I can hardly conceive them. I don't wanna exploit them – just see with my own eyes."

He's right. I do need to learn to trust him, because this little speech sounds like crap to me. Do I risk it? Do I show him this new space? And what if I find he's just spinning me a line and next thing I know the Powers That Be are moving in. He has helped me this far considering how much of a pain I must be to deal with. It would be good to be free to talk to someone about it, to share it all. I just don't know.

"If I'm going to meet these aliens I'm going to need a wingman."

"How long you been waitin to use that one?"

"It just came to me."

"Really?"

Using the speakers on my laptop I play the synthetic drum track and my synthetic drum along with it. Unless Corbie finds another way through, without access to this he's not going anywhere without me.

In the technological Otherworld it is close to dawn. Corbie stands on my shoulder, stunned into silence. The mounds of webbing still lie in the Gardens where the Tent City is. There's something wrong about me being Virgil. I've barely visited here myself. I head towards the Tree of Life, if that's what it is here.

Now my eye is a little more sensitive to it I see that the other trees, and even the grass underfoot, have an inner flow moving through circuitry or optic fibre. I can't be certain whether it's data, pure energy, or something else. Everything looks organic, but is actually synthetic.

The Upper World is a world of intellect, of control, or Nous. The Lower World is one of bodily appetite, of wild indulgence, of animal lust, or Epithymia. There was a third part of the psyche, Thymos, which corresponds to emotions, passions and thinking. I don't know if it fits this place. Thymos could be the Middle World. But I think that the Middle World is just a reflection of the Living World, a vast lobby to the other Worlds.

It doesn't make sense at first that the seeming spiritual side of technology is connected with emotion and passion. But technology has always been about passion, and emotion. People lust after these objects, covet them, connect to them and with them better sometimes than with other humans. We've fed ourselves tales of cold robots and unfeeling machines performing acts of murder that humans have shown themselves quite capable of equalling without them.

The aliens, the explorers, that I've met are made from inorganic matter but have the same problems with spirit and soul. Perhaps we distrust our technology as we distrust our emotions and passions. That's why we've never really explored this side of the spirit world any more than the living world.

Perhaps this is not a matter of a spiritual side to technology so much as the emotional, passionate side of life is being expressed through mechanical and informatic form.

"What the holy fuck is that?" Corbie says. He's seen the Tree.

Beams of light pulse into the tree, others are emitted from it. The light is almost invisible as this world wakes up. I can hear a high pitched modulation, like an old dial-up modem communicating with a server. The smell of fresh plastic is strong.

"That's pretty much what I said when I saw it."

"Seriously, Dude. What in the name of all that is holy is that twisted abomination?"

"Abomination? It is exactly what it looks like, the Tree of Life, but made from inorganic matter. It is transmitting data, I think. Energy too, probably. No different to what the one you're used to does. Of course this could be the Tree of Knowledge instead."

Then it hits me. I feel that cold draining feeling. Illumination. Never a truer word spoken in jest. The Tree of Knowledge is exactly what this is. The partner to the Tree of Life. We eat its fruit daily. This space is the spiritual reflection of knowledge. Somehow our shamans have been divorced from this as much as the alien explorers had been from life.

So where did I go last time I came here? The Upper or Lower World of this Tree, or somewhere else entirely? Another Underworld? If we go back maybe I'll get a better idea.

"It's an abomination. They've taken the Tree of Life and grafted electronics into it."

"I don't see that. It's a different Tree. It has what it needs – data ports. This has been here since the beginning. We've maybe fallen in and out of love with it, but this feels more like where I was being called to. Information, data, is just as much part of us as life. Look at DNA. It's a code. Data."

"I'll accept that it's part of the Living World, but this is the spiritual world."

"There's no communication in the spirit worlds? No information. No data. Why do you think my GPS system works? Maybe it isn't just a visual projection of my mind working; maybe I'm tapping into this place too."

"I'm not convinced."

"So apart from an abomination, what is this then?"

"It's an attack, if not a corruption by some force," Corbie says. "Those aliens of yours takin over from another angle. They've body snatched the entire Tree of Life."

"It was like this before I met them. You should listen to yourself. That's not an explanation for what is in front of you. It's just paranoia."

"No, Man. This is all that technology crap slippin in and undermining nature. We need to fight this."

"I never took you for a back to the Stone Age type. Though, come to think of it, that's when we know we started using tools. Technology. So I guess you're more a back to the primordial ooze type. Knowledge has been with us since the beginning. Mind, Body and Spirit, right? The Living World is Body, the Otherworld connected to the Tree of Life is Spirit. Maybe this is Mind. Crick saw the serpent of DNA while tripping on LSD. They're linked together like DNA itself. Wrapped round each other, forming the third part, life."

"I didn't say we had to throw our technology in the sea. I just think this isn't nature, Man. The spirit world is natural and untainted. It's a reflection of the past when things were in balance."

"It's that Hippy shit that gives the New Age movement its new recruits and a bad name. All this yearning for some mythical golden age of peace and harmony while sticking your heads in the sand and denying what's actually in front of you.

"The spirit world reflects the Living World you told me. That's why sooner or later there'll be a revolution. You were right, but the revolution is not that socialism will free the spirits from slavery, but that we recognise the Tree of Knowledge as well as the Tree of Life."

Corbie drops his shoulders. "It's just too much for me."

"You want to see just how deep the rabbit hole goes?"

"I don't think I can handle it."

"I thought you wanted the bloody doors blown off your mind?"

"Fuck, man," Corbie says. "That was when I was alive and young and foolish."

"None of us are getting any younger. Adapt or die."

He seems to perk up. "Fuck it. Let's go."

We walk over to the round plate, the circles of light begin to pulse and we beam to another world. Mind, spirit. I don't think it matters.

This other place has transformed since I was last here. The plant-like structures appear to have linked together and become buildings. Large cubes of black glass with that inner pulse. Christmas trees petrified in obsidian. More of these plants now appear throughout the desert, growing, changing, morphing as though they were living calculators. The morning light makes them all cast long shadows on the sandy ground.

Is each grain internally a nanoscopic processor? Sand already formed to be the building blocks of information pathways.

"What do you think?" I say.

Corbie jumps from my shoulder, flaps and glides round in a wide circle. "This isn't bringin the walls down, but it's a full-scale siege."

"Shall I call the aliens?"

"Okay." He doesn't sound too sure.

I root around in my pocket and I'm pleased to find the smooth pebble. I don't know what else to do with it, so I just hold it in my hand and think of a Hello message.

Time moves in odd ways in the spirit world, but it feels like a long time passes. From the dark spaces behind the obsidian blocks I feel attention.

"I guess they're not comin. Let's go," Corbie says.

"You know as soon as you say that they'll appear. It's like making tea when you're waiting for someone. Soon as the kettle boils, they turn up." I had counted on them answering their own device. I didn't find the way back last time. We wait some more, until even I give up. I look over the pebble to see if there are any designs on it or an indication a signal has been sent. Nothing. "Okay. Let's go. I don't know what's lurking out there, but I think it wants to try us for lunch. Thing is I don't know how to get back."

"What do you mean you don't know how to get back?"

"I didn't find the beam point last time," I say. "The aliens took me home. I did tell you this."

"You haven't figured out where it is then?"

"Why don't you try getting a bird's eye view? See what you can find while dodging the light beams. I'll see if the plate is covered with sand or something."

Perhaps there's a call box round here and the pebble is a coin. I walk over to the nearest obsidian cube and move the pebble close to the surface. A number of pinpoints of colour shine deep in the lustre of the pebble. The cube surface echoes with some lights of its own, but both items go dark again.

I try to pinpoint the exact spot where we landed. Having not gone far the impressions of my footsteps are clear in the sand, even if they have collapsed into shapeless shallow hollows. I brush some sand to one side, and then move more using my hands as shovels. Down and down I dig, but there's no sign of another beam plate. Maybe there just isn't one.

Corbie swoops down from on high. "Dig up anythin?"

"No. See anything?"

"Nada. We're in deep shit aren't we?"

"We need to find a way back. There can't be only one way to go and then you're stuck."

"You can try wakin up in the Living World. It's a long shot. Could be harmful too. Might leave shards behind you have to come back for."

"Sounds like an option when we've done everything else. I'll try imagining myself back through the beam and home." I don't move. "This is stupid. Why build a door that only goes one way?"

"To selectively remove the gullible and stupid."

"That includes you too, you know."

"Don't I just?"

"Ahh. If this is going to work anywhere – Computer, locate the nearest door back to the Tree of Knowledge." A window opens in front of me. There's nothing there. It has a frame but is otherwise empty. Shit. Why even open at all? Then a beacon appears in the top-down map. A large arrow points the way across the landscape.

Following the route amongst abacus fronds and black glass cubes, I'm knocked to the ground. A large weight rests on me. I feel light headed and sleepy. It's warm and comfortable and I'm wrapped in a soft duvet. In my day dream there's the image of teeth, of a creature in the jungle, hunting. I need to push this weight off. It feels like someone put a dead giant on top of me. I can't move and I'm getting tired. I bend one leg and lever myself over. I'm on top of a heavy object, but I'm still wrapped in the duvet. I try to stand but my limbs are held together. I wake up. This is not a duvet. Something like a furry octopus with a wolf's head is under me, its arms around me. I yell out in shock and revulsion.

It throws me over its head. I land on the sand. I pick up a handful of the stuff to throw in its face. The sand becomes ordered in my fist. It forms a bar like a roll of pennies. I imagine it like the handle on a sword and a familiar beam of light emerges from the top end. I swing it down on to the limbs of the octo-wolf and the beam slices through. The thing roars in pain and I feel it loosen its grip. I swipe at it again as it tries to knock the hilt from my hand. Again the light cuts through. It lets go and scrambles off on its remaining limbs into the dark places. If it makes a sound, I can't hear it.

I stand up and brush myself down. Small silvered grains fall back to join the others on the ground. A bird stands in front of me, except it isn't a real bird, it's like it's made from black barbed-wire or something. A pointy mesh surface of a bird. I don't know where I am either. It looks like I wandered onto the set of an episode of Star Trek. I expect a green lizard man, or one of those pointy-eared guys with pointy eyebrows to appear. I know I should know the name, but it's just...gone. Why am I here? This must be some kind of dream.

"How you doin? That looked...," the bird says.

A talking bird sculpture with an American accent. This really must be a dream. "I'm okay, thanks. How are you?" I decide to play along.

"You don't sound okay," it says.

"Really? How should I sound then?" I say.

"Well, more like you. Crazy with a side of sarcasm."

"That sounds more like you." Perhaps I can figure out his name without asking.

"I've just picked it up from the master."

Does he mean me, or someone else? "Where are we, again?"

"I thought you knew," the bird says. "I followed you here, remember." It cocks its head to one side and looks at me closely with one beady eye.

I know where I am alright. Dad was right. Oh God, please don't let him be right. I'm in some institution. I've really cracked properly. This is all in my head.

What do I remember? I'm Nikolai Munro. I work in the IT department of a bank. If we use department and bank very loosely. I'm married with two kids. Kathryn is my wife. Lucas is my son. I don't know my daughter's name. I can't even remember her face. Do I really have a daughter? If that's not true, what about my wife, my son? I don't think I can bear that. I'm sure it's true. How can it not be? Yet I remember having sex with a nature goddess. Was that really me, a dream, a fantasy, a delusion, a film I saw once? What was her name? I remember Egyptian gods and being tortured in caverns of fire. A vast concentration camp of the dead. Tents. I live in a tent. I had pneumonia. Rachael saved me. Sam. My daughter is Samantha. They're Romulans. The bird is Corbie. I'm a shaman. I live in a tunnel in a tent in a garden in Glasgow.

Shit. That was scary. My heart is beating overtime. My forehead is wet with sweat. "Pi is three point one four one five nine."

"Pie is *à la mode.*"

"Why can't you just say with ice-cream?"

"Ah, my contrary boy is back," Corbie says. "Thought I'd lost you there."

"I know I'd lost you. Couldn't remember much at all. That thing was eating my memories." I slump against a nearby cube. My legs feel weak and rubbery. I feel shaky and hollow, like I need to eat. My breathing is still fast, but my heart is slowing.

"All the more reason to get out of here then and not come back. Where was that beam plate you found?"

"It was over there somewhere. But I think I have a better solution." It is still a few more minutes before I feel I can begin. I build a low mound of silvery sand and touching the edge I will it to form a beaming point. The sand remains lifeless and inert. What the hell is it with this place? Nothing works like you think it should. Did I just imagine the light sword? Or was it the stress?

"Better hurry, Man. Something big is coming. I think that thing is bringing its dad."

I glance up and see a large shadow moving. I'm not going through that again and I have no strength left to fight another one. Placing my hands on both sides of the sand mound, I try again to will it to form a beam plate. There's a ripple across the surface. Then, like a drum skin with dust on it, struck the right way, the surface turns into a series of concentric rings. The silicon starts to fuse together when I'm drowned in light. I can't see anything but white.

I look up, but can't see anything outside this spotlight. Then the light switches off and I'm left with an afterimage blinding me further. I'd run, but I'd probably break a leg running into something. When my sight returns I see a strange jellyfish shaped craft hovering overhead.

"I think this is our lift," I say.

"Better late than never," Corbie says.

I'm actually disappointed I didn't get to see if my beam plate would work. I disperse the mound with my foot.

The craft lowers a ramp and Opening Flower is waiting for us. I lead the way and Corbie lands on my shoulder.

"We are pleased to meet you again." Opening Flower indicates the way deeper into the craft. "It took us some time to come back when we received your signal."

"I didn't mean to take you away from your business." I don't know why I thought they would turn up quickly.

"We were not busy. We are happy to find time to share experiences with you."

We are led into the central console area. Amazing Mesa and Eroding Blade are still lying on the couches. They look like they're waiting for the dentist to see them. "What sort of medical facilities do you have on this ship?" I say. Perhaps they can help me with Stevie. Aliens always have advanced magical medical abilities in the movies after all.

"Are you hurt?" It feels like Opening Flower is studying me intently.

"Not really. I was attacked by some kind of eight legged wolf thing but I think I got my memories back."

"Let us check." Before I can explain fully what my reasons for asking were, Opening Flower has pushed me against a wall and I feel a weird tingling sensation which turns into that creepy back of the neck feeling. "There is a small chance you have lost some memories permanently. It does not look like they will be important. Small details, one or two early ones."

"I have a person, a patient, who is sick, in my Living World. I didn't know if you could help me heal him. He has a brain tumour."

Eroding Blade joins us as though he'd only just noticed we'd arrived. "Our system can cure most ailments in our bodies. But we are not made from carbon-based molecules. We could do a scan and try to determine poor material from functional. It will take a while to determine the differences and the procedure will not be without risk."

"That's a risk we'd be willing to take." I've not asked Stevie but I know what his eyes were telling me. "What can I do to return the favour?"

"We would not expect anything in return. The procedure itself will help us learn much about organic life with souls."

"I really appreciate your help. I still feel I owe you a favour."

"Man, are you sure?" Corbies whisper is rough in my ear. "They could learn to build weapons to wipe us out."

I turn away and pretend to look at the wall I was pushed against. "They already have a flying space craft that moves between worlds," I say. "Besides, they just scanned me. They already know everything they need to break our meat sacks into basic atoms."

"Good points well made."

"How will we do this? Can I bring my patient to you or can you come into the Living World?"

"That is an interesting question," Amazing Mesa says, joining the conversation from his couch. "It is possible we can scan without entering your physical space. To us there is no difference between them, so we should be able to appear there. Give this patient your token when you return and we should be able to find him. We will scan him and then try to enter your physical space when the calculations are complete."

Once again we are left beside the Tree of Knowledge and I leave the trance feeling like a wreck. My muscles all feel cramped. I feel old and emotional.

Shit.

I forgot to sort out Brutus.

I hobble up the rusted steps and over to Janice's tent. Brutus darts past me and I have a mess to clean up. So wrapped up in my own crap I forgot to help the dog. He comes back when I get the food ready which is a small blessing. Only one more day to go and I feel like I've really screwed up. Picking up dogs turds is easy. Getting the stain and smell out of the tent is going to be impossible. It stinks of dog anyway but this is off the scale. Not quite a dead Albert but pretty bad. Walking

Brutus back to my camp, I get some cleaning cloths and some soap. He starts barking when Stevie appears out of the gloom of the tunnel.

"I told you no dogs near my stuff."

"It's alright, Stevie. He'll be gone in a minute," I say. "Here, take this. Keep it on you for the next few days. It'll help with the problem you asked me to fix."

Stevie looks at the small flat stone, turning it over in his hand. He sniffs it. I hope it doesn't smell of dog shit. He hides it amongst his layers of clothes and nods at me. "Get that dog out of here."

I clean up the mess as best I can and swear to never let this happen again.

"Aye it's a real bitch isn't it?"

I turn to see a spry man with a shaggy beard watching me. "What's that?" He's like a garden gnome come to life. Could he be a gnome? Stranger stuff has happened to me lately.

"Looking after another's animals, so," he says.

"Yeah. Wish I hadn't agreed to it."

"I'm Joe Graham. I live just opposite, so."

"Pleased to meet you Joe. I'm Nik. I used to be up at the end there. Now I'm in the tunnel. I'd shake your hand but I'd rather clean it first."

"Ah, yes. You got sick, didn't you? Got taken away. Glad to see you're better. That spot was a wee bit exposed, so."

"Thank you. I better go wash up. Good to meet you."

"Sure," Joe says. "What are you doing with yourself, so?"

"I'm training to be a shaman and doing IT services. What about you?"

"A shaman? That explains the drumming. I didn't realise anyone was still doing that. I may have need of your services, so."

"You need me to look at your laptop?" That's usually the first thing anyone wants you to do. "Have you tried turning it off and on again?"

"Oh, yes. Very funny, Nik. No. It's handy you being a shaman and all. I need help with spirits," Joe says. "Looks like you're the man for me. What were the chances of that, so?"

"Well, I..." I don't know what to say. What are the chances of that? "Is it urgent? I could come by after I feed the dog tomorrow."

"No. Not so urgent. Why don't we talk when you're free of looking after Janice's things, so?"

"Okay. I'll speak to you on Thursday."

"A good evening to you, Nik."

"And you, Joe." I still don't know where he came from. I clean my hands in the freezing water of the toilet block and I still need to eat. I don't think I have the strength to go see Midori.

Chapter 18

In the evening I'm just too tired to think about shamanising after I've walked Brutus. My body is sore, my muscles ache and I'm just so, so tired. I get something to eat and sit in my tent idly surfing the web. The weather outlook is not good. Looks like it'll go below minus twenty here in Glasgow. A record low. If we thought it was bad recently, it will seem like a tropical holiday in comparison. My phone rings; Rachael. Am I really afraid of a new relationship, of not being in control? Did I really want out of my marriage but couldn't say so to Kathryn? Was I ashamed, but of how I really felt not our financial circumstances? "Hey, good to hear from you."

"Hey, yourself."

"You got your marking done?"

"Nearly just a few more jotters to go through. Feeling better?"

"Yeah. Just bone deep tired."

"I keep trying to feed you up, and then you go and fast for a few days."

"Not eating much is a surprisingly hard habit to get out of." I hear shuffling around and some grumbling outside. Just Stevie coming back from wherever he goes to.

"Look, I'm sorry I wasn't more enthusiastic on Sunday. It was early and I didn't sleep well."

"I should've left it til later, let you lie in. We can't all be early birds."

"How's it going exploring strange new worlds?"

"Going where no one has gone before."

"You should avoid the green skinned alien babes."

"I think I'm more Spock than Kirk."

"Let me know when it's mating season then. Can't have your blood boiling can we?"

"That's very altruistic of you."

"I'm sure I'd get something out of it."

I'm pleased Rachael is back to her normal self but I'm feeling sick with guilt. I leave her and run into the arms of another woman. It may all be in my head, but I'm a coward when it comes to real life. "When I get my final papers through we should celebrate." How romantic, Kolya.

"I thought you'd be drowning your sorrows."

"It has been suggested to me I wanted out a long time ago, but didn't have the balls to say so. I should take the freedom I'm granted and move on."

"I hope you'd be able to tell me if you wanted out."

"I already live in a tent. If I move to another country I'm sure you'll get the hint."

"I'd track your ass down and shoot you if you did that to me."

The line goes bad as Rachael is saying something – it's all chopped up into fragments. The lamp in the tent begins to fade. I hear Stevie cry out, shock more than pain, like he's having a bad dream. Then the lamp burns bright and I can't see anything but the light.

I fumble my way out into the tunnel. The light is here too. The aliens. It can only be. I can't find Stevie next to the tent, but I can barely see. I try to get out of the light. The golden beam is oppressive and my eyes ache. The light still fills the tunnel, but along on the platform I'm out of it. Looking up through the air vent I see a bright jellyfish shape, luminescent strands running across the surface and trailing out over Great Western Road. The tendrils pulse with colours.

A smile sneaks across my face.

I stagger up the steps and push through the spindly undergrowth into the park. Any question of this just being a vision is gone. The light from the craft casts long shadows behind the tents and twenty or so people stand, staring. People have left their cars and are gazing up, the changing traffic signals paling into insignificance when compared to the vivid iridescence of the ship.

The smile turns into a grin. I did this. Finally something went right.

Coming out of their initial surprise I see hands reaching for mobile phones. Some to film, some to call. There can be no doubt where the column of gold is aimed.

Then it comes down on me. What have I done now? Stumbling from one folly to the next I seem to have no concept of the consequences of my actions. Stevie better be okay.

I realise I'm freezing, having crawled out of the tent without my coat. I still have my phone clamped in my hand. The call is dead. I hope Rachael sees this on the news and doesn't think I hung up on her.

The golden light ends, shadows snap into darkness. The ship looks brighter and more beautiful. Then it simply fades.

I head back down to the tunnel. Stevie is lying on his cardboard bed holding his head, a smear of blood beneath his nose. Has this been another of my foolish ideas? Another dead person I should have done something more for? "Stevie?"

Stevie moans, nothing coherent. He sits up, illuminated by the glow from the light in my tent. He looks at me. I see a change in his eyes. He no longer looks like he's trapped inside himself. He's fully present. "Got any painkillers? My head is killing me."

I come back with a blister pack and some water. Stevie pops out two and takes a swig from the bottle. "Thanks."

"No trouble."

"Space alien abduction? That's the best you could do?" He's smiling.

"Yeah. Sorry about that. I think half the planet will know about it by morning."

"Not from me," Stevie says. "I was asleep. Didn't see a thing, Ossifer."

As if on cue, I hear sirens coming from, well, everywhere, it seems. Even down here we can see the reflected flash of blue and red as they converge.

"Maybe you should find somewhere safer to recover."

"And leave you to face the circus on your own?" Stevie says. "After what you did to me? No chance."

"Thanks."

"No trouble." Stevie laughs. It's weird to hear it. "I was a lawyer once, had a wife and kids. Buggered if I know if they'd even know me now. Hell, I can't even remember the last time I remembered them. But the law." Stevie taps his head. "It's all here again, now."

"I doubt it'll come to that."

"What's the scout motto? Be prepared. You had any media training? No, didn't think so. Keep it short. Sound-bite size. Say what you want to say. Not what they ask you."

I'm amazed. "Slow down. You sound like you're on Speed. I'm glad you're not yelling at me to move my stuff, but, man, take it easy. You've only just, I'm guessing, had parts of your brain removed or lasered or something. You should rest a bit."

"Nikki, I've spent God knows how long fucked in the head. I've been on the longest vacation. What year is it by the way? I'm not resting ever again."

There are footsteps on the metal stairs. It's the police. Their flashlights dance across the platform. "Be careful," I say. "Those steps are rusted through in places." When they get to the bottom the beams are turned on us. I'm dazzled again.

"What are you doing down here?" one of them says.

"I live here."

"I see." He lowers his torch. "You realise you're open to a charge of trespassing."

"If I may?" Stevie steps forward, crooked arm shielding his eyes from the beam on him. "There is no law of trespass in Scotland."

"Ah. We got a smartarse," says the second cop. "That's not strictly true. But I'm not the landlord and frankly it'd be pretty hard to show you were damaging the place." He lowers his beam. "I wouldn't bet you're making it better."

"Did you see anything unusual this evening?" first cop says.

I close the gap now it looks like these two aren't about to give us any serious grief. "What do you mean by unusual?"

Cop One shrugs. "Anything you consider odd."

"No, I was in my tent. Although I was on the phone when the signal got all choppy. It's surprisingly good down here. Must have been half an hour ago."

"What about you Robinson Crusoe?" Cop One says.

Stevie shuffles up behind me. I'm not sure if he's acting or if he's moving out of muscle habit. "I was sleeping."

"Are you alright?" Cop Two says. "Your nose is bleeding."

I turn to Stevie. Fresh blood gleams on his fingers. "Ah, shit. Not again. I'll be all right." He sinks to his knees.

"Shit, Stevie." I catch him in my arms as he collapses. Hang in there, man.

Cop Two gets on his phone. "Despatch can you send the medics down into the tunnel. We have an unconscious male, bleeding from his nose. I'll meet them up top to show them the way." He leaves.

Cop One comes over and puts Stevie in a recovery position on his side. "You got a blanket or something?"

I get back, pulling my coat on, and see two guys in fluorescent jackets negotiate a gurney down the broken stairs. I put my sleeping bag over Stevie, who's still breathing.

The paramedics trundle along the platform. "Ah didnae even know there wis a station here," one says.

"The station rooms burned down in the seventies, well before my time never mind yours. So what happened?"

The younger paramedic starts checking Stevie over.

"He collapsed with a nose bleed just after we arrived," Cop One says, standing up.

"Do you know anything else?"

Cop One looks at me.

"He was a guy who showed up here almost incoherent, about a week ago," I say. "Said I was camping in his spot and not much more. I think he had a brain tumour."

"He was complaining of headaches, had nosebleeds, something like that?" The paramedic's tone suggests I have no medical training so what do I know. He's right.

"No. I had..." It feels stupid to say it out loud. Corbie and the others understand. I feel my face get hot. Fucks sake, Kol'ka, this isn't about you. "I had a dream. And in it I saw what I thought was a tumour inside his head. I told him about it, but he didn't confirm or deny it."

The paramedics glance at each other. I can't tell what the subtext is.

"Anyway, this evening it was like he was suddenly a different person. He was chatty, happy. He asked me for some painkillers. That was just before the police officers arrived."

"So this was after the neon jellyfish in the sky?"

"Yeah."

Cop Two turns on me. "So you saw that then?"

Shit. Me and my big mouth. "Yeah."

"That didn't count as unusual to you?"

"Ah think we should take him in." The paramedic examining Stevie interrupts.

"He can't pay for that and I've no money either." I feel a cold dread rising in me, almost a panic. What can I do?

"We can still help in emergencies, you know."

"Can I come with him?"

"I think you've still got some questions to answer." Cop Two moves in front of me.

"Like what? I didn't want to say anything about the goddamn spaceship in case you thought I was a nutter."

"Who said anything about a spaceship? So you saw aliens too?"

"See what I mean? I thought it was a spaceship like out of Close Encounters. I didn't see any aliens. What more do you want from me? Can we take this guy to get some medical care?"

"Okay. Calm down, sir," Cop One says. "I'm just trying to get a picture of what just happened from all the witnesses I can find. Did you record it?"

"No. I didn't. I just saw this beam of light, well was blinded by it. Came out of the tunnel and saw the whatever it was."

The paramedics place Stevie onto the gurney and head back up the steps.

"Do you know anything more about this guy?"

"He told me he used to be a lawyer. He said his name was Stevie."

"Okay, thanks. We may come back and have another chat. Any other way we can contact you."

Giving him my number, I realise he's not writing anything down. He doesn't need to. There's a camera and microphone fitted to his uniform. It's all recorded. Voice recognition will have transcribed it all. Walking CCTV.

I run to check on Brutus, and Janice's things, before I catch up with the paramedics as they take the gurney through the gates. Loads of people are still milling about, but the cops have got the traffic moving again. Two fire engines are parked up on the pavement along Queen Margaret Drive, lights still flashing. I climb into the ambulance for the short journey to the Western A&E.

We seem to wait in the cubicle forever. They wheel Stevie away for scans and he hasn't yet returned to consciousness when they come back. I've retold almost all the events I can. I want to tell them the tumour has been removed by aliens I summoned from the spirit world, but I'm afraid. Not that they won't believe me, that goes without saying. More that I'll get locked up for practicing medicine without a license, or for some other thing like they used to shut down the psychics and mediums. You're no offense as a witch – it's the trade descriptions act you've got to look out for.

A woman not wearing blues comes in. A young man follows her round the curtain. She is startled to see me, shocked to see Stevie. "Sorry. I didn't expect anyone else here," she says. The man stares at Stevie then returns his eyes to his phone screen. She's late forties I guess. Tanned, healthy, well-dressed, expensive hair do, rich perfume. If I was in Paris she'd be the average middle-aged woman on the street. In Glasgow it's another matter.

"You must be Mrs Stevie" I say. "I'm Nik."

"Stevie? No, Rutherford. Glinda. But yes, I'm Stephen's wife. Technically ex-wife. We had him declared dead last year." She looks at Stevie more closely. Holds his heavy hand in hers, checks to see he's still breathing, checks his pulse, then peels up his eyelids. She lifts the short sleeve of the hospital gown they changed him into revealing a small skull tattoo. "It may have been only a little premature. Where was he?"

"I don't know what you mean, Linda."

"Glinda." Her look tells me not to take the piss. So much for her bedside manner. "Where did you find him?"

"He was with me, up in the Botanics. We were lucky. The emergency services were already there en-masse."

"Have they told you anything yet?"

"No. Just done scans." Should I tell her about the tumour? "I didn't really expect them to tell me anything. Surprised they let me in here."

"So, Nik, what's your story?"

"Financial collapse, bankruptcy, divorce, tent city."

"Banker," the boy says, like he's swearing and laughs. Maybe he's younger than I thought.

"Physicist, actually," I say. "Far worse."

"What?" he says.

Glinda continues as through there's been no interruption. "And what do you know about my husband?"

"Nothing really. I only met him a few days ago. Claimed I nicked his sleeping space. He wasn't very chatty."

"He must have told you about us," she says. "How did the police know to call?"

"He told me he used to be a lawyer, but that was only a few hours ago. He was a different man."

A doctor comes in before Glinda can interrogate me further. What kind of sick parents name a child after a Good Witch?

"You're, er, Stevie's family?" the Doctor says.

"Stephen's. Yes."

"I can go." I stand up.

"It's okay. Please, stay." Glinda waves me back.

"Alright then," continues the doctor. "It appears that Stephen has been suffering from cancer. His blood tests show a tumour is present in his body. The CT scan we did looking for it showed an absence in his brain."

"Absence?" Glinda says. "What kind of absence?"

"I'm just getting to that. If the tumour was in his brain, it is not there anymore. I have to say that we wouldn't have operated on it. It was advanced and the tissues we would have had to remove would have been considered too much. So far as we can tell, the tumour was removed surgically and probably recently. Clearly he did not have his skull opened to do this. Frankly, we're at a loss as to how it could have happened. It's like it was just beamed out of his head. As with anyone who has been in such a severe state he will need post-surgery care and there will need to be tests to see if the cancer hasn't spread to other parts of his body. There will always be a chance that a tumour could return at the site."

Glinda sits down on the edge of the bed. "Thank you, Doctor. Can we take him home?"

"I think it would be best if we kept him in for observation. If you want to arrange transport to another hospital, that's okay. Otherwise, we'll move him shortly to the Beatson, up the road." He leaves us. Stevie stays asleep.

"What do you know about this?" She stares at me.

"You wouldn't believe me if I told you."

"Try me."

"I'm a shaman. I asked the spirits for help. This evening they did that."

"I thought you said you were a physicist?" says the boy looking up from his phone for a moment.

"The glowing mushroom on TV?" Glinda says. "That's why you now look like the cat that got the cream. I don't whether to believe you or slap you."

I shrug and then yawn. The ache from my bones hasn't gone, but at least it's warm in here. "I'm going to get some sleep. I've got work in the morning. Stevie knows where to find me. I'm sure he'll pull through and I'm glad you'd not forgotten him."

As I walk up Byres Road I realise I should have grabbed another jumper as I pull my coat tighter round me.

Chapter 19

In the night I have to put on a jumper and trousers and I still struggle to keep warm. I'm sorely tempted to get up and go to the hotel over the road and beg some space in the kitchen or somewhere hot and out of the way. I know in my cold aching bones that none of us will last up top unless we've got Arctic quality tents and maybe some heating gas. How explorers at the poles survive I don't know, but I bet it isn't with tents bought from a supermarket for ten quid or hand outs from NGOs usually used in sub-Saharan Africa. I'd light my stove but I'm worried I'd kick it over in my sleep. Even with us all down in the tunnels, pitched in the middle and with the ends closed over with boards I don't know if we'd make it. So far as I can tell it's our only option as I don't see too many wanting to share tent space.

I awake again shivering a few hours later. I make some weak tea and go back to sleep until my alarm wakes me. We need action today. I check in with work remotely and make breakfast.

Frost flakes disintegrate into a fine mist when I unzip the tent flap. I'm glad Stevie is in the hospital as I don't know if he'd have made it through the night out here. Everything is covered in a thick frost and it even extends a few metres into the tunnel. It sparkles in the early morning light. The sky is clear and blue.

Should I call Rachael and see if she'll take me in for a couple of days? It would be a lot to ask. Things are delicate enough as it is. I don't owe the locals anything, but if we're going to avoid several deaths and maybe start to build a real community here then we need to act together.

There are still chunks of snow that haven't melted. Now they're like treacherous ice rocks, sharp and hard. I shatter a few and try not to slip on some of the ice underfoot. Brutus is fine when I look in on him. He'd buried himself amongst Janice's clothes but he's up for a walk and a sniff about. The air makes my lungs clench it's so cold then great billows of steam burst out. Each breath leeches away some energy. I don't think I've much fat left to burn. Any serious work and I'm going to need serious fuel.

There's no water moving in the toilet block, so I can't flush and I can't wash my hands. Washing anything else had already made me think twice. I leave feeling slightly soiled.

Borrowing a pan and a spoon from Janice, I start beating the bottom. It's an unwelcome way to be woken, especially as the excitement of the night before must have kept everyone up late. Heads poke out of tents and tell me to piss off. When I don't stop bodies emerge before quickly returning for more layers. Eventually a surly crowd gathers round. Still not everyone, but I feel forced to stop under the glares.

"I don't know if you've seen the news, or the weather reports, but tonight is going to be the coldest night on record here. Below minus twenty they think." No apologies we need to get down to business. "If we move down into the tunnels below we'll be less exposed. Our heat will stay in and if we cover up the entrances this will help. We don't have much time."

"That's whit ye goat us up fur? Gies a break. Ah thought it wis somethin important."

"Minus twenty. You think you won't freeze to death. Albert died of hypothermia only a few weeks ago when the weather was comparatively mild."

"He was an old man. We'll be fine. I'll just put on some socks and jumper like I did last night."

"Last night it was minus eight, maybe minus ten."

"What dae you ken aboot the cald anyway?"

"I can tell when there's a danger. We're living behind thin plastic. It would be freezing inside a house. Seriously, do you want to die?"

"Look we've heard what you've got to say. We're going to take our chances. We move from here they may not let us back."

"Okay. If any of you change your minds I'm happy to lend a hand." I can't believe they would rather freeze than move their stuff.

I order a large cooked breakfast from Sindi who almost faints in mock shock. "Did your aunt just die and leave you her fortune?"

"I wish. I don't fancy my chances of making it through the night on an empty stomach."

"You've a few hours yet. All this'll be gone by then."

"I may come back for more later."

"Shame my sofa's already taken."

"That would be like staying at the Ritz."

"Steady on, the Hilton maybe."

I'm surprised how hard it is to finish the sausages, bacon, fried eggs, French toast, beans, fried mushrooms, fried tomato, tattie scone and black pudding. Sindi even brings me a fresh tea to help wash it down. I swear my stomach is sticking out like I'm pregnant.

With the sun up, it would be warm if it wasn't for the thin wind whipping up from the Clyde. I search round the back of shops for empty boxes and newspaper.

Corbie glides down from the blue and sits on the lid of a dumpster. "Jack Frost nippin at your toes?" I'm getting used to him just coming and going. We need our space.

"I tried to get them to join me in the tunnel, but they weren't interested."

"Maybe if you made the place respectable. Put up some lights, got some nice flowers."

"I just feel responsible somehow, after Albert...I could've done something."

"There's no point cryin over spilt milk and all that."

"Could I ask the spirits for help?"

"It's kinda your job."

"I don't know. Ask the spirits of cold to keep away or spirits of summer to warm the place up?"

"It's worth a shot." Corbie shrugs.

"You're not filling me with confidence."

"You're not fillin me with confidence."

"What's the problem?"

"Shouldn't you know this stuff by now? I mean why you askin me? Get on with it if you think it's right."

"If that's the best advice you're going to give me then I don't why you've bothered showing up." But he stays and watches me pull on my shaman outfit. I'm just pulling on the jeans when I hear footsteps along the platform. Just what I need.

"Hello, anyone here?" A woman's voice. Doesn't sound like anyone I know. I can hear a second person too.

I finish doing up the buttons and come out of the tunnel onto the platform. A woman in a heavy quilted coat, jeans and hiking boots is coming towards me with a guy balancing a professional video camera on his shoulder. I consider heading out the back of the tunnel, but she sees me first.

"Hello. They said I'd find you down here," she says, offering a gloved hand, brusque and all business.

"Hi. Who said that?" I don't think the camera's on but I'm wary anyway.

"Some of the, er, residents up top," she says.

Revenge no doubt for their rude awakening. "I see. What else did they say?"

"That you're a magician, that you cast spells and summon demons, like the neon jellyfish last night."

"I think they're pulling your leg."

"Why are you wearing that strange outfit?"

"Who are you?"

"I'm Shona McFadzean, Alba Today. This is Mike, my cameraman." Mike mimes tipping a hat at me with his spare hand.

"Alba Today?"

"We're a digital-only news channel covering Scotland and Scottish Affairs."

Corbie jumps up onto my shoulder. "You don't wanna talk to reporters, man," he says.

"What do you broadcast the other 23 hours?" I say.

She cracks a smile. "Adverts for shortbread and teacakes. I've heard them all before, Mister...?"

"Nik. Nik Munro."

"You didn't answer my question, Nik."

"I'm training to be a shaman," I say. "This is my uniform."

"So you are a magician."

"I don't cast spells or summon demons. I don't make love potions or Voodoo dolls."

"What do you do?"

"What is it you want, Ms McFadzean?"

"We were looking to interview people who had witnessed last night's event. Some of your neighbours suggested you might have seen it. One or two did go so far as to accuse you of causing it."

I shrug, recalling the conversation with the cops last night. "I was in my tent reading. I got a call on my phone and it cut out as my lamp started flickering. Shortly after that the guy who was crashing down here got sick and fortunately some cops had come down asking the same question."

"You're not very good at answering questions, are you?"

"I'm not very good at giving you the answers you're looking for."

"How did you get into the shaman business? I can't imagine anyone's really been practising it for a few hundred years now."

Corbie chuckles like he's shifting phlegm. "Hah. Shows what she knows."

"Shamanism is alive and well. Sometimes the state carts kids off to the psych ward, sometimes they support it. Everyone needs help. I'm a spiritual plumber."

"You don't make it sound very glamorous."

"It's a discipline of pain and blood. No one really wants your help except when they're desperate."

"Like Ghostbusters?"

I smile. "I ain't afraid of no ghosts."

"You see dead people?"

"Not here, in the Living World. I don't see any spirits here at all. But they live in everything. The bricks of the tunnel, the plants here between the tracks, in that camera, or your phone."

"Animism, right?"

"Shamanism is as old school as it gets," I say. "Shamans made the cave paintings."

"How can you know that? They didn't write anything down."

I laugh. "Of course they did. They used the walls didn't they? The first graffiti artists, the first psychedelic users, the first cross-dressers. Shamans are the real bad boys, the original outsiders."

Mike whispers something in Shona's ear. She nods. "Look, this is fascinating and all, but it's bloody freezing down here and we've got a story to file. Any chance we could pick this up again sometime. Maybe in a café?"

"I'll think about it. Can you leave me out of whatever you broadcast? I'm supposed to be at work right now instead of trying to keep my neighbours from turning into icicles."

"If you agree to an interview, then I'll think about it."

Crap. "Ok. When you blackmail me like that, what choice do I have?"

"I'll be in touch."

"You shouldn't have done that," Corbie says.

"Without my job I can't eat and then there'd be no shamanic activity at all."

In the jungle riot of the Lower World I head towards Midori's pool. If anyone can point me to the right place for the elemental spirits I hope it's her. I also need to find something for Janice's cough before she gets back. I'm not sure why I'm bothering to help though.

Midori is sitting beside the river in a pool of moonlight. Some of her leaves look jet black, on others the veins are silvered. She stands and walks over. The sensuous sway of her hips brings back an echo of the pleasure that being with her brought me. She leans in close to me and I can smell a heavy intoxicating mix of woods, jasmine and rose. I feel her hand sneak beneath my coat and under my shirt. My skin tingles and I wish Corbie wasn't here.

"Where have you been?" Midori says.

I feel a sharp scratch across my stomach and another along my cheek. I cry out in shock and pain as I feel blood seep down my face. Corbie takes to the sky.

I try to get away but I'm embraced by vines and roots and see fury on Midori's face.

"In the Living World, Midori. Where do you think?" The hawthorn point in front of my eye has my whole attention.

"We made love and then you just abandoned me." She snarls at me.

Corbie flaps back down but keeps his distance. "Please tell me you didn't?" he says.

Just what I need – a spirit going all bunny-boiler on me. "Midori, I'm sorry. I wanted to come and see you, but I was busy trying to help people. This is the first chance I've had, and I'm here."

"Oh jeez. You did, didn't you?" Corbie says. "You fuckin idiot. Is there nothin you can't fuck up?"

Midori changes, like sunshine appearing through a storm cloud. "You have nothing to apologise for." The bonds snake away, the thorns retract. "I forgot that you have other responsibilities."

"I promise that I'll come and see you as often as I can." Idiot why are you making promises?

Midori licks the blood from my face. I see a Venus flytrap snap over a careless fly. A leg sticks out between the jaws. Slow digestion awaits. "What have you been doing?" she whispers in my ear.

"I helped a man with his cancer, and now I'm hoping to prevent my neighbours from freezing tonight. And I need to find a cure for a dry cough. Do you know where I can find the spirits of winter or summer or fire or some way to keep an area warm?"

Midori steps back and I miss her heat already. The tip of my tongue aches. "That doesn't sound like it would take up a lot of your time."

"I have to eat, go to work and do all of that too. Can you help me find the right spirits?"

Midori sighs like wind through a field of wheat. "Some of these elementals work in opposition. Show too much favour or ignore one group the others may get upset. Ask Winter and Frost spirits to ease off first, see if that works. A blended tea of Echinacea, Thyme and Peppermint will help the cough. Who is it for?"

"A woman in the camp." I don't even think first.

"A woman? Who is she?" The sun retreats behind the cloud. The thorns are out again. "Is she another lover of yours."

"She isn't my lover," I say. "I'm helping her, like I help everyone. You can't get jealous every time I need to help fifty two per cent of humanity."

The sun reappears, a little shy. "I know," she says.

"Where will I find the Winter and Frost spirits?"

"Head that way as far as you can go." She points the way. I have no idea if it is North or South.

"You could come with us?"

"No. I couldn't."

"Okay. I'll see you soon."

In the moonlight she looks like a weeping willow on the banks of the pool.

I walk through the jungle until it becomes a more sparse savannah, big cats watching as we pass. Herds of deer and cattle chew the long grasses. The savannah changes to a more familiar temperate landscape of rolling downs and deciduous woods and I wonder if The Hunt is nearby. All the while Corbie is nagging at me, "What were you thinkin?"

I finally snap. "I wasn't thinking at all. It was lust. Have you been up close to her? Your mind doesn't work right."

"It was probably that first kiss," Corbie says. "Your apology is gonna cost you more than you know. I told you to be careful."

"You also admired how I got out of the diplomatic problem too. I thought she bit my tongue but now I wonder if she didn't spike me somehow."

"She has a unique way of forgin alliances, I tell you."

"We'd already agreed to help each other before anything like that happened."

"Is that what your head thinks or your dick?"

The temperate zone changes to thick boggy tundra, evergreens and stunted bushes struggle to hold on and the temperature drops. I see snow glinting in the moonlight and I wrap my coat about me but the thin wind ferrets its way past all my defences.

Wisps of the white stuff sliver down to us on the wind before we reach the snow line. The going is tough and I don't have breath for argument or the strength to knock Corbie off his human perch. The direction, if we've stayed true, heads upward towards icy crags. If I have to climb, I'll be in trouble.

The ice sheet is black and a deep eerie blue. A huge wall that spans a valley. The ice groans and a deep cracking sound leads to large chunks falling off and splintering on the hard ground in front of the glacier. I walk along, hunched over, expecting to be brained or impaled at any moment, until I find a tunnel. It is a blessing to be out of the wind, but I don't feel secure going deep. Inside the ice walls there are figures, I'm sure of it. Darkened outlines of shaped ice, frozen within the glacier. Frost giants, angular shard beings, a conquered army or one waiting to be set free, I don't know. But if we think this is winter now, what would it be like with spirits like this loose in the land? It is still late summer in the spirit lands.

I can hear a high pitched chittering sound, like locusts, or the slicing of ice skates on a pond, coming from up ahead. We stumble into a large cavity, like an amphitheatre. Along the tiers a number of creatures gleam like knives. If the sound of the glacier was to come from smaller bodies of ice it would sound like this. I hope I'm not interrupting parliament.

In the centre of the amphitheatre is a short humanoid ice sculpture, if the artist had chosen to represent the frozen bones of a glass nightmare.

The chittering sound quietens down. The sculpture moves and points its head in our direction. I'm reminded of the aliens' heads, as this too looks like a 3D fractal geometry; ice planes with an ever smaller set of melted blobs eaten into their surfaces and edges. Are the aliens truly that, or are they spirits of some natural process?

I clear my throat. "My apologies for interrupting. I was looking for help from the spirits of Winter and Frost."

There is a hiss from the small fractal ice figure, like snow grains blowing over rock. In a voice like cracking glass the figure responds. "What do you wants warmblood?"

"I would like an area in the Living World to be left alone for the next two days."

"Impossible."

"Nothing is impossible. If you want to help you can. If not I'll find another way, but someone else will get the tribute."

"You offer tributes? To us?"

"Of course. The favour of a powerful shaman is useful, surely?" I turn to Corbie and ask in a whisper "Why don't they expect tribute? I thought everyone wanted something round here."

"I don't think anyone usually comes here looking for them to make significant changes. Weather patterns shiftin have long term consequences, the butterfly effect, you know, and they're showy."

"You're saying we shouldn't do this?"

"I'm sayin there'll be big after effects. And it may cost you."

"What are you offering us?" In my head he's Jack Frost, if Frost was a vicious cutpurse.

What would ice creatures want? Do they desire warmth or symbols of cold? What am I prepared to sacrifice for people who won't listen in an act that will draw even more attention to me if I'm not careful?

While I think this through I feel the pressure of interest from the assembled elementals and I'm amazed to feel beads of sweat appear on my brow. It's the usual dilemma – I don't want to give away too much. I start with something trivial. "I will sacrifice fine wine and liquor – I will offer you libation once a week for three months."

"That is nothing. You want us to act, to change much."

"No I want you to change a little. Make it not so cold. Clearly if it was not cold at all this would be very hard for you to do."

"It is not so difficult."

Ha! These guys must be out of practice. "If it is of so little effort to you, why should it be at great cost to me?" Frost screams and I have to cover my ears. Some of the elementals look restless. They rub the shards that are their forelimbs together, making a keening ringing. "How about a small animal sacrifice once a month for four months?" I say.

"This is not enough," Frost says. "We need hot blood."

"The sacrifices will give you hot blood."

"We wants blood now."

"That's a big ask," Corbie whispers in my ear. "Are you sure this is gonna be worth it?"

How much blood is enough? "If I give it to you now, how do I know you will do as I ask?"

"A pact is a pact, Shaman. Your blood, our words."

I don't know how this will work, or what it will do to me back in the Living World. I step forward and open my thumb on one of Frost's edges. A smear of darkness is left on him. The blood wells up and drips onto the floor of the cavern hissing where it melts the ice. Soon a small pool forms lined with frozen blood. My thumb just keeps bleeding, big heavy drops splash into the pool. I've had bad cuts before, I sliced my hand on a tin lid once, but I've never needed to get stitches. This just keeps on dripping. I feel light headed and sink to my knees.

"Enough," Corbie crawks at me.

I feel the restlessness amongst the elementals. I realise my eyes are shut. The pool looks like a small lake to me now. I come round and sit up lifting my hand out of the blood lake with my other hand. It looks blue. I push the thumb against the frozen ground and it congeals the blood.

"Thank you, Shaman. Our deal is agreed."

I crawl back toward the tunnel and the mouth of the glacier. Behind me I hear the elementals swarm down to the pool. I imagine them diving in, revelling in my life's blood.

"Quick." Corbie pecks at me. "Imagine yourself back in your body. Now."

I imagine myself back at my tent and feel the rush as I flow back through tundra, taiga, savannah and jungle, past the Tree of Life and home to my body.

My arm is whole, there is no cut, but it is blue and the thumb tip is numb from frost bite. I need to get warm. I try to stand but my legs are dead. There is tingling in my toes. I am thrown by a deep shiver. Making it upright, I stumble to the stairs and eventually, leaning on bins and lampposts along the way, get back to the café.

Sindi knows something is wrong straight away and helps me to a seat. My feet, hands and arm start to come back to life and I cry out startling the other customers. A hot towel is brought to me and I wrap my hands in it. A cup of tea is left in front of me while the paying clientele are placated. I try to lift it with my good arm, but my grip is so unsteady I think twice about spilling hot tea on myself.

"What have you been doing to yourself?" Sindi sits down opposite me. Her boss, the cook, hovers in the background.

"I don't want you getting into any trouble on my account."

"Let me worry about that, will you?"

"I'm sorry. I didn't know where else to go."

"I told you, don't worry about it."

A deep shiver racks through me. "If it at all works out, then I've saved a few people."

"At what cost? You're no use to anyone dead. We should get you to the hospital. You should be wearing some proper clothes in this weather too. I've not seen you in this get up before."

"Everything has a price. It's just a question of whether you're prepared to pay it." I feel able to lift the mug of tea in my hands. The liquid almost scalds me on the way down and the heat in my stomach makes me start, but soon it spreads out. My hands and toes continue to tingle but the pain starts to subside. There is a large white blister on my thumb where I had cut myself in Frost's cavern. "I'm a shaman, Sindi. This is my uniform."

"You speak to spirits, huh? What does my Great Aunt Mhairi want?"

I laugh. "I'm not a spiritualist, but she wants you to go back to work before you get fired in a difficult jobs climate." Even I can tell that a few customers want to place an order, which at least means I haven't scared them away.

After a while the tingling in my hands subsides and my arm gets some use back in it. There's still a nagging itching in my feet and I'll have to be careful with them. I order a hot sandwich and start to feel human again after nearly two hours in the café. Corbie hasn't said a word, just sat and looked at me. I don't know if he's trying to see something or if he doesn't want me to appear mad by talking to myself in public.

I go to the loo, surprised and pleased I can stand up ok. On the back of that success I feel ready to go back to the tunnel and move my tent deeper into it.

Janice is back in the camp. "Thanks for looking after Brutus. I hope he wasn't too much trouble."

"No. He was fine. Are you sure you won't come down into the tunnel, just for the night."

"No, Nik. This pitch is all I have. I saw what happened when you left. I'll be fine. How much fucking colder can it get?"

I've nearly killed myself to help prove them right. "I got a tea recipe for you. Sorry I've not had a chance to get the ingredients." I tell her which herbs Midori recommended.

What have I got myself into? Should I have used some kind of protection? If my blood can be consumed in the spirit world then maybe my sperm is viable too?

It is hard to do some of the fine movements I need to move the tent – lifting out and resetting guy lines and pitons. Not strictly necessary with internal frame tents, but they add some stability. I arrange some of the large cardboard boxes I got from the supermarket over the tent like I'm building a fort. It is a bit shaky but hopefully will add another insulating layer. In my current condition I really should call Rachael, even Kathryn, and beg some crash space for a couple of nights, but I just can't bring myself to do it. Although after last night I really ought to call Rachael back anyway, but she'll still be teaching right now. I need to stay to see if this works, if the loss was worth it. I don't know if the spirits will include where I am when it comes to keeping it cool rather than Baltic.

Corbie is still following me around like a lost duckling when he breaks his unusual silence. "I'm really proud of you. You know that right?"

"For what? Fucking a tree woman? Asking aliens to invade the Living World to cure a dead man? Being the bitch of some kinked spirits?"

"Shut up and take a compliment for once," he says. "I'm proud of how you may not have taken to this life like a duck to water, but you made it your own. You've shown real initiative, real courage, not pussied out on makin real sacrifice. I didn't know if you'd make it, but I think you're gonna do great."

"Well, thanks." I don't know what else to say. I hadn't expected this from Corbie.

"I don't think you need me anymore," he says.

"What?" I'm surprised at how this brings a sudden lump to my throat, a panicked shock. It's like being dumped for the first time, out of the blue. "Let's not be too hasty. Someone needs to stop me dropping atomic bombs in the spirit world. I'm sure there's plenty you still have to show me."

"I got nothin you can't find out for yourself. You've already found places I didn't even know existed. You don't really need me to point you to the Diaspora of Hells and Heavens, the Desert of Dreams, or the Seelie Court."

"Okay, that may be true," I say. "But who can I talk to about all this?"

"You've already been getting friendly with the locals."

"Very droll. We both know I can't really trust her."

"I'll catch up with you from time to time. Now go get some totem spirits on your side."

"Gotta catch em all."

"I'll see you around," Corbie says.

"It's been good working with you."

I check through my things. I need to make sure I have as much fuel, water and insulation that I can get. I check through it again. I'm as prepared for tonight as I'm going to be. I check in with the work systems. Perhaps there's something I can do there. In theory the servers are insulated from the outside world, and usually the issue is if it gets too hot. It's unlikely there are any water pipes that might burst going through or over those rooms and if so I don't know which idiot designed the building that way or at least left them going through there when they put the computers in.

I check the news and there are plenty of shaky handheld images of the jellyfish. I should check in on Stevie, see how he's doing. There's a few articles talking about how Arctic it's going to be tonight and tomorrow. Then my stomach hits the floor. There I am on Alba Today looking like a right eejit. A short film clip under the heading "Whatever Happened to the Shaman?" A couple of jokes from the studio host about Mr C back in the nineties and a brief bit about how the neon jellyfish is being blamed on my casting spells by the local campers and most of my interview. I pray to God that no one watches this. Especially anyone who employs me. How could she do this to me? We had an agreement. I'm not so worried about the publicity. I met more than a few reporters when everything crashed. I need my job or I'm royally fucked. I want to punch something. Preferably a reporter's face.

My face is hot and almost seconds after Corbie's left I have no one to turn to. My thumb throbs and my toes are still tingling. At least I can feel them now. I'd love just to throw it all in and walk away, but this is all I have now, isn't it? It's taken over. But how do I make a living from being a shaman?

Maybe I can become a minor celebrity, have a few turns on some reality shows, a book deal, a photo shoot in a bikini. Come back to my tunnel in between times and keep some ingrates from killing themselves.

Rachael calls. I hesitate then accept. "Aren't you at work?"

"It's playtime. Besides, I just saw you on the TV. Glad to see you're still alive, although that explains you hanging up on me."

"I didn't hang up. EM radiation from the aliens must have knocked the call out. You watch Alba Today?"

"Never heard of it," Rachael says. "You're on the BBC."

Fuck. "A big thing or a soundbite?" I pick up my laptop and load the site. There's another article there. How can anyone not spot this?

"It was a couple of minutes."

I see they've mirrored the same video. Isn't there some rule about copying people's stuff? I'm sure the BBC couldn't afford to license another company's news or need to. "I sure hope my bosses don't see it."

"You looked fine. A little odd maybe, but we all know you're that."

"I'm supposed to be at work. How would you feel if someone interviewed you in a pub when you were supposed to be off sick?"

"Shit. I thought you just kind of worked from home."

"As a backup, yeah."

"I'm sure it'll be fine. They'll have a laugh, give you a warning. Nothing more serious than that."

"I hope so." I want to explain how nervous this makes me. I want to talk about Corbie leaving. I wish I could ask her for a bed for the night.

"Where were we before we got interrupted?"

"That seems like a long long time ago. I think you were going to track me down and kill me if I left the country. I off course disappear into other worlds on a regular basis, but I hope you realise that's part of the package."

"Man with tent, talking invisible animal and a tendency to visit other worlds. It's a singles ad that writes itself."

"I really should get round to updating my status to 'It's Complicated'."

"Not to 'Seeing someone'?"

"After the weekend I wasn't sure I was."

"I promised you time. It's my own fault if I moved too fast."

I don't know how I'm going to juggle Midori's feelings. Is it even possible? I committed myself to trying to get back in touch with the real world, but the spirit world has its thorns in me. Maybe I don't need Midori as an ally, but I sure as hell don't want her as an enemy. I don't know how I'm going to get out of this situation. There are some people who wouldn't care, would take their cake and eat it. I just can't do that. Now that Midori is as real to me as Kathryn and the kids I can't treat her any differently. "That's kind of what I'd hoped to talk to you about. Should have talked to you about it on Saturday. My situation isn't easy in either world, but over there I got into some trouble. My trust was taken advantage of and I was hurt, physically. Well, it felt physical. That's why I wasn't myself. It was a serious attack and I tried to just leave it behind but this stuff follows me back into the Living World."

"What happened?"

"I was trying to find a cure for Stevie's cancer and some spirits told me they could help. They chose to demonstrate their proposed surgery techniques on me without asking first."

"Are you wounded? Do you need to visit a hospital?"

"In my body I'm fine. I've not noticed any problems in the spirit world either. Maybe I shouldn't tell you about these things. No point getting you upset."

"If it's going to affect us, if you come back hurt, then I should know. Is there anything else?"

"I may lose a thumb from frost bite, and a creature stole my memory, but I think I got most of it back."

"Since Saturday?"

"I don't remember anything else."

"You need to slow down a bit or you'll be dead by next week. I'm sure the powers that be aren't interested in you not being alive to do your job."

"The spirits are very hungry."

"A few scraps may be better than nothing. You don't owe them a feast. You're the one in charge."

"I'll remember to boss them around when I next go over there."

"Too right." I hear the bell go in the background. "I should go."

"Thanks for calling."

"Maybe we can catch up properly at the weekend." She hangs up.

I could go to the office now. Make sure everything will be okay in person. Part of me says that will make me appear guilty. I should carry on and if something happens, react to that.

I don't know what to do about the press. We did get some training when things turned bad in my old job, but just a few minutes. I don't know if it's better to face it head on or hope it just goes away as the wacky story of the day.

Out in the tunnel it doesn't seem so cold. It probably helps that I moved into the middle. As I head towards the entrance though it still feels warmer than it did yesterday. There's no frost on the platform and the snow in the middle is forming pools around the ruined plants. I go up to the park and the ground is spongy with water. It's still daytime; this could be the warm front before the storm. They really will hang me for a sorcerer if the coldest night ever only happens outside the park gates. I guess that's another thing I'll leave worrying about until it happens.

I had anticipated a long day of work. It's mid-afternoon and I've nothing to do. I'm as ready as I'm going to be. All I need to do now is have a hot dinner and it's too soon for that. I could go spend time with Midori, try and ease my way out of that difficulty, or even find the aliens and thank them for their help, but I feel it will be better to keep what reserves my sparse body has for tonight.

I return to my tent and try to read, check on the servers, run a few system checks, make sure my equipment is as charged up as possible and that my stove is still working. Eventually I feel it is late enough to eat. It's starting to stay light for longer. I feel embarrassed to go to the café after my scene there earlier so I get a couple of supersized burger meals, something I wouldn't normally have without the kids to help eat them and Kathryn to help pay for them. I'm so full after that I feel uncomfortable and have to resist the urge to walk it off.

Byres Road is cold and dark, but I feel the difference as soon as I enter the Gardens. It is much warmer here. I open my coat to prevent a build-up of sweat. The plumbing is working again in the toilet block. I don't need to crawl into my sleeping bag as it's still quite pleasant in my tent. I watch the damn footage of myself too many times. I look like a right idiot and sound worse.

Chapter 20

At some point I fall asleep, soundly too, as my alarm wakes me. I'm half in half out of my sleeping bag, like it's summer. My thumb aches and it looks a bit black near the tip. I'll go to work and then see about getting it looked at by a medic. I know I'm going to lose it – at least to the first joint. It's going to make typing weird for a while.

Outside the air is crisp and damp. There's no snow anywhere in the Gardens and the tent city looks more like it has seen a downpour than a freeze. All the cars in Queen Margaret Drive have a thick rind of frost on them. Grime coated snow banks still separate the parking spaces from the road proper. The dome of the Kibble Palace is frost free. The toilet block is functioning, the water cool but not bracing.

I'm pleased that it has worked, even if it is only for one night. I don't think anyone could explain this away as a unique microclimate. Passing through the gates is like moving into another world. It is harsh in Glasgow, like the arctic cave I met Frost in. Inside the Gardens it is almost tropical in comparison. You could get thermal shock jumping between the two.

On my way to work I see that a number of my neighbours are alive and coping with an unexpected sogginess. I try not laugh as really it's all my fault.

I can't bring myself to open the email. It sits there, the little icon a pristine envelope. The first line preview says almost all of it.

Dear Mr Munro,
We would like you to attend a performance review meeting on Friday
at 11am in

Performance review, eh? How well I did in front of the cameras will be critiqued. Will the benefits agency accept "Tunnel in the Botanic Gardens" as a suitable home address? At least I won't need any heating or lighting. I'll do a deal with some elementals and they'll keep me right. Soon as I work out what an information spirit looks like and how I can communicate with it I'll get my internet access upgraded. So all I need to worry about is food. Guess I can sort out my own hydroponics system or something like that. Convince some plant spirits to help me out with that. Who needs the real world?

I do my diagnostics and a close visual inspection of the server room in case of leaks or worse some frost forming overnight as water condensed on cold metals and plastic. It's all clear though because I've done my job and looked after this place. It hasn't gone down once on my watch.

In the A&E at the Western I wait behind dozens of people who all caught mild frostbite or don't know what chilblains are. The doctor looks at my thumb. The black blister is getting larger. Apparently it's only second degree frost bite and I'll be fine in a month. As is often the case I'm made to feel like I wasted someone's time. I know I wasted mine. At least it doesn't hurt.

What do I do with myself? The immediate crisis has been taken care of. I think I need to thank a few people. Not least Corbie. It would be good to see how Stevie is doing. I walk through an icy world, a long and cautious journey, to Gartnavel Hospital and then to the Beatson Centre round the back.

The reception is bright and cheerful without overdoing it. I hesitate before asking. What if Glinda took him someplace else? I'm sure there's a private clinic they could afford. What if Stevie is angry with me for bringing his family back to him? I'd be overjoyed to see mine, but he stayed away for years. He was dead to them. Were they dead to him? Did he spy on them to see how they were doing?

Stevie is in Ward B1. I'm out of visiting hours but they let me in anyway. They recognise me from the news which is embarrassing as it gives me some kind of minor celebrity status.

Stevie is awake and reading from a tablet. There's a still frame of me under a headline. He laughs when he sees me. "Hey big man, how you doing?"

"Nearly lost my arm," I say and give him a thumbs-up with the black blister wrapped in bandages.

He sits up, sliding on the sheets. "Those alien bastards."

"Just your normal everyday ice spirits." I shrug.

"The only place for them is in a good whiskey."

"How are you getting on?"

His grin is painful. "They've done more probing and prodding than our friends. There was some internal bleeding but they fixed it with a bit of keyhole surgery." He shows me the shaved area on the back of his head with a white bandage stuck to it. "I should be okay. Complete remission. No metastasized sites. No major brain centres affected. Fucking miracle apparently."

"Any explanation?"

"I keep telling them you did it." He laughs. "With your Bowie knife and some chanting."

"Don't pull my leg."

"It's true. None of them believed me until they saw the item on the news. Now they just look at me funny."

"How's Glinda?"

"She's taking it well. I reckon she thought I'd run off with an intern or advocate and not looked back."

A nurse discretely clears his throat.

"Looks like my time is up. You know where to find me."

"Hey, don't be a stranger. I owe you a wee dram."

"Since I'm about to get the sack tomorrow I'll have plenty of time to take you up on that."

"Wish I could help you with that, but I don't think they'll let me out in time."

It takes forever to get back to the Gardens. They're still mushy. I get the impression a lot of people have been tramping around in the station area and my tunnel. Nothing appears to be missing from my tent, but I'm a bit pissed off none the less. I don't feel entirely comfortable going into the Otherworld if people are going to be able to prod and poke my body while I'm away. It has always been a risk, but there's a difference between a chance and a near certainty.

Opening Flower and her companions arrive much quicker than last time. The infovores stayed away but I feel much more exposed without Corbie here. He wasn't much use in a fight but at least he was an extra set of eyes.

"The procedure was a success." Opening Flower says, making it sound somewhere between a question and a statement.

The hint of uncertainty is a surprise. "I spoke to Stevie earlier on, he was fine. There was a small problem with some bleeding so he ended up in hospital, but the upside is he was reunited with his family. Thank you all for helping me with this."

"It was useful to us," Eroding Blade says. "You have our thanks too."

"Did you find it?"

"We don't understand."

"The soul. That's what you were looking for wasn't it?"

"Our data remains inconclusive, but aligns with what we know of ourselves."

I laugh. "I'll take that as a yes then."

Eroding Blade inclines his head slightly. "We would be pleased to meet with you further."

"I'd like to get to know you guys better too. I'd love to see your home world."

"Perhaps that can be arranged," Opening Flower says, sounding happy.

Midori's hiding something. I've never seen her stay submerged in her pool before. This worries me. I'm already nervous after our last meeting. "How are we going to move against the Powers That Be?" she says.

"My passion for a fight has faded over the last few days," I say. "I'm still angry at being manipulated and my family hurt. Revenge is best served cold. I need more time. Without Corbie I need to find spirits to work with."

"I am glad you chose to work with me," she says. "But I'm disappointed. The purpose of our alliance is, in part, to do something about the Great Spirits."

"And we will, in time. Just not right now. I've only been doing this a few weeks and I've barely made it through alive. I have a lot to cope with in the Living World right now too. Food I eat here will not sustain my body. There's something else we need to discuss. You were very hurt and angry last time I was here. I didn't feel we could talk properly."

Midori frowns. "Say what you want. We are allies, are we not?"

"Our...intimacy was wonderful. I enjoyed being with you. But now you've been acting like a jealous girlfriend. We hadn't made any commitments to one another. I have ties to people in the Living World. My ex-wife, my kids, and there's a woman I like."

"You want to make an alliance with someone over me."

"See that's what I'm trying to say. We slept together, now you're threatened by every other woman in my life. That's not acceptable."

"And what about me? What about my feelings, my needs?"

"I'm not denying them. But you don't own me anymore than I do you. Sex one time, and let's be honest you drugged me, is not a relationship. I work in the spiritual world, but I need a life in the Living World too. Otherwise I can't be a shaman."

"You have responsibilities here too."

"Exactly. I have feet in both worlds."

Midori emerges from the pool. At first I think it is just the water bending the light. Then I know I'm in trouble. She stretches her arms below her distended belly like she's carry a basket. Is it possible to be surprised and unsurprised at the same time? What is even in there? I feel slightly ill.

"And I take all my responsibilities seriously," I say.

"I'm glad to hear it."

"When are you due?"

"In another day or two."

It had only been a couple of days. How is this even possible? "How can I help?"

"I'm sure simply having a father around to show some guidance will be enough," she says. "But I expect your undivided attention."

"That's not going to happen. I'll support you in any way I can, but you can't lay claim to my time."

"It is so nice to see you've grown a backbone. You'll need it when you lead our children against the Great Spirits."

"Okay. Corbie was right. You really are crazy." I'm starting to think of any number of cheap horror flicks.

"I'm helping us both. You need spirits to aid you. What better than your own family?"

"We're a family now? Nuclear, no doubt. I like you but this is all a bit too much, too fast."

"I can give you more than any mere human woman. I won't age. I'll never die."

"Now you try the sales pitch for a long term relationship. We should get to know one another better, spend time learning about one another. We started down that road, but I've been under the influence, and your behaviour is possessive and beyond creepy."

"How can you not love the mother of your children?"

It's like talking to an immortal pregnant teenager. "If I was younger you'd have me walking up the aisle. But I've already been married. I have kids. I know how this works. I've picked up their puke, cleaned their soiled clothes and watched them walk for the first time. I'm also being divorced by their mother. Having kids together doesn't obligate me to love you."

Midori slumps to the ground groaning and holding her stomach. I scramble down beside her but she looks at me with such hate her feeble push is enough for me to move back. She rises into a squat in the sand on the banks of the pool. I see her stomach bulge and throb. Is this normal? Is she early? I don't want her to come to harm, or the kids, whatever they might be.

A sharp angular shape thrusts up distending her skin. She cries out. Another pushes up and the leafy skin of her abdomen tears like paper. I see a beak poking through. Another tear forms further down and as the two tears head towards each other her body bursts open in a torrent of wings and a shimmer of fins. The birds flee into the air, the fishes flop and jump and slide into the pool. Balls of wet fur fall into the sand from the ruined cavity of Midori's belly. They mewl and finding legs scamper into the nearest dark spaces.

Midori lets out a deep cry. I don't know if it is relief or sadness. I feel disgusted that I had anything to play in this. Her abdomen closes over with folds of leaves and petals.

"Are you okay?"

Midori laughs. "Never been better."

"Those are our children?"

"Don't worry, shaman. None of us need your support." She rises up to stand and wades into the water.

I watch until the ripples fade.

Sitting up I nearly head-butt a camera. "What the fuck?" There's a crowd in the tunnel and I'm in an island of light. Several other cameras are pointing at me and a number of people lurk beyond the dazzle. I ask the question even though I know the answer. "What do you want?"

"Are you responsible for the neon jellyfish hoax?"

"How did you make the Gardens warmer than the rest of Glasgow? Did you use magic?"

"How long have you been a necromancer?"

I nearly respond to that one. Remember; don't accept the premise of the question. "I'm an IT worker trying to get by like hard working people everywhere." Spoken like a true politician. Have they talked to

Kathryn? Have they hassled my kids? She'll never let me see them again.

"Can you answer our questions, please, Mr Munro?"

"You'll have to forgive me I've just woken up."

"Do you like sleeping in a tunnel?"

"How have you been finding it?" This gets a few laughs. I head towards the light. The geese follow. If I answer their questions will it make it worse? Or will they go away and the story will die. I wish I'd done more media training. I'm glad to get out, get some space. I'm still shocked by what I saw Midori do. Was that a regular occurrence for her or was my sperm was required? Meantime I need to be careful. The press will warp anything I say.

On the platform I turn to the pack, most of them are still inside the gloom of the tunnel. I'm out in the light. The sky is ice blue, the sunlight crisp and golden. Sometimes there's a performer in me trying to break out. I see the beaks tear open Midori from within.

"Last time I spoke to the press I thought I'd made an agreement. That promise wasn't worth the paper it was printed on. Now I'm going to lose my job.

"Look at where I live. You've seen it. I can't go much lower. Without my job I'm going to be raiding the skips round the back of the supermarket just to get something to eat. You've all got roofs over your heads. Maybe you've got kids to feed too. All I'm asking for is a little respect, and a little restraint. I think I know what you want to ask me about. I wish I had answers for you. I only have more questions.

"Being a shaman is a calling not a choice. You can fight the call, but you won't survive. My family have suffered already. Please, I beg you, leave them alone. I've not been able to save my marriage as a consequence of the call. Leave my kids out of this. You speak to my family and we'll see if I have any necromantic powers or not. Can I trust you to agree to that much? If so, I'll answer your questions."

They're stunned for a moment. Maybe the sunlight shining off a spanner has them dazed. Someone says yes. I look at them, they drop their eyes. Someone else says I agree. They can't hold my gaze either.

"It's simple. If you believe I can change the weather at my whim or conjure up strange glowing things in the night sky then you can only imagine what other powers I have. And I'm asking you to respect my family's privacy. If you don't believe it then you damn well better hope that you're right."

Some of the reporters break ranks and walk past me. A few remain, including the two who wouldn't look me in the eye.

"I don't care if what you print is the truth. I don't care if you believe me. I just ask that I'm the only person you interview in my family. I'm taking a huge leap of trust here. Who has the first question?"

"You said before that you interact with spirits on behalf of other people. What are these spirits like?"

"Some of them are just like animals, some of them are plants, and some are simple objects like eight sided polygons. A few look like mythical beings. Some are quite beyond anything I'd seen before." I laugh. "I nearly said alien, but I don't know if that means anything anymore."

"What do you mean?"

"I can't say that they come from other planets."

"Was the spacecraft being here your fault?"

"I didn't see any spacecraft."

"What did you see?"

"I was in my tent reading. When my light failed I came out and saw the same glowing thing in the sky you all did."

"Did you have anything to do with it being here?"

"I think my neighbours have had a big laugh at all our expense. I encouraged them to move down here to be warmer when the antici-pated cold weather came. They didn't appreciate me waking them up early yesterday morning and seem to have decided to play a prank on all of us."

"What about the warm weather?"

"That was my solution to my neighbour's reluctance to move."

"You got spirits to make it warmer?"

"I asked spirits not to make it so cold. It seems that they were a little overzealous. Alternatively, there are special geothermal or microclimate conditions that made it warmer here than the rest of the city for the last two days." I feel my thumb itching terribly and have to resist the urge to scratch it.

I spend an hour answering every question they can throw at me. Eventually they get bored and leave. Am I a deluded religious freak, a new prophet for a new age, or nobody at all, a complete waste of time? I'll read all about it tomorrow with everyone else.

The rest of the day is preparation for tomorrow's lynching. I'm on shaky ground, but I did my job, day and night. I can't see how they can fire me.

I peek under the bandage on my thumb. The white sets off the creeping black well. I think it is starting to smell.

Chapter 21

"You're looking smart. The usual?" Sindi smiles at me like nothing happened two days ago.

"I've got an interview. And yes, please."

"New job, eh. You leaving us for bigger things?"

"Sadly I'm trying to keep my existing job."

"Shit. You never seem to get an even break."

"Look. I wanted to thank you properly for helping me out the other day." I release the money for my bacon roll and tea.

"We'd go out of business if we let our customers die on us."

Sitting outside the shared meeting room in the building I know I'm too early. My employers haven't even made it in yet.

"Just go in and wait." Jill on reception nods at the door.

The screen is on and live. I don't know why I thought there'd be direct human interaction. They introduce themselves. Blah from HR, Y from ICT Services, Damien my line manager, a couple of other folks in the shadows. PR people?

"Your conduct has been fine." "We think you've done a great job." "We appreciate the contribution you've made to the company."

There have been some who had suggested my appearance on TV during working hours could constitute bringing the company into ill-repute. This would be a gross misdemeanour worthy of immediate dismissal. Other, wiser, people have suggested that being seen to persecute someone for their religious beliefs or trying to help the community would be seen in a much poorer light. It is just pure coincidence that they are having to streamline the company further and I'm one of those having to be let go. They have prepared a fair, some would say generous, redundancy package of six month's pay plus notice and holiday pay, but with immediate loss of all other benefits.

I reckon with no more support payments and staying in my tent that could last me a year, probably longer. I'm pissed off. I can't believe despite the smoke and mirrors that they're actually firing me. I'm also relieved. It used to be all I had, but it was starting to feel like a millstone round my neck.

I sign some pieces of paper, hand my pass to Jill and walk into the bitter morning air. Fuck em all.

All through the meeting I was increasingly glad they weren't in the room with me. My thumb has that sweet smell of rotting meat. I knew yesterday that it needed to go, despite what the doctor said. They didn't just need blood from me. They took my flesh too. I need to take care of this.

In my tunnel I have gauze, bandages, clean water, a flat rock, a scalpel edged kitchen knife and my gas stove hissing blue. I unwrap my thumb. The material sticks to a moist patch and I feel my flesh rotate as I pull. I hold back my breakfast.

It is as black as all my sins, purple round the edges, swollen with pus and other fluid.

I don't think this is going to work. I should have bought a hatchet instead.

I bring up Rachael's number on my phone. All I have to do is hit the Call button.

With my hand flat on the stone, I extend my thumb out at ninety degrees. I heat the blade in the flames. With the tip on the stone, I rest the blade along the big joint. The bastards are only getting the end, nothing more. I lift the blade using the point as a pivot, like a paper guillotine. There's no room for hesitation. I slam down the blade with all my strength. It slices through skin and gets caught in the joint of the bone. Electric blue hits my forehead. I see stars.

When I come back I'm still kneeling before the stone. A pool of blood surrounds my thumb, the knife quivers with every move. The blackened tip of my thumb is half on half off. I turn my hand so the blade faces the stone. I reach for a loose brick in the floor of the tunnel. I try again to prise it free. It feels too heavy to lift. Too solid.

The brick comes down on the blade. Shards of red ceramic join the blood. I feel like I'm operating myself on remote control. I plunge my hand in the water washing off the gore and brick dust. I thrust it into the flame. I smell like bacon. I put my blackened half thumb back into the water. Then my thumb comes back to life and I scream out. It echoes down the tunnel and bounces back to me.

Lovely faithful Rachael is slapping me awake. My thumb is on fire and my stomach is groaning. I shiver hard. The gas stove is out. The blood on the stone is gone. Where is the rotten end of my thumb? The fingers of my other hand are bent round my phone.

Midori is standing out in the light beneath the air vents amongst the first shoots of spring. How is that possible? My head feels thick and heavy. It's hard to think. If the aliens could come through why not her too?

"I got your call." Rachael stands up. "Or maybe it was hers. My colleagues heard my phone constantly ringing in the staff room. There was some weird message. At first, just you begging for help, then a woman starts calling me a traitor. It was a hard decision to come here. After what you said about your wife getting weird calls, I didn't know what to think. I'm surprised you're not in a pool of your own blood. Are you really suicidal?"

Am I? I stay out in all conditions. I don't eat. I get sick and run away from the hospital. I give myself severe frostbite. I cut off my own thumb. After I lose my job. "You'd think I'd do a better job."

"Who was the woman?"

"You can't see her?"

Rachael turns around. "Who?"

I sit up, and then stand. My thumb is a mess. I go to a spot midway between the two women. "This is Midori. She is a powerful spirit. An ally."

"Oh, I'm just an ally am I?" Midori says.

"What are you doing here?" I say.

"Like Corbie?" Rachael says. "I can hear her. Is there something in the brambles?"

"I heard your scream," says Midori. "I wouldn't want my ally coming to harm, now would I?"

Rachael can see and hear Midori? Is this really happening? I don't want to lose Rachael. I've already told Midori how things were between us. "Thank you for looking out for me," I say.

"Why is this friend of yours calling me a traitor?"

Honestly has never been the best policy. I've been as honest as I can all my life. Look where it got me. If I have a hope of anything with Rachael though I need to tell her.

"You're a traitor because we have an alliance," Midori says. "You're trying to come between us and form your own alliance. I can't let that happen."

"What the hell is she talking about?"

"I told her that I was seeing you, trying to have a proper relationship," I say. "That I needed to keep myself grounded in the Living World. As she says, we had agreed to an alliance."

"Exactly what kind of alliance?" Rachael says.

"He's my husband," Midori says.

"What?" I say.

"You got married?" Rachael says.

"First I heard about it. Since when am I your husband?"

"We agreed an alliance and we consummated it," Midori says. "That makes you my husband."

"That wasn't the nature of our agreement," I say.

"You consummated it?" Rachael says. "You had sex with this woman? When did this happen?"

"It was like having an erotic dream," I say. "It wasn't real."

"I had babies," Midori smiles. "It was real enough."

"I'm out of here," Rachael says.

"Don't go, please. I'm trying to make this work."

"This is too fucking much to ask, Nik. Mutilation, killing yourself, I could maybe get used to that. Spirit wives. No fucking chance."

"Rachael, please. We can find a way to make this work. I need you. But I need Midori's help too."

"No. This is too fucked up," Rachael says. "Don't call me."

"Rachael."

She leaves, feet ringing on the steps.

"I'll see you around, lover." Midori laughs and fades from view.

I can't stand anymore. I'm on my knees looking up into the clear blue sky. The moon is already visible.

I have no job, no partner, no income, no house, and no friends. Blood is seeping through the bandage on my thumb.

Then I see it. I missed it before. A pyramid of food cans, just in front of the tunnel.

I don't know how they got here or when. Must have been while I was getting fired.

I get some painkillers from my bag, but I need more water, my throat is dry and I can't swallow. I climb the rusted steps and walk through the Tent City. Someone calls my name. I turn and they wave. Perhaps we're a community after all?

I lift my injured hand without thinking and wave back. I feel the blood rush into my thumb when I lower it, it throbs with each pulse.

This was how it started, in pain and mutilation, and this is how it goes; I'm a wounded man now, a shaman.

About the Author

Richard grew up with the threat of mutually assured destruction, and public information films haunted by the robed Spirit of Dark and Lonely Water. His earliest reading included folk tales about plucky country folk fooling the Devil, alongside the heroes and creatures of Greek and Norse myth. In time he discovered the works of Stephen King, Clive Barker, and H.P. Lovecraft.

In his early teens Richard started storytelling, including scripting a zombie movie one summer in which the local kids all had parts. Much of his effort went into running roleplaying games, and eventually he started writing short stories too.

Going to university in Glasgow, he studied Laser Physics; a misguided attempt to enter the world of special effects. Richard joined a number of clubs and societies, running the Science Fiction and Roleplaying clubs, and eventually moving up to be President of Clubs and Societies, showing his natural gift for organising and planning. After his undergraduate degree completed, he chose to continue studying for a PhD, growing and characterising crystals; creating materials that had never previously existed. Continuing to write and roleplay, Richard joined the local branch of live action group The Camarilla in its early days, in time becoming the local storyteller. From there he helped grow the society throughout Scotland, and took on the role of Regional Storyteller.

After completing his PhD, he moved to Dublin, working for Guinness, the Ulster Bank, and a software company where he wrote scripts for training environments teaching the user Word, Project, and other Microsoft products. While in Ireland, Richard started a new national Camarilla group, eventually passing this on and moving up to work on storytelling at an International level, working with countries across Europe, and the USA.

Returning to Scotland, Richard began working in a series of small technology SMEs, which led to redundancy every couple of years, but he went up through the ranks and became Managing Director of a medical device company, launching new products in the UK and abroad. Unfortunately, the economic crash also took the company with it. Leading to a return to the academic sector where Richard worked on behalf of all of Scotland's Physics departments, encouraging business to take an interest in the varied research output.

During this time, Richard joined the Glasgow SF Writers Circle, having left The Camarilla and pursuing writing with a commercial aim, which matched the ethos of the GSFWC. With the support of the Circle he has completed a number of novels and had several short stories published in a range of magazines and anthologies.

Currently, Richard is working at the University of Glasgow, managing multi-million research projects and continues to write. He is married, with two cats.